KATHY

Linda Sole

This first world edition published in Great Britain 2003 by
SEVERN HOUSE PUBLISHERS LTD of
9–15 High Street, Sutton, Surrey SM1 1DF.
This first world edition published in the USA 2004 by
SEVERN HOUSE PUBLISHERS INC of
595 Madison Avenue, New York, N.Y. 10022.

British Library Cataloguing in Publication Data

Sole, Linda
     Kathy
     1.   World War, 1914-1918 - Medical care - Fiction
     2.   London (England) - Social conditions - Fiction
     3.   Domestic fiction
     I.   Title
     823.9'14 [F]

     ISBN 0-7278-5869-6

Typeset by Palimpsest Book Production Ltd.,
Polmont, Stirlingshire, Scotland.
Printed and bound in Great Britain by
MPG Books Ltd., Bodmin, Cornwall.

KATHY

Recent Titles by Linda Sole from Severn House

THE TIES THAT BIND
THE BONDS THAT BREAK
THE HEARTS THAT HOLD

THE ROSE ARCH
A CORNISH ROSE
A ROSE IN WINTER

BRIDGET
FLAME CHILD
A SONG FOR ATHENA

One

'How is your grandmother today, Kathy?' Bridget Robinson called to me as I was leaving the shop at the corner of Farthing Lane and had paused to greet her. 'I heard she wasn't well.'

'She seems better again now. The doctor thinks it was just a chill, but he says she should take things easier.'

'Well, I'm glad she's getting over it, whatever it was. I'll pop in and see her later if I can manage it.'

'She would enjoy that . . .' I hesitated, then went on in a rush: 'Gran often talks about you, Bridget. She says things would have been different if Da had married you.'

Bridget gave me an understanding smile and I knew she must have heard the latest tale about my father, but she wouldn't embarrass me by mentioning it. Bridget's husband Joe was a rich man these days and owned most of the property in the lane, including the small general store we all used at the corner. Some people were a bit jealous of his success, but most agreed that he was generous in his support of local people, and everyone liked Bridget.

'She's just the same as she always was,' Gran had told me more than once. 'Ernie Cole was a fool, that's what I say. He had his chance with her and threw it away – that's your father all over. Never knows what's good for him. I warned him when he married that woman – but he wouldn't listen to me and look what it got him! He's never been the same since.'

Why did Gran dislike my mother so much? What had

1

she done that caused both Gran and my father to scowl if I mentioned her name?

I often wondered why my mother had run away soon after I was born, but when I asked questions about her Gran shook her head.

'Best you don't know child. It wasn't your fault – and you've been a blessin' to me.'

Jean Cole had been as good as a mother to me, loving me and making sure that I never went without anything if she could help it, though I suspected she sometimes had help with money from a source she wouldn't reveal.

A Londoner through and through, she had lived in the same house since marrying at the age of seventeen, moving only three houses when she left her home to start her married life. Our lane was just across from the St Katherine's Docks, which were now a part of the larger London Docks, but when they were first built almost a whole parish, including the old hospital of St. Katherine's, had been pulled down to make way for them.

'Well, I must get on,' Bridget said, her voice breaking into my thoughts. 'Our Tom is coming for a meal this evening. He's a doctor with the Army, you know, but they didn't send him to France with the troops because of that bit of bother he had when he was a lad. Not that it troubles him now. In fact, he thinks he may never have had consumption at all, just an infection of the lungs. He knows all about that sort of thing now, our Tom – and he says the doctors made a lot of mistakes in the early days.'

'You'll be glad to see your brother, I expect.'

'Yes, I shall. Tom is busy so we don't see him as often as we'd like – but at least he keeps in touch. I haven't heard from Jamie for ages. He was in America the last time he wrote and doing well, but that was years ago . . .'

She frowned, her eyes full of shadows as if she were remembering an old sadness. I knew there was some story about Jamie O'Rourke having gone away after his girl was killed in a fire on the eve of their wedding, but I didn't know the details.

'Give my best wishes to your grandmother, Kathy love – and if you need anythin' you know where to come.'

'Thanks, Bridget,' I said. 'I'll tell Gran you asked after her.'

She smiled, nodded and moved on, seeming to have something on her mind. I thought it might be to do with her elder brother Jamie and wondered if Gran would tell me the whole story if I asked.

I was reflective as I walked on. If my father had married Bridget I would be her daughter and Amy Robinson would have been my younger sister – or perhaps I wouldn't have been around at all. A sigh escaped me as I thought that I would have liked Bridget as a mother, but it was hard to believe that my father had ever wanted to marry her. He always seemed to dislike her, though it was her husband he really hated.

'You stay away from that Bridget O'Rourke and her 'usband,' he'd said to me time and again when I was a child after Bridget had given me a treat of some kind, as she often did. 'That bleedin' Joe Robinson is too clever for 'is own good!'

It was odd that he should call Bridget by her maiden name, but then my father was a law unto himself. He hadn't been so bad when I was a small child. I could remember him taking me up on his shoulders to carry me down the lane when he was in a good mood, and there had been occasional visits to the fair and one never-to-be forgotten trip on the train to Southend as a treat for my tenth birthday. There had always been enough money in the house for food and rent then; it was only since Da's accident that he'd turned sullen and taken to the drink.

He'd been a driver for Mr Dawson at the brewery, and proud of the wagons he drove with their magnificent horses and shining harness, but he wasn't capable of loading or unloading the drays now. Mr Dawson had kept him on in the brewery, because with the onset of the war he had been short of men, but of late he had been given only the more menial of jobs to do and was forever complaining about his employer.

'You mustn't mind your da, Kathy love,' Gran had told me when he came home full of the drink, swearing and yelling the house down. 'He's in pain from his leg – and he's a disappointed man. He's not had a fair deal from life, your da.'

'What do you mean, Gran?' I'd asked but she only shook her head as she always did when I asked questions about things she didn't want to tell me. Her silence only made me more curious.

What had happened to my father to make him so bitter? Was it just that my mother had gone off and left him when I was a baby? Yet it was Gran who had had all the trouble of bringing me up, and she wasn't bitter.

'Wait up, Kathy Cole! I want a word with yer . . .'

I turned as I heard the sound of running feet behind me and hesitated, recognizing at once the man who had called out to me. It was Billy Ryan, Maggie Ryan's youngest son. He was twenty-six going on seven and I was seventeen, but he'd been after me since I'd left school and started work at the glove factory. Billy had worked there too as a foreman for a while, but he'd joined up as soon as war was declared, one of the first to do so in our street. Before he went away he'd told me to wait for him, because he was going to marry me one day.

'Oh, so you're back,' I said, not smiling at him. I wasn't at all sure how I felt about Billy Ryan. He had always been a cocky lad and people whispered that he'd been in a bit of trouble a couple of times and was lucky he hadn't been up in front of the magistrates. 'Did the Army throw you out then?'

'You haven't changed,' Billy replied and grinned at me. 'Glad to see me then are yer, Kathy girl?'

'I'm indifferent either way,' I said with a shrug of my shoulders and he gave a hoot of laughter.

'Swallowed a dictionary this mornin', did yer?' Billy's parents were Irish, and still spoke with a soft Irish accent but Billy had lived in London all his life and sounded like a cockney. He wasn't in the least put out by my manner and despite myself I warmed to him. He had a nice smile and he wasn't bad looking, his hair dark and wavy and his eyes a melting chocolate brown. He had smartened up and I supposed the Army had done that for him; his boots were polished so fine you could see your face in them. 'Fancy going to the Pally this evenin' then?'

I stared at him in silence for a moment or two. My father wouldn't be pleased if I went out with Billy, but then he didn't like any of the people in Farthing Lane these days. Gran would encourage me to go. She said I didn't get out with other young people often enough.

'I like dancin',' I said at last. 'But I'm not sure I should go with you, Billy Ryan. You might try to take advantage.'

'God's honest truth I'd never do that to yer, Kathy,' Billy said and he sounded sincere. 'It ain't just 'cos you're the prettiest girl in the lanes with that lovely hair o' yourn and them big eyes. You're the girl I'm goin' ter marry one day, and I respect yer. I swear on me 'onour that I won't put a finger out of place. I won't even kiss yer unless you agree, lass. Cross me 'eart and 'ope ter die.'

I wasn't surprised by his answer. Billy had told everyone for years that he was going to marry me one day. It had been a joke amongst my school friends, but looking at him now I almost believed him.

'I'll come then,' I said making up my mind. 'I'll meet you outside the brewery at seven.'

'I was goin' ter call fer yer proper, Kathy. We might as well start out right.'

'Me da might not like me going with you,' I said doubt-fully. 'But perhaps you're right. Call for me at seven then –

that will please Gran anyway. She says no one shows her any respect these days.'

'I've got every respect for Mrs Cole,' Billy said. 'She's been good to you, lass – just the way I shall be when we're wed.'

'And who said I was goin' to marry you? Sayin' I'll come to the Pally with you doesn't mean I'll marry you, Billy Ryan.'

He grinned at me cheekily. 'First things first, Kathy. Yer don't know me yet, but you'll soon change your mind when yer see how generous I can be. I'll be there at seven so don't keep me waitin'!'

I glared at him, almost sorry that I had agreed to go out with him that evening. Just who did he think he was? I nearly told him to forget it but something held me back. I was seventeen and I hadn't had a regular boyfriend yet. I'd been dancing at the Pally with other girls and their brothers, and a few of my dance partners had made a pass at me. I hadn't let any of them kiss me. It annoyed me because one or two of them had seemed to imagine that I would be easy and I didn't see why. I wasn't a flirt and I had never been out with a man on my own.

Once I'd heard some boys whispering about my mother and laughing in a nasty way, and it had made me wonder. Why should people laugh about Grace Cole in that way – and why did the men sometimes look at me oddly? I wasn't a tart and I had never given anyone cause to think it.

It was a mystery, and it would never be solved until I could get some answers about my mother – but no one would tell me anything.

I made up my mind to ask Gran about it again when I got home. Surely I had a right to know the whole story?

'Well, I suppose you are old enough to know the truth,' Gran said when I took a cup of tea up to her in bed and told her what was on my mind and why. 'It might be best if you know – especially if you're goin' ter start courtin'.'

She had her pink bed shawl about her shoulders, and the patchwork quilt she had made with her own hands as a young woman was pulled up tight about her. Even on a warm day the old house seemed cold and draughty, and in winter we often needed a fire in the bedrooms.

'I'm only goin' dancin' with him, Gran.'

'Yes – but these things lead to somethin' more in time,' Gran said. She was looking tired and I knew her illness had dragged her down, but at least she was beginning to improve. 'Grace was no better than she ought ter be, Kathy. Yer da wasn't the first with her by a long way . . .' She hesitated as though she wanted to say more and then shook her head. 'And she went off and left yer as a baby – that's reason enough fer me to dislike her. Some folks might think you will likely turn out the same way. They don't know yer the way I do, love.'

'Is that why . . . ?' My cheeks were bright with fire as I looked at her. 'Does Billy Ryan think I'm that way, too? Is that why he wants to take me dancin'?'

'No, I don't think so,' Gran replied. 'Billy is a bit of a cheeky devil, and he doesn't always know which is the right side of the law – but he is fond of you, Kathy. Even when you were fifteen he was always 'ere tryin' ter get yer ter to go out with 'im. If I thought he wouldn't treat yer right I wouldn't let yer go.'

'Do you mind if I go, Gran? Can you manage without me?'

'Of course I can, Kathy. I'll be fine tucked up in me bed. Leave yer da a cold supper on the table – though God knows what time 'e'll get 'ome. Just be sure that Billy brings you 'ome by half past ten – and if he does try anythin', give him a slap round his ear.'

'He promised he wouldn't,' I said and bent to kiss her cheek, which felt papery soft and dry. The sheets were clean on that day and smelled of soap, as she did herself after I'd helped her to wash. 'He says he respects me too much.'

'Then I'm sure 'e means it,' Gran said and smiled lovingly as she reached up to touch my cheek. 'You're a good girl, Kathy, and bright. You did well at school and you speak better than most round 'ere – better than yer da or me. I should like ter see yer make somethin' of yerself. Don't get into trouble and rush in ter marriage, love. Look at Bridget Robinson. Her mother was a drunken slut, but Bridget was smart – like you. They say she does all Joe's bookwork fer 'im, and she's got a couple of market stalls 'erself. Likes sellin' flowers, Bridget does. I should like yer to settle with a good man like Joe Robinson – so you just be careful. Billy Ryan is all right, but make sure 'e's what you really want afore yer settle on 'im.'

'I'm not thinkin' of marryin' yet, Gran,' I said and laughed as I flicked back my hair, which was a dark honey blonde and set off eyes Gran always said were green like a cat's. 'I'm too young to train as a nurse yet, but that's what I'd like to do. I keep thinkin' about all those young men getting hurt so bad over there . . .' I sighed. 'When is it all going to end, Gran? I think it's terrible that all our boys end up gettin' killed in the trenches.'

'We all feel the same, Kathy,' Gran said. 'It's a wicked shame that it happened at all, that's what I think – decent folk shooting at each other. Bridget's eldest son is out there fighting, and she told me that he wrote to her about the first Christmas of the war, when the German soldiers and the British played football together in no-man's-land between the trenches. She said her Jonathan thought the Germans were just like us then; they didn't want to fight and kill people. It's all the fault of them what started it – the Kaiser and politicians.'

'Well, I don't suppose we shall solve anythin' by talkin',' I said. 'But if the war isn't over when I'm eighteen I shall join the Voluntary Aid Detachment as a nurse.'

'That's what I like to hear,' Gran said approvingly. 'My girl has a bit of ambition – not like her father. You stick to your guns, my girl, and don't you let anyone talk yer out of it.'

We had been at the Pally for a couple of hours, and the dance floor was crowded with young men and women. Most of the men were in uniform, and the girls were all wearing pretty dresses. I knew some of them from school, and several of them were working in the munitions factory or voluntary organizations. We had been dancing most of the time and I was enjoying myself as Billy was fun to be with. However, I was very much aware of the war and that I had done nothing to help except knit a few socks and roll some bandages. So when Billy went off to fetch us another drink I spoke to a girl called Valerie Green about being a nurse.

'It's hard work, Kathy,' she told me. 'I've just come back from three months in France and the conditions were awful. The men are crawling with lice when they come in after weeks in the trenches, and there's never enough of anything to go round. I asked to be transferred back home.'

'But you like being a nurse, don't you?'

'It's all right I suppose . . .'

I would have asked her more questions about nursing but Billy came back with our drinks and she walked off.

'Port and lemon you said, Kathy?'

'Yes please.' I took a sip. 'Oh, that's lovely. Not too strong.'

Billy grinned. 'I didn't think you were a hardened drinker so I told them to put plenty of lemonade in.' He took a swig of his beer. 'Are yer enjoyin' yerself then, Kathy?'

'Yes, thanks.' I finished my drink and put the glass down. 'I'm goin' to the cloakroom. It's nearly ten o'clock, Billy. We'll have time for one more dance before we go, won't we?'

'Just about. Mustn't be late back though or your gran won't trust me to take you out again.'

I smiled as I moved away from him, knowing that the gift of chocolates he'd brought for Gran when he called to pick me up earlier had gone a long way to winning her over. He had also brought a little posy of flowers for me.

'Now that's a lad who knows how to come courtin',' Gran had whispered to me as I'd kissed her goodbye.

I was beginning to think Billy was a decent lad and that I quite liked him. He'd given me a good night out and I was feeling relaxed and happy as I made my way back to him after visiting the cloakroom. It was then that someone grabbed my arm roughly, making me swing round to look at him in alarm.

'What are you doing?'

My heart had begun to thud wildly. I didn't know this man to speak to, though I'd noticed him standing with the crowd of rowdies at the bar on a couple of occasions. He was one of the lads who seemed to come to the Pally just to drink and stare at the girls.

''Ave a drink wiv me, luv?'

'No, thank you. I'm with someone.'

'That bleedin' Billy Ryan. He ain't no good to yer, Kathy. You come outside wiv me and I'll show yer wot's wot.'

His expression made me feel sick deep down inside, and I tried to pull away but his grip tightened on my arm, his fingers digging painfully into my flesh. People were looking at us, some of them frowning, others grinning as if it were amusing.

'Let me go please. I don't want to come with you – you are very rude.'

'Rude, am I? Hoity-toighty bitch! Yer no better than yer ma was and she were anybody's.'

'You shut your dirty mouth!'

I pulled sharply away from him and after a tussle he let go of my arm, but then as I tried to move away he caught me about the waist. His intentions were obvious but I was determined that this brute should not maul or kiss me. I gave him a kick on the shins and he swore, raising his right arm to hit me. A cry of alarm escaped me but before I could do anything I felt someone pull me roughly away from his hold and Billy was there.

'You take your filthy paws off my girl!' he said and the look on his face was so savage that I was startled. He looked capable of anything at that moment. 'I'll teach you some manners, Sam Cotton.'

'You and whose bleedin' army?'

'I don't need no 'elp,' Billy said and launched himself at my assailant in a fury.

In another moment they were at it full pelt, punching and jostling. Billy seemed as if he wanted to murder the other man, and I drew back in horror as girls started screaming and the men formed a sort of semicircle around them, yelling encouragement.

'Give it to 'im, Billy. Kill the bugger!'

'Hit him, Sam. Give the bastard one for me.'

'Billy, *don't*!' I cried, feeling horrified as I watched them slugging it out. It was quickly clear that Billy had the advantage and as his fists slammed into Sam Cotton's chin he went down. The next second Billy was sitting astride him, hitting him in the face over and over again. 'That's enough . . . please. Stop it, Billy. You will kill him.'

It was so awful. Everyone was aware of what was going on, and I felt terribly embarrassed, as if it was all somehow my fault.

'I thought you were taking a risk coming with him,' a voice said at my elbow. 'Billy Ryan has a bit of a reputation . . .'

'What do you mean?' I glanced at Valerie Green. 'Billy's all right.'

'He used to hang around with a rough crowd.' She shrugged her shoulders. 'It's nothing to do with me, but you wouldn't catch me going around with him.'

She walked away without giving me a chance to answer, but my attention was abruptly transferred back to the fight, which had ended as swiftly as it had begun. The owner of the dance hall had sent in his bouncers and they hauled Billy off his vanquished victim, dragging him to the door to eject him despite his protests that Sam Cotton had started the fight.

'Come on, Kathy,' he yelled over his shoulder. 'We're leaving.'

I followed hurriedly behind him, my cheeks flushed with embarrassment as I heard laughter and jeering. Now that the fight was over people were relieved and amused, but I felt hot with shame.

Billy was wiping blood from his mouth when I joined him outside the hall. He looked at me uncertainly, sensing my mood. 'I couldn't let him insult yer like that, Kathy.'

'You didn't have to start a fight. You could have simply told him to leave me alone.'

'Swine like that needs teachin' a lesson. I'm 'andy with me fists. That will learn 'im and a few others not to mess with my girl.'

There was a look of satisfaction in his eyes that made me angry. 'You think you're clever, don't you, Billy Ryan? Well, I don't. I hate being made a show of and that's what you've done. Everyone will laugh behind my back.'

'Yer don't want ter worry about what folks say. 'Sides, I weren't 'avin' that bleedin' Sam Cotton bad mouthin' my girl.'

'I'm not your girl!' I glared at him. 'You don't imagine I'd go out with you again after that?'

I started to walk away from him. I was smarting because of the insulting way Sam Cotton had behaved towards me, and also Valerie Green's remarks about Billy. She was a year or so older and I'd known and liked her at school; it pricked my pride to know she thought me a fool for going out with him, especially as I had a sneaking suspicion she might be right.

Billy followed behind me. 'Don't be like this, Kathy. I'm sorry the evening was spoiled, but it wasn't my fault. Sam Cotton is a docker. He couldn't join up because they said he was needed on the docks – and some of us called him a coward. He hates anyone in uniform, especially me. That's why he went after yer like that.'

'He implied my mother was . . .' I choked back a sob.

'Don't matter what she were,' Billy said swiftly. 'You ain't like 'er, Kathy, and any man with sense knows that. Don't be mad at me. I only did it fer you.'

I stopped walking and looked at him. 'Was she a tart – my mother? Tell me the truth, Billy. I really need to know.'

'I remember talk when she married your da . . .' Billy frowned. 'I were only a lad and me best mate were ill. Tom O'Rourke went away about that time and I were angry at the world because I thought he were goin' ter die. I didn't take much notice of anythin' else, but I know me ma thought Ernie Cole was a fool to marry 'er. Sorry, lass. I can't tell yer much more. Ma knows it all but whether she'd tell yer . . .' He shrugged his shoulders. 'I shouldn't let it worry yer, Kathy. No one who knows yer thinks you're like that.'

I looked at him unhappily. It wasn't Billy's fault that the unpleasant incident with Sam Cotton had happened. He had defended me and I supposed I ought to be grateful.

'You shouldn't have kept on hitting him like that, Billy. I thought you were going to kill him.'

'I might 'ave if they 'adn't dragged me off 'im,' he admitted. The look in his eyes told me he wasn't quite so proud of himself now. 'He made me see red, Kathy. No one treats you like that when I'm around.' He reached out and stroked my cheek with the tips of his fingers. 'You're special to me. Don't you ever forget that.'

'Oh, Billy . . .' I was moved by something in his voice and manner and didn't resist as he bent his head and gently kissed me. It was just a brief touch of his lips against mine but it made me feel odd. 'Please don't, Billy. Not yet. I'm not angry with you now, but I don't know how I feel. I'm not ready to think about—'

He placed a finger to my lips. 'Yer don't 'ave to say anythin', Kathy love. I don't want ter rush yer. It wouldn't be fair to marry yer while this bleedin' war's goin' on. Yer don't want ter be a widow before you're a wife.'

'Billy!' I went cold all over. 'Don't say that. Nothing is going to happen to you.'

'Not if I can bleedin' 'elp it!' He grinned at me. 'I've got too much ter come 'ome for. You are goin' ter wait fer me, ain't yer, Kathy?'

'Don't swear so much,' I reproved with a little smile. 'Da swears somethin' terrible when he's drunk and Gran hates it.'

'I'll try to remember,' he said. 'You will be my girl, Kathy – please?'

'I'm not giving you my word yet, Billy. But if you promise not to get into any more fights I might go out with you again.'

'We'll go to the pictures tomorrow if yer like. There's one of them Mack Sennett films on – the Keystone Kops, I think. Or we could go to a music hall if you'd rather. I've only got three days' leave, Kathy, so we might as well make the most of it.'

'Yes, all right,' I agreed. 'But remember, I'm not promising anythin' yet.'

I thought about Billy when I was lying in bed that night. In the past I'd heard rumours about him getting into bad company, and I'd been very upset by the fight at the dance hall, but maybe he'd had to let off steam. All our men were under terrible strain out there, and Billy was no different from anyone else. I liked his smile and easy manner, and as I finally fell asleep I realized that I was looking forward to meeting him the next day.

I saw Billy twice more before he went back to his unit. We visited a music hall and saw Gertrude Lawrence and Jack Buchanan, joining in as the audience sang along with songs that had become so popular since the beginning of the war. On his last afternoon we went for a walk by the river and then had a drink in the pub.

14

Kathy

It was a pleasant day despite the cool breeze and a lot of people were out walking about, making the most of the fine weather. The Sally Army was playing hymns outside the pub, and a group of children were marching after them banging on drums made out of old biscuit tins.

Billy looked at me anxiously as we lingered over our drinks. 'You won't go and marry anyone else, will yer?'

'I'm not planning on it, Billy. I want to be a nurse when I can – to do something to help. I think of the war and about what's happening out there all the time. All those lads getting killed and hurt.'

I had been reading the news about German submarines sinking ships, and the tremendous numbers of casualties at the Front, and it made me feel guilty for being safe at home when so many others were being killed.

Billy nodded, a serious expression on his face. 'It's bad, lass, real bad. We don't talk about it much when we're home on leave, but it's a nightmare for the men. I've visited mates in the field hospitals out there, and those nurses are angels. I'd be proud for my girl to be one of them, so if that's what you want to do I shan't stand in yer way.'

Hearing the emotion in his voice I felt closer to him than ever before.

'When will it be over, Billy? It's more than three years since it started. Surely it can't drag on much longer – can it?'

'I wish I knew. Most of us who were out there at the start are sick of it – them what are left, that is. I'm one of the lucky ones. I've only 'ad a couple of scratches but I've seen some of me mates catch it. Us veterans 'ave to look out fer the young uns. Most of the new recruits they're sendin' us now are still wet behind the ears.'

'It must be awful.' I looked at him with sympathy, realizing for perhaps the first time how bad it must really be for the men in the trenches, seeing their friends get hurt. 'You will take care, Billy? I shouldn't like anythin' to happen to you.'

'I'm an old 'and at it now,' he said and grinned. 'It's a matter of keeping your head down. Run away to fight another day and don't be a hero – that's what I say.'

'Oh, Billy . . .' I laughed. 'I can't see you runnin' away from a fight.'

'You're never goin' ter let me forget the other night are yer?'

'Is your lip still sore?' I asked and shook my head at him. Now that I'd had time to think about things I felt more pleased than angry that Billy had stuck up for me. I didn't approve of fighting, of course, but it was nice that he'd cared so much.

'Nah. It were just a little cut. I could kiss yer – if yer like?'

'We'll see. I think you'd better walk me home now or you'll be late for your train – and Da will be back for his tea soon.'

So far my luck had held and my father hadn't questioned me about my going out with Billy Ryan. I wasn't sure that he knew. Even if he'd noticed I wasn't around, he'd probably just assumed I was out with friends.

Billy finished his drink and stood, holding out his hand to me. I took it and we left the pub together, strolling through the lanes, which looked brighter than usual in the warm sunshine. In the distance we could hear the rattle of the trams and a hooter from one of the ships blasting off somewhere on the river. I'd heard that morning that an American ship had made its way here safely, bringing much-needed supplies to a country that was gradually running short of almost everything.

When we reached my doorstep, Billy lingered uncertainly. He was reluctant to leave and I knew he was waiting for the kiss I'd half promised him.

'Oh, go on then,' I said and moved towards him. 'You can kiss me if you like.'

Billy smiled, reached out and drew me close to him. His kiss this time was much deeper and lasted longer than the first. I felt him shudder as he at last released me and I was trembling too. I gazed up at him wondering what emotion had made me feel so shivery inside.

'You felt somethin' too, didn't yer, lass?' Billy asked, looking down into my eyes. 'I love yer, Kathy. I 'ave fer years. Wait fer me because I don't think I could bear it out there if I thought yer were kissin' another bloke.' His tone and expression were so sincere that I was moved.

'I like you a lot, Billy,' I whispered feeling breathless. 'I can't promise that I'll marry you, but I'll think about you – and I don't often go out with blokes. You're the first I've let kiss me.'

'Will yer write to me, Kathy? Ma will tell yer where if yer ask.'

'I might now and then,' I said. 'Take care of yourself, Billy. We'll see how we feel next time you come home.'

'Fair enough,' he said and that cocky grin spread across his face. 'You're my girl, Kathy Cole – whether you know it or not – and I'll be claiming you when I get back.'

I smiled, but didn't answer him, and I lingered on the doorstep to watch as he strolled down the lane. Billy's kiss had certainly shaken me, but I still wasn't ready to give him an answer.

I waved as Billy turned to look at me from the corner of the lane, and then I went into the house. I was smiling to myself, about to go upstairs when a yell of rage startled me and my father shot out of the kitchen and grabbed my arm.

'You sly slut!' he growled at me, his fingers digging deep into the flesh of my upper arm. 'So that's what you've been up ter behind me back!'

'Leave off, Da, you're hurtin' me,' I cried and pulled back from him. 'What's the matter with you? I've only been out for a drink with a friend.'

'You've been out three times with that bleedin' Billy Ryan,' he muttered, his face puce with temper. 'And don't lie to me, girl, because you were seen by one of me mates.'

17

'Billy is all right,' I said rubbing at my arm where he'd hurt me. 'We went out a few times because he was on leave – but we didn't do anythin' wrong. Billy respects me. He wants to marry me.'

'I 'eard about the fight down the Pally,' Da shouted, his face working furiously. 'Makin' a show of 'imself and you with 'im. No daughter of mine is goin' around with a bloke like that.'

'Billy was defending my honour,' I said. 'Someone tried to maul me and called me names – said I was like my mother.' I looked at him defiantly. 'Besides, you're always getting into a brawl when you've been drinking. They threw you out of the Feathers last week and told you not to go back.'

Da raised his hand and struck me a heavy blow across the face, catching my lip. I gave a cry and jerked back as I tasted blood, gazing at him in horror. He had given me a clip of the ear in passing a few times when I was a child, but he'd never hit me like that before.

'You shouldn't have done that,' I said. 'You had no right to hit me like that.' I felt like crying but I was determined not to let him see me weep.

'That will teach you to cheek me,' he muttered a sullen look in his eyes. 'Your mother was a cheat and a whore – and I'll kill yer afore I let you go the same way. You mind what I say, Kathy. See that Billy Ryan again and you'll be sorry.'

He pushed past me and went out of the front door, slamming it behind him. For a moment I stood staring after him feeling shocked and numb. His rages and tempers had never really frightened me before, but now I wasn't sure what he might do next.

Two

I tossed restlessly through most of that night, sleeping hardly at all. My face hurt where my father had hit me, but it was my pride and my sense of justice that had been hurt the most. I knew I had to change things, because I wasn't going to let myself be beaten and used like so many of the women I knew. By the morning I had made up my mind.

'It's a bit desperate, Kathy,' Gran said as I finished telling her my thoughts after breakfast. She was sitting by the fire, warming her hands round a mug of scalding hot tea, her expression anxious. 'Ernie will come round in time. There's no need for yer to go rushing off like this because of a quarrel. Besides, didn't yer tell me yer had to be eighteen to enrol in the VADs? You're not old enough until your next birthday – and that's months away.'

'He hit me, Gran.' My face bore a purple bruise to prove it and I'd lain awake all night thinking about what my life would be like if I continued to go on as before. 'If I stay here he might do it again. I've seen women in the lanes that get beaten regularly on a Saturday night, and I'm never going to let a man do that to me. I look old enough to pass for eighteen, you know I do – and if they want proof I'll tell them we've lost my certificate. Lots of people I know would have difficulty proving their exact age.'

Gran acknowledged the truth of my words. In an area like ours some people didn't even bother to register the birth of a child. The narrow lanes around Dawson's Brewery had been almost a slum for years, though they were a much

19

nicer place to live now due to the influence of Joe Robinson. Not content with improving the properties he owned, he had campaigned for the old warehouses that had harboured rats and vagrants to be pulled down. There was a stretch of grass in their place by the river now and the kids played there after school. Most of the houses in the lanes had running water and inside lavatories too.

'I've never known exactly how old I am,' Gran said, looking at me sadly as she leaned forward to poke up the fire. I'd been up early to black lead the grate and scrub the stone floor, which was covered with several peg rugs Gran had made from scraps of material. 'I'll miss yer if you go, Kathy – but maybe it's for the best. Ernie's temper gets worse all the time. If he doesn't watch out Mr Dawson will get rid of him altogether, and then where will we be?'

'He only keeps him on because he thinks he was to blame for the accident. At least that's what Da says.'

'That's daft talk. Ernie has only himself to blame. He was drunk and he didn't watch what he was doing with that load. It was his own fault it slipped and caught him, breaking his leg. The break never healed properly, that's the pity of it.' Gran sighed and looked at me. 'When are you goin'?'

'It might as well be today,' I said and immediately felt guilty as I saw her expression of shock. 'That's if you're feeling well enough to manage? I could stay a few days longer if you need me?'

She shook her head. 'I'm better, Kathy. I shall miss yer, girl, but I won't stand in your way if it's what yer want – and maybe it's for the best. I should think them hospital folk will be glad of a bit of 'elp. They need all the nurses they can get from what I 'ear of things.'

'That's how I feel,' I said and kissed her cheek. 'I know I shan't be much use for a start, but I'm willing to do whatever they want and I don't mind hard work.'

'There will be 'ell to pay when Ernie knows you've gone,

but never mind that, Kathy. I'll give 'im a piece of me mind fer what he done to you.'

'Don't upset yourself over it, Gran.' I touched the bruise gingerly with one finger. 'It doesn't hurt so much now and it will soon go.'

I felt guilty as I looked at her sitting there in her chair by the kitchen range, the fire blazing and putting out so much heat it was almost unbearable on a warm day like today unless you kept the yard door open. The fire and tiny oven beside it was Gran's only method of cooking and there was usually a pot bubbling away on the top all day.

She *was* much better again now, but she wasn't a young woman and I knew she would miss my help around the house. I didn't like deserting her, yet I knew I had to get away for a while. For years I'd been aware that there was some mystery surrounding my mother, and my father's harsh remarks about her had hurt me as much as the blow to my face. He'd seemed to hate her and, for a moment as he'd looked at me, I'd felt he hated me too.

It was hurtful to have my mother's shame thrown at me like that, to feel that everyone was expecting me to behave in the same way, and I wanted to go right away from the lanes. Somewhere I wasn't known. Somewhere I could be myself and hold my head up high.

There was another life away from the lanes, and this was my opportunity to find it, to make something of myself. I knew that if I didn't take my chance now, I never would.

'So you want to be a nurse, Miss Cole?' The rather severe-looking woman behind the desk stared at me in what could only be described as a disapproving manner. 'And what makes you imagine you have the qualifications for such an important task?'

I had waited several days to get this interview and I was feeling anxious as she glanced down at my application again. If she turned me down I didn't know what I was going to do.

'I know I've got a lot to learn, miss,' I replied, meeting her forbidding gaze as steadily as I could. 'But I'm a quick learner and I don't mind how hard I work.'

'Are you indeed?' She drummed her fingers on the top of the battered-looking desk. 'Well, we shall see. You have already been accepted into the VADs, but it is up to me whether I recommend you for the nursing branch or something else.' She glanced at the papers in front of her. 'You give your age as eighteen last birthday – you are a very young eighteen, Miss Cole.'

'Am I?' She waited for me to elaborate but I didn't, lying wasn't my strong point. I had a feeling this woman would know if I tried. 'I'll work really hard, miss.'

She continued to look at me thoughtfully for some minutes.

'Yes, I think perhaps you will.' She nodded as though making up her mind. 'Very well, I'm going to put you forward. You will be sent to a hospital just outside London where they have a shortage of staff at present, and more patients than they can cope with, I'm afraid. It's under the authority of the Military and the patients are all wounded personnel from one of the Armed Forces. You understand that at first you will be doing all the menial jobs the trained nurses just don't have time for?'

'Yes, miss. All I want to do is help – whatever it is.'

'Then I shall not deny you the chance to serve, Miss Cole. Goodness knows, we need enthusiastic young women badly enough.' She stamped a paper and handed it to me. 'Take this to the desk on your way out. You will be provided with your ticket and all the necessary paperwork. You will be required to report to the duty officer on Monday morning without fail.'

'Thank you.' I took the paper she gave me gratefully, giving her a smile of thanks. 'Thank you so much for passing me.'

'Don't let me down, Miss Cole.' She gave me a wintry

smile. 'And I should let your birth certificate remain lost if I were you.'

The look in her eyes told me she had not been convinced that I was eighteen, but circumstances were such that she was willing to accept almost anyone she felt could be trusted to work and behave decently.

It wasn't surprising with the way things had been going for the past eighteen months or more. The numbers of casualties, both dead and wounded, had been rising steadily as the fighting intensified and the hospitals were stretched to breaking point.

I had no illusions as I joined the queue at the recruitment agency's reception desk. There was nothing glamorous about the job I had taken on. I was more likely to find myself emptying and scrubbing endless bedpans than smoothing the brow of a brave soldier, but at least I would feel needed and wanted. It was a chance for me, a chance to get away from the lanes and the past.

The memory of that quarrel with my father was still hurtful, but I'd made up my mind to put it behind me and look to the future. It was going to take years of hard work, but one day I would be able to call myself a nurse. I wanted to make something of myself.

'Have you been accepted for nursing training too?'

I turned as the girl spoke behind me. She was several inches shorter than me, not much more than five foot five or six at most, whereas I was nearer five foot eight, but as I looked down into blue eyes that sparkled with fun I liked her immediately. She was pretty, had soft fair hair that curled about her face appealingly, and she was clearly very excited.

'Yes – it was touch and go for a while, though; Miss Martin thought I might not be up to the work, but she accepted me in the end. I've been passed to train as a nurse, though I don't suppose I'll do much of that for a while.'

'No – but it will be worthwhile in the end,' she replied.

'Miss Martin was a bit of an old battleaxe, wasn't she? At first she said I would never stand up to the work because I'm too delicate. I told her I can eat and work like a horse, and that if she didn't pass me I'd give a false name and try again until I did get someone to pass me. That made her stare, I can tell you.' A giggle escaped her. 'Mind you, I don't suppose she had much choice really. They need girls so badly and they get an awful lot who fall by the wayside – find they can't stand the hours or the work – or simply collapse under the strain. That's what my cousin says anyway, and she has been in the Service from day one.' She held her hand out. 'I'm Alice Bowyer by the way. Ally for short.'

'Kathy Cole.' I shook her hand. 'I'm being sent to a hospital just outside London – Military-controlled, she said.'

'Me too,' Ally agreed. 'They're short of staff there. Joan says they get most of the worst cases – badly burned or crippled by loss of limbs, long-term patients, I think. They've usually been in other hospitals for some weeks or even months, poor devils. Joan says that some of them will never be fit to go home.'

'That's such a shame. My friend was telling me it's much worse out there than most of us know. The papers don't tell us the half of it, according to Billy.'

'Probably wouldn't dare.' She gave me a little push forward. 'It's your turn next. Will you wait for me? We can go for a cup of tea or something.'

'Oh yes, I should like that. We shall be able to travel together, I expect.'

Ally nodded and gave me another push. The woman behind the counter took my paper and gave me a sheaf of leaflets with my instructions and information, and a small brown packet containing a ticket for the bus.

'You'll be one of fifteen personnel catching the bus,' she told me. 'Be there on time or you'll be left behind. They don't wait for stragglers. Miss it and you'll have to make your own way.'

I thanked her and moved aside while Ally was given identical instructions. She grimaced as she joined me.

'Anyone would think we were school children,' she muttered. 'I don't know why they couldn't give us the money and let us get there ourselves.'

'We might take their money and run. Besides, it is a Military hospital and they probably want to control things their way – make sure we're not spies or something. We might be German soldiers dressed up as girls . . .'

Ally laughed. 'Daft! I thought you looked my sort. Where shall we go for a chat? I don't know this part of London too well – I'm from the other side of the river, down Finsbury way. My father has a business there and we live near the shop. Let's get something to eat, shall we? I'm starving.'

'There's a little teashop I've been using just up the road. It's not bad and they make everything themselves.'

'Do you live near here?' She looked at me curiously.

'I've got a room in the next street. It's temporary – just until we go.' I hesitated; then: 'I had a row with my father and walked out last week.'

'Oh, poor you,' Ally said and linked her arm through mine. 'My parents have been really good to me. They were expecting me to work in the shop – Dad owns a grocery business – but I told them I thought it was important to give something back to the men who were giving so much for us and they agreed.'

Ally was obviously from a better class of home than my own, but she was prepared to be friendly and it would be nice to have at least one friend in this venture.

'Your family sounds nice. I–I don't have a mother, just Gran and my father. Gran is lovely, but my father has a temper. He hit me after an argument so I left before he could do it again.'

'Good for you!' Ally hugged my arm and gave me a look of approval. 'I hate that sort of brutality. I'm glad you left home, Kathy. I think we shall be good friends.'

25

'I think so too.'

Ally smiled. 'You spoke about your friend just now. Is he a soldier?'

'Yes. His name is Billy Ryan. He's asked me to marry him, but I haven't said I will yet. I want to learn to be a nurse first – and there's no sense in planning anything until the war is over.'

'That's just how I feel,' she agreed. 'I've got a special friend too. His name is Mike Saunders. He's just been promoted to sergeant. In his last letter he said he wants to get married when this is all over, but we've agreed not to rush things.'

'Are you in love with him?' I asked her shyly. Ally nodded, a little smile of satisfaction on her mouth. I continued, feeling I could open up to her now, 'I'm not sure how I feel about Billy. I like him – and he makes me feel odd, sort of excited, when he kisses me – but I don't know if I love him enough to marry him.'

'Wait until you are sure,' Ally advised. 'There's nothing worse than being married to the wrong man. You remember me mentioning my cousin Joan?' I nodded. 'Well, she is divorced . . .'

'Never!' I stared at her in amazement.

Ally nodded solemnly. 'It caused terrible trouble in the family. But Joan said he was making her life a misery and she left him. He divorced her. He's something in the city and rich. She got absolutely nothing because he claimed she was unfaithful to him. Joan didn't care as long as she got away from him. She applied to be a nurse and then the war happened.'

Ally's sophisticated talk of divorce was an eye-opener for me. It just wouldn't have been thought of where I lived, but I was beginning to realize that the world was very different away from the lanes. A rush of excitement made me glad I had taken my courage in both hands and walked out when I did – and that I had found a new friend.

'She sounds wonderful – your cousin.'

'Joan has a lot of courage,' Ally replied seriously. 'My father says she's one of the new modern women who will emerge when this war is over. He thinks it can't be long before women are allowed to at least vote for who they want in Parliament. Joan is ahead of her time. If she hadn't wanted to be a nurse she would probably have tried to stand for Parliament herself.'

I stared at her in amazement. 'Can women do that?'

Ally shook her head. 'Not yet but one day they will – and if she lives to see it my cousin will be one of the first to join the men on the hustings.' She laughed at my look of disbelief. 'I can see I am going to have to educate you about your rights, Kathy – but for the moment I want my tea!'

The hospital was the most amazing place I had ever seen. Both Ally and I were speechless as the bus finally pulled up in the courtyard of Beckwith House.

'Good heavens,' Ally said in an awed whisper. 'We've done all right for ourselves here, Kathy. This must have been someone's private house before the war. And what a house! Mind you, I wouldn't want to live here, stuck out in the wilds like this. When they said it was outside London I didn't expect it to be this far.'

'I expect that is because they like to keep the location as secret as possible; no doubt that's why they brought us here instead of giving us the money to find our own way. It's huge, isn't it – and that's without all those temporary buildings they've put up in the grounds.'

'You mean those tin shacks we passed?' Ally grimaced. 'I'll bet you that's where they put us.'

'Well, I don't suppose we'll be staying in the main house; that's sure to be needed for the men.'

'They come first, of course.'

'Pay attention please!'

An officious-looking man in uniform was trying to line us all up. We stopped talking and waited for directions.

'Nursing recruits are to report to the Dower House. Orderlies and outside staff come with me.'

'They get the tin huts,' Ally said and grinned. 'Where do you suppose the Dower House is? Hey – where are we supposed to go? Some of us are new around here, you know. We're not all mind readers!' She got a glare from the sergeant in charge of new arrivals, but there was a murmur of agreement from some of the other girls.

'Follow that path.' He pointed to the right. 'The one between the shrubbery there. Someone will look after you when you get there. Right! Sort yourselves out, I haven't got all day. Everyone other than nursing recruits come with me.'

'Poor devils,' I whispered to Ally as several women and a couple of elderly men trooped after him. 'He's a real bully. I'm glad I'm not in his charge.' I picked up my case. 'We'd better try to find the Dower House.'

'Not very welcoming are they?'

Ally and I both turned as we heard the bored but extremely cultured voice behind us. The girl who had spoken had black hair and grey eyes and she was beautiful. Not just pretty or attractive but 'knock 'em dead' gorgeous, and the dress she was wearing looked as if it had come straight from the pages of an expensive fashion magazine.

'It's all such a bore, isn't it?' she said smiling wryly now that she had secured our attention. She offered her hand to me and I took it thinking she seemed nice enough in her way. 'I'm Eleanor Ross, by the way.'

'I'm Kathy and this is Ally – Alice Bowyer.'

'I'm not in the least bored,' Ally retorted with a sparkle in her eyes. I could sense her hostility towards the other girl immediately. 'Why did you join if you didn't want to come?'

'Daddy insisted,' she replied and pulled a face. 'It's good for his public image to have a daughter doing her bit. I'm lucky. He chased my poor brother into the Navy as soon as this stupid war started. Paul hates every moment of it. He's a talented musician and that's all he wants to do, but he wasn't given a choice.'

'What does *Daddy* do?' Ally asked in an acid tone.

'He's a parliamentary secretary,' Eleanor replied. 'Very patriotic and filthy rich. One daren't refuse to do as he asks or one might be cut off without a penny.'

'And that would be dreadful for one, wouldn't it?' Ally glared at her with dislike. 'Come on, Kathy. We don't want to bother with her sort. She doesn't belong with the rest of us.'

Ally took my arm and marched me away down the path some of the other girls had already taken. I glanced back at Eleanor Ross feeling a bit sorry for her. She looked unhappy and was vainly struggling with three heavy suitcases. I was considering whether to risk Ally's disapproval and help her when a young man in a white coat approached Eleanor. He was good-looking, tall, had dark hair and clean-cut features that immediately triggered something in my memory.

'Let me give you a hand?' he offered. 'You'll never get all this stuff to the Dower House alone. You've brought rather a lot, haven't you?'

'I wasn't sure what I would need.' She gave him a flashing smile. 'This is very kind of you, Mr . . .?'

'Dr,' he corrected. 'I'm not a consultant so you call me doctor – Tom O'Rourke off duty.'

Ally had looked back to see what had caught my interest. She scowled as she saw the very attractive man speaking to Eleanor.

'Trust her to get her claws into a terrific-looking bloke five minutes after we get here! That sort always know how to get their own way.'

'I think I know him,' I said as we started walking again. I could hear Eleanor talking to Dr Tom O'Rourke as they followed behind, though I couldn't quite catch what they were saying because they were trailing some way back down the path. 'I'm not sure, because I haven't seen him for ages, but I think he used to live near me at home. I know his sister well. She's always been really nice to me, because she delivered me when I was born.'

Ally gave me a curious glance. 'You'll have to introduce me when you get a chance. We can't let Miss Stuck Up Madam get all the best men, can we?'

'What about your boyfriend? I thought you were thinking about marrying him?'

'That's when the war is over,' she said and grinned naughtily. 'I intend to have some fun in the meantime. Mike doesn't expect me to sit at home and twiddle my thumbs every night – and if he does he's mistaken.'

I smiled and let the subject drop. I was in no position to introduce her to Tom O'Rourke. He probably wouldn't remember me. I was still a snotty-nosed kid at school when he'd gone off to college. I remembered people talking about it, saying he was lucky to be alive because of the illness he'd had in childhood. The family was well liked and they had all wished him luck. He'd obviously done all right for himself, and it was an odd sort of coincidence me coming to train at this particular hospital.

I forgot about Dr O'Rourke as we arrived at the Dower House to find it a scene of friendly chaos and confusion. When some of the fuss had died down, we discovered that there were only three rooms to accommodate ten newcomers. It meant that we would be three to a bedroom and one of us was going to have to share with the senior nurses, which was something no one seemed to want to do, hence the argument.

The first girls to arrive had sorted themselves out apart from one girl who was looking for two others to share. She looked at us uncertainly as we signed the register.

'Will you share with me?' she asked. 'There's one other girl to come but she hasn't turned up yet.'

'Oh, she's busy chatting to one of the doctors,' Ally

said. 'Yes, we'll share – won't we, Kathy? What's your name?'

'Sally – Sally Baker,' she said and looked relieved. 'I don't want to go in with the seniors. They are bound to be superior and look down on us, especially those who were nursing before the war. Apparently, they think we're all useless.'

'I suppose we are for a start,' I said. 'We've got to learn, Sally – but I agree it is better to be with other recruits. We can all cry on each other's shoulder when Matron ticks us off.'

'Yes, that's what I thought.' She smiled shyly. 'I'm so nervous – are you? I'm sure I shall make lots of mistakes, and I do want to do well. I've got two brothers in the Army, and a . . . friend.'

'We've all got someone out there,' Ally said. 'But even if we hadn't, we would want to help. I hope they are going to let us do something useful and not just scrub floors.'

'There will be plenty of that,' Sally said. 'I've got the key. Shall we go up now and see what the room is like?'

Ally followed her to the foot of the stairs. I glanced back and saw that Eleanor Ross had just arrived and was being told the situation. She caught up with me as I began to climb the stairs.

'You couldn't give me a hand with one of these cases, Kathy?'

'Yes, of course.' I took the case she offered; it was very heavy and I grimaced. 'What on earth have you got in here?'

'Clothes and books,' she said and looked apologetic. 'I thought it might be as well to have something to read in the evenings. It's bound to be deadly dull. Dr O'Rourke says there's a Military base a few miles down the road and they give a dance every month and invite us over, but apart from that there's nothing much. Just a trip to the pub or dinner if you're lucky, and the occasional film show over at the base again. But that's bound to be something we've seen in London months ago, of course.'

31

'I expect we'll be too busy and too tired to think about anything else for a while anyway,' I said and laughed as I saw her expression. 'Oh, poor Eleanor. This is awful for you, isn't it? It really wasn't fair of your father to make you do this.'

I was surprised to see a faint flush in her cheeks.

'Take no notice of my moaning, Kathy. I don't mean half of what I say. I expect I shall enjoy it all once I get started – and it's probably time I did something for someone else. Daddy says I'm spoiled and I expect he's perfectly right.'

At the top of the stairs we paused and she thanked me for my help before we parted. 'I can manage these now, thanks. I hope we'll be friends?' she said hesitantly. 'I know your friend Ally doesn't approve of me.'

'Ally's all right. She'll change her mind when she gets to know you.'

We parted and I hurried after the others. The room was furnished with three beds, each with a small cupboard for our possessions, and a rather spotty mirror on the wall.

Ally had already bagged the bed at the far end. Sally asked me which of the other two I wanted and I told her to take her pick. She chose the middle, which left me near the door.

'What made you lag behind with that stuck-up Ross woman?' Ally asked with a frown. I sensed that she would rather have had me sleeping next to her and was annoyed that I had let Sally choose. 'You should've let her carry her own cases.'

'I didn't mind. She isn't so bad really. It's just that she feels awkward and strange in a new place.'

'Don't we all?' Sally chirped in. 'I felt like a fish out of water until you two turned up. I've never been anywhere like this before. Whoever owns it must be rich, a bit different to where I live, I can tell you.' Ally immediately started to ask her questions about her life and family, and the subject was turned. We had time only to finish unpacking our things before a girl in the heavy, ugly uniform of the VADs came to fetch us.

'My name is Nurse Millie Smith and I've been sent to show you around,' she said with a cheerful smile. 'You will all be issued with uniforms and Matron will give you a welcoming speech at three – so you had better look sharp.'

Millie's arrival effectively cut short all small talk. We hurried after her as she rounded up all the new recruits and led us first to a large room where we collected our kit. Then, once we had sorted ourselves out, and amidst a great deal of moaning and laughter, dressed in the unflattering clothes we'd been given, she took us on a whirlwind tour of the main building.

As we'd first thought, it had once been a beautiful private home but was now forlorn, stripped down to bare walls and very basic. The wards had been painted in dark cream and green gloss paint, though the bedrooms allocated to certain patients seemed to have more home comforts.

'The men in the private rooms are probably going to be here for ages,' Millie explained as she gave us a peep into one that was presently empty. 'This belonged to a Major Robinson – he died yesterday. We're expecting a new patient this evening.'

'Do many of the patients die?'

Millie looked at me in silence for a moment, considering my question. 'We get some deaths. You have to remember, these men are seriously ill or they wouldn't be here – but most have been given life-saving treatment before they are brought to us. Our patients are here to rest and recover from the terrible ordeal they've suffered. Some will leave eventually – others will survive but never be well enough to go home.'

'That's sad,' one of the other girls said. 'Will they always have to stay here?'

'Here – or another nursing home. A private one, probably, if their family can afford it. Some of the patients are officers, but we get men from the ranks as well.'

'So I should hope,' Ally muttered beside me. 'Where do we work?'

'Matron will explain,' Millie replied. 'I'm just here to show you where everything is so that you don't get lost.'

We were shown the way to the operating theatre, though not allowed inside it. Millie warned us that there were strict restrictions about entering the sterile areas.

'New recruits spend most of their time fetching and carrying on the wards, attending lectures – and of course your favourite place, the sluice room. You'll get to know that very well, I promise you.'

Groans and laughter greeted this announcement but nobody really minded. We were here to help wherever we could. Already we were banding together, feeling a shared interest in doing our very best for the unfortunate men who had been brought to this place.

We visited the common room, where some of the patients had congregated, and had our first glimpses of the appalling injuries these men had suffered. Some had lost limbs, others had burns to their faces and hands, but these were the luckier ones who had begun to recover and we were warned that we would see much worse in the private rooms.

'Who have you brought us now, Millie love? More lambs to the slaughter?'

A soldier in striped pyjamas with his army coat over the top came up to us on crutches. He had lost a leg from the knee down but was grinning cheerfully, apparently unconcerned by his loss. He looked all the new recruits over, his eyes coming eventually to rest on me.

'Lovely despite that awful dress,' he said. 'Eyes a man could drown in. I'm Sergeant Steve Harley – what do they call you other than beautiful?'

'Kathy,' I replied. 'But they don't call me beautiful.'

'Blind or mad,' he quipped with a grin. 'Want to be my partner for the bath chair race this weekend?'

'Yes – what is it?'

Sergeant Harley chuckled. 'Lucky girl! You get to push me right round the house faster than any of the others in the line-up – and let me tell you, I shall expect to win.'

'I'll do my best.' I glanced at Millie. 'If it's allowed?'

'Provided you're not on duty,' she said. 'Matron frowns on such activities, of course, but the doctors are usually there to cheer us on. I shall be taking part myself.'

'You're on then,' I told Sergeant Harley. 'Provided I'm not on duty when it happens.'

'You can get someone to switch,' he told me. 'Ask Millie, she knows how to get round the rules.'

'I'll let you know,' I said and followed the group as they moved on.

After our visit to the common room we all had a late lunch in the canteen, which was used by both the doctors and nurses. The food wasn't exactly like home cooking but it was just about edible and the tea was hot and strong, just like Gran made it.

'Awful!' Ally complained as she picked at her shepherd's pie but Eleanor Ross cleared her plate and said it was no worse than their cook served up at home. I wasn't sure whether she was just putting on a brave face or not.

Lunch over, we had half an hour to ourselves before being taken to Matron's welcome talk. She was a large woman with iron-grey hair and a stern manner, and her speech was more of a lecture than a welcome. We were told that we were expected to work hard and behave ourselves, then warned not to be late on duty.

'You will find a duty roster at the Dower House,' she told us. 'It is up to you to check where to report and at what time. Recruits who arrive late for duty will be reprimanded. We expect certain standards from all our nursing staff. Please make sure you keep to them.'

'Phew – she's a right old battleaxe,' Ally said as we were at last released to settle in, having been told we were now free for the rest of the day. 'I wouldn't want to get on the wrong side of her!'

'No, nor me.'

Matron was strict, but I supposed she had to be. She had a lot of young women under her charge, and that couldn't be easy at the best of times. I just hoped I wouldn't do anything to displease her.

I was pleased to see that I was working on Saturday morning and then free until six in the evening on Sunday.

'Oh good, that means I can push Sergeant Harley in the race. It starts at four on Sunday afternoon so that gives me plenty of time to get ready.'

'More fool you,' Ally retorted. 'It's going to be hard work. Rather you than me.'

She pulled a face but I got the idea that she was a bit miffed because I'd been picked to take part and she hadn't.

The next few days were the most hectic of my life. We worked seven-hour shifts on the wards fetching and carrying for the nurses and patients, but we also had to take turns scrubbing endless floors. On Friday I came off duty at five feeling tired after three hours in the sluice room. I was looking forward to putting my feet up before supper but as I was about to leave the main building someone called to me.

'Miss Cole, could I have a word please?'

I stopped and turned, staring in surprise as a doctor came sprinting up to me. For a moment I was afraid I'd done something wrong and then I saw he was smiling – and that I knew him. It was a long time since I'd seen him in the lanes and I hadn't been sure when I heard him talking to Eleanor Ross, but now I was certain.

'Yes, Dr O'Rourke? Is there something you wanted?'

'You *are* Kathy Cole . . . little Kathy from the lanes,' he said. 'What a nice surprise to find you here. When Sergeant Harley told me about the girl who had offered to help him,

I wondered if it could possibly be the same person. Bridget wrote in her last letter that she'd heard you had joined the Service. How are you getting on?'

'Oh, managing,' I said and smiled ruefully. I wasn't sure that I liked being remembered as little Kathy from the lanes. 'I knew it was going to be hard work but we never seem to stop.'

He nodded, eyes bright with amusement. 'They work you girls hard; it's part of the initiation. But at least you'll have some fun on Sunday. Sergeant Harley wanted to be sure you were still up for it?'

'Oh yes. I was going to pop in this evening and have a word with him, find out what it's all about.'

'It's sheer nonsense,' he replied. 'But some of them take it seriously and the competition is fierce.' He arched his brows, which I'd noticed were fine and nicely shaped. He was very attractive altogether and his smile was somehow easing my tiredness. 'Have you ever pushed one of those chairs?'

'Yes. I had to take a patient down to the common room yesterday. It wasn't easy . . . those chairs can be awkward to manoeuvre.'

'No, they aren't easy, and you'll find it much worse round the building, especially on the gravel. My advice is to take it slowly for that part and put a spurt on when you get back to hard ground. Otherwise you might get bogged down.'

'Thanks. I'll remember. It was good of you to give me some advice, doctor. Sergeant Harley told me he expects to win so I want to do my best for him.'

'Yes, mustn't let the patients down. They will all be watching the outcome eagerly.' He smiled and nodded, his bluish grey eyes studying me thoughtfully. 'I shall be there to cheer you on, Kathy. Good luck.'

'Thank you, Doctor.'

'Right then. Get off and put your feet up for a while.'

His smile made my heart jump with excitement, and I felt pleased that he had taken the trouble to seek me out and wish me luck. Suddenly, I was looking forward to the race on Sunday and what might come after it . . .

Three

'Come on, Kathy!' I heard Ally's voice screaming above the others as I turned the last corner with my chair and patient still intact despite a bumpy ride. We were lagging behind the leader, who had seemed to fly over the first part of the course. 'Don't let them beat you!'

'Push harder,' Sergeant Harley urged me on as we saw our quarry just ahead. 'We'll catch them if you put your back into it, Kathy. Come on, don't give up. Why are you slowing down?'

'We've got to cross that gravel yet . . .'

Ahead of us I could see Nurse Peters struggling to get through the loose gravel. She had glanced at me over her shoulder and then plunged in recklessly, obviously fearing that I was about to catch up with her, and now the wheels of her chair had become embedded in the gravel just as Tom O'Rourke had warned.

I entered the stretch of gravel gingerly. Nurse Peters was digging at the gravel that had bunched beneath the wheels of her chair with her bare hands and I noticed that the chair she was using had small wheel arches and looked hopelessly stuck.

'Put a move on,' Sergeant Harley said. 'She's getting it free . . .'

'We have to go carefully – and if she rushes she'll get stuck again.'

Nurse Peters scowled as I wheeled my chair carefully past her. It took patience to maintain my slow pace until we were through the gravel and on to solid ground again, and then, to the sound of cheering, I started to push for all I was worth.

Nurses, patients, and quite a few doctors were at the finishing line urging us on. I was breathing hard, feeling the strain of pushing a considerable weight for some distance. Behind me, I could hear the sound of pursuing feet and the rattle of Nurse Peters' chair. Then I heard a crashing noise and looked back to see her chair collapse as a wheel came off, but another nurse was coming up fast behind her and I had to put a spurt on to keep my lead. Then we were at the finishing line and I felt a surge of triumph as I realized we had won.

'Well done, Cole,' I heard praise on the lips of others. 'It's about time someone else won. Nurse Peters has had it her own way for too long.'

'Clever girl, Kathy,' Sergeant Harley said. 'I didn't think about the gravel trap.'

'That was brilliant, Kathy.'

'Well done, Kathy.'

I swung round as I heard Tom O'Rourke's voice. He was smiling at me, obviously pleased with the result.

'I took your advice, Doctor.'

'I knew you'd had help.' Nurse Peters looked at me half-admiringly and half-annoyed. 'But it was a good race. I shall know to watch out for you in future.'

'There's always next time,' I said. 'It was a good race . . . fun.'

'We're having a few drinks in the common room,' Sergeant Harley said. 'You'll come and celebrate, won't you, Kathy?'

'I shall have to stick to lemonade. I'm on duty in an hour. I mustn't be late.'

'Plenty of time. You've got to celebrate your victory.'

It was an excited group who trouped into the common room to toast the victory. I hadn't realized quite how important the event was and I was amazed by all the fuss everyone made of me. The praise for my tactics was overwhelming and I glowed from all the attention while feeling a bit of a cheat. After all, it was Tom O'Rourke who had told me about the gravel trap. He had watched the race but didn't seem to have joined the celebrations, which left me feeling slightly disappointed.

It was half an hour after the race when the laughter in the common room suddenly stilled. Everyone was gazing towards the door and following the general direction my heart jerked as I saw Matron standing there watching us.

'So much noise,' she said. 'You are disturbing my patients, ladies and gentlemen, and some of you are needed on duty.'

Her eyes seemed to dwell on me with what I fancied was disapproval as she spoke, and then she turned and walked out leaving a hushed silence behind her.

'Spoilsport,' someone muttered resentfully but the party atmosphere had gone.

'I'd better go,' I said, glancing at Sergeant Harley. 'I'm on duty soon and I dare not be late.'

'Come and visit me soon. We might have a drink or something. I owe you a night out, Nurse Cole.'

'I'm not a nurse yet. Just a volunteer.' I smiled at him. 'It was good fun. I'm glad we won. And I shall come to see you when I can.'

I hurried away to my room to change and tidy myself. My hair had worked loose from the tight roll I usually wore for duty and my face was flushed. It wasn't surprising that Matron had looked so disapproving. My appearance wasn't up to the standards she expected from her staff.

As I made my way back towards the main building I saw Dr O'Rourke coming towards me and my heart began to thump with excitement.

'Back to work and sanity now, Kathy?'

'Yes, Doctor. It was fun but I'm on duty soon.'

'It cheers the patients up,' he said. 'Even those who can't get to watch like to bet on the outcome. You're the first probationer to win.'

'Only because you told me how.'

'Oh no, it was courage and determination,' he replied easily. 'But we might go for a drink to celebrate one evening when we're both free?' His suggestion surprised me so much that I didn't answer immediately. 'Talk about old times, what's happening in the lanes . . . ?'

'Oh . . . Yes, thank you.' I blushed and my knees went oddly weak. 'Yes, I should like that. I'm free on Wednesday or Friday evening this week.'

'I'm free on Wednesday so we'll make it then. Pick you up outside the Dower House at seven. OK?'

'Yes, lovely.' My mouth was dry with excitement. 'I'd better go . . .'

'Yes. Go on then, and don't worry so much, Kathy. Matron doesn't bite.'

'She might,' I said, remembering her expression. 'Bye now.'

After we had parted I had to hurry. There were still five minutes before I was due on my ward but Sister expected us to be early and would look pointedly at her watch if we were a second over our time. I was hardly going to make it. Fearing a reprimand, I began to run.

'What are you doing? Running in corridors is strictly forbidden!'

I stopped and swung round guiltily at the sound of Matron's voice, waiting in trepidation for her approach. Now I was in for it!

'I'm sorry, Matron. I was delayed and didn't want to be late.'

Her brow furrowed. 'Rules are there for a purpose, Miss Cole. You could endanger a patient by careless behaviour. Always take your time and think what you are doing. Remember that in future.'

'Yes, Matron. I am very sorry.'

'Very well. I shall not punish you this time, but do not let success go to your head, Miss Cole. You are here to work and everything else comes second to that duty – do you understand?'

'Yes, Matron.'

'Go along now or you will be late.'

I turned and began to walk at a sedate pace towards the ward, feeling her eyes boring into my back. She must think I was a harum-scarum girl with little or no sense.

'And congratulations on winning, Miss Cole.'

I heard her voice as I turned the corner but did not dare to look back. Had she really said those words or was I dreaming?

Sister Norton glanced up from her desk as I entered the ward. She glanced at her watch and frowned but said nothing about the fact that I was three minutes late.

'The patient in number five requested a bedpan some minutes ago. Make sure that he is comfortable, Miss Cole.'

'Yes, Sister.'

I hurried off to do her bidding, knowing that I had a black mark against me. Matron had warned me and I would need to work extra hard to scrub out any idea that I had let my success in the race go to my head.

'You're the first VAD ever to win,' Ally said to me the next morning at breakfast. 'Apparently most get bogged down in the gravel – especially those who haven't entered before. Nurse Peters is blaming her chair. She says it was just bad luck that she got stuck, and that you had help, but that's sour grapes.'

'She was OK to me. Anyway, I was told to be careful in the gravel so I did have help of a kind.'

'Who told you – Dr O'Rourke?' Ally raised her brows at me. 'You'll have Eleanor Ross breathing fire down your neck. She thinks he's her property because he took her out one night.'

'He's asked me out for a drink on Wednesday.'

'You're joking?' Ally stared at me and then chuckled. 'That really will upset Miss Hoity-Toity.'

'I don't see why. It's just a drink to talk about people we both know. I told you he used to live in Farthing Lane.'

'I thought he went off to a fancy school when you were just a kid?'

'Yes, he did – but he visits his sister now and then. I didn't think he would remember me. I was surprised when he wished me luck before the race.'

'Well, well . . .' Ally looked mischievous. 'You're a dark horse, Kathy Cole.'

'It's just a drink,' I giggled as she looked disbelieving. 'But yes, I do like him – quite a lot.'

'You watch it, Kathy! Men who look as good as Dr O'Rourke aren't to be trusted. Besides, what about Billy Ryan? I thought he'd asked you to marry him?'

'Yes, he did – but I didn't say I would.'

'You didn't say you wouldn't either.'

'No . . .' I shook my head at her. 'It's just a drink, Ally. Dr O'Rourke isn't interested in me that way. He's just being friendly, that's all.'

'We'll see.' She grinned wickedly. 'You be careful, Kathy, that's all I'm saying.'

'Well, if I had any idea of grandeur this morning's duty will knock it out of me. I'm scrubbing floors.'

'Poor you,' Ally said. 'I've got seven hours on the ward and lectures all afternoon.'

We both attended lectures, which were more absorbing than we'd imagined as they dealt with the practical side of nursing rather than theory. We were shown how to read thermometers and had our first go at taking each other's pulse. We were also given detailed instructions in recognizing signs of serious distress in patients.

'Now that *was* interesting,' Ally remarked as we left the lecture room afterwards. 'For the first time I really felt that I was being trained as a nurse and not just used as a skivvy.'

I felt just as she did, although it all seemed a little daunting.

There was much more to nursing than I had imagined at the beginning.

'There's such a long way to go. But at least we've made a start. I'm going to read up all the information I can about the vital signs in the pamphlets they gave us. I know we shan't be expected to deal with a crisis ourselves for years, but you never know when you might see something that ought to be reported to a senior nurse.'

Ally nodded, looking serious. 'There was a death on our ward this morning. The dreadful thing is I'd been having a joke with him earlier. He had had both legs amputated but I thought he was getting over it. He was talking about getting false limbs and looking forward to going home – and then when I came back from the sluice room there was a crowd around his bed.'

She looked upset and I put an arm about her waist. 'I'm sure they did all they could, Ally.'

'Yes, they did what they could, but it was so sudden – a blood clot, apparently. Sister told me it often happens after a serious operation.' She frowned. 'Maybe if I'd known what to look for when I was talking to him earlier . . . ?'

'You can't blame yourself. There were experienced nurses and doctors looking after him. If they weren't aware of anything wrong, how could you be?'

'Of course I couldn't, but it's sad, isn't it?'

'Yes, it's very sad.' I squeezed her waist. 'Come on, let's go and have a cup of tea to cheer ourselves up. You'll never guess what I managed to buy in the village shop on Saturday morning – a packet of shortbread biscuits. If you promise to stop moping, I'll share them with you.'

'You're a good friend, Kathy,' she said, cheering up. 'You were lucky. When I asked for biscuits they said they hadn't got any.'

'Well, it's knowing how to ask,' I said and grinned at her. 'The old man who serves there calls me sweetheart. I think he fancies me a bit.'

'He's old enough to be your granddad,' Ally said but she was laughing, her good humour restored.

'You look lovely,' Ally declared as I fidgeted with my dress for the umpteenth time while getting ready for my date with Tom O'Rourke. 'Besides, I thought you said this was just a drink to talk about old times and not important?'

'Of course it isn't, but I want to look my best.'

'You always look good,' Ally said. 'You've got the perfect English rose complexion and your hair is a lovely colour. You can see it's natural and not dyed.'

'Yes, I'm lucky with my hair.' I gave it a little pat. 'I never have to do much with it. After a wash it just waves naturally.'

'Well, don't gloat. Just because you're going out with the best-looking fellow in the place.'

She was grinning at me but I caught a faint note of envy in her voice. Ally had already been out with three different men since our arrival, but moaned that she hadn't really enjoyed herself with any of them.

'Don't worry,' I told her. 'You'll find someone you like soon.'

'I'm not sure . . .' She bit her lip anxiously. 'It's daft, but I can't help thinking about Mike the whole time. He usually writes as soon as he gets back to his base, but he hasn't this time. I'm worried about him, Kathy. Supposing he's been hurt – or killed?'

'Perhaps he's just been too busy to write,' I suggested. 'If there was bad news someone would let you know.'

'Yes, I expect you're right. I'm being silly.' She pulled a face. 'Go on then, you lucky thing. Go and meet Dr O'Rourke. And stop looking so nervous!'

'I'll try.' I gave her a quick hug. 'You try to stop worrying about Mike.'

She grinned and shook her head as I left. I went downstairs and saw Tom O'Rourke standing just outside the front door. It was a pleasant summer evening and he was wearing beige slacks, a brown shirt, a deep fawn sweater slung over his shoulder. I thought he looked like a star from the movies and my heart did a rapid somersault.

'Kathy,' he murmured, his eyes going over me with approval. 'You look . . . very nice. That colour blue suits you.'

I was wearing a simple blue dress with a tucked bodice, short sleeves and a white collar. It was good to get out of uniform for a while, but I knew the dress was a bit girlish. I'd had it new just before I left home and the style wasn't what I would have chosen for myself, but I hadn't been able to get myself anything new yet. Ally had spoken of us spending our first leave together at her home, and I intended to buy some more suitable clothes, but that wouldn't be for ages.

'I thought we would walk to the village.' Something flickered in Tom's eyes as they went over me. 'You hardly look old enough to drink in the pub, Kathy.'

'It's just this dress. Gran bought it for me. It's too childish but it's my best.'

He nodded and smiled. 'Very pretty. You look older in your uniform.'

I bit my lip as I sensed a withdrawal in him and realized he wasn't pleased by the way I looked. Perhaps I should have worn my hair up instead of letting it hang loose? It was too late now. I should just have to hope my youthful appearance hadn't put him off completely.

'Have you written to Mrs Cole yet?' he asked as we began to walk in the direction of the village. 'Bridget told me that she was worried because she hadn't heard.'

There was a note of reprimand in his voice that touched a nerve. Did he imagine I was an irresponsible child? The evening I'd been anticipating so eagerly had suddenly become disappointing. He had said it was just a drink to talk about people we both knew but I had expected more than this somehow. I'd thought there was something between us. Now he seemed to have become the grand doctor figure being kind to a new recruit.

That was exactly what I was, of course, but I'd hoped for a very different outcome to the evening. We spent half an hour talking about people in the lanes, and then progressed to the hospital. He became passionate then and I glimpsed a man I could admire as he spoke about his work and hopes.

By nine o'clock he had me back outside the Dower House.

'It was a pleasant evening, Kathy,' he said offering me his hand. We shook hands as if we were polite strangers. 'We must do it again one day.'

'Yes. Thank you, Dr O'Rourke.'

He frowned, hesitated as though wanting to say more, then turned and walked off in the direction of the hospital. So that was that then! My heart flopped all the way to my boots as I stood watching him. He simply wasn't interested in me as a woman. In fact he thought of me as a child.

Ally looked surprised when I walked in.

'You're back early? I thought you would be ages yet.'

'I told you – it was just a friendly gesture. I'm a kid he used to see in the lane years ago.'

'It's that dress,' Ally said. 'It's too young for you. I would've lent you something but mine wouldn't fit.'

'I don't suppose it would have made any difference. He remembers me as a kid from down the lane and always will.'

'Well, there's plenty more fish in the sea. Sally says there's a dance on next Saturday in the village hall. We'll see if we can borrow a dress for you and we'll all go.'

Ally's attitude was the right one, of course. She seemed to have got over her personal worries for the time being, but I was still smarting from my disappointment that evening.

Eleanor Ross came up trumps over the dress. She was on duty that evening and gave me a choice of three, because, as she said, she wouldn't be needing them herself.

'I brought far too much with me,' she told me with a wry look. 'But maybe these will come in useful after all. Try them all on and see which one suits you best, Kathy.'

'May I really?'

'Yes, of course. I never say what I don't mean. The green silk is lovely on, but the yellow brocade might suit you better. I'm not sure about the black.'

The black dress was fabulous, very slinky and cut close to the body. It had tiny shoulder straps, the bodice heavily beaded with jet. I knew at once that it suited me, but it was very sophisticated and so obviously expensive that I was afraid to choose it.

I finally settled on the green silk. It was a simple dress cut low on the shoulders with tiny puffed sleeves and a full skirt that just flirted above my ankles. No doubt it had cost almost as much as the black dress, but I sensed that Eleanor was pleased I hadn't chosen her favourite.

'That one looks really good on you, Kathy,' she said. 'We're very much the same size but I could put a couple of tucks in the bodice for you.'

'Won't that spoil your dress for you?'

'No – besides, you may want to borrow it again. I've got loads more at home.'

Eleanor had never made any secret of her father's wealth, but it was hard to imagine anyone having a wardrobe full of clothes like these. I felt privileged to be wearing the green dress for the dance that evening, but a little anxious in case I should spoil it.

Several of the nurses and VADs were going as a group. Someone had fixed up a bus to take the party, and twenty of us piled into it. The men were mostly junior doctors, though there was also one of the porters and two flying officers, who had received burns to their faces and hands but were recovering now. The scars they would bear for the rest of their lives were terrible but the girls had all seen worse cases and no one took any notice. For these particular officers a dance in the village was the first step towards going home and a normal life.

One of them had become engaged to a nurse who had looked after him from the beginning. It was against the rules for nurses to marry, of course, but Julia Lane would be leaving when her fiancé was well enough to go home, and then they planned to marry. Their romance had pleased everyone, because in the midst of all the pain and suffering in the hospital it proved that life went on and sometimes people found happiness again.

We were certainly a merry group that evening, chattering and laughing all the way to the dance. Held in the village hall, it had been put on especially for the hospital crowd and the local people had taken trouble to decorate the place with flowers and streamers, making a rather dreary room look bright. A refreshment bar providing soft drinks, tea and beer had been set up at one end.

The dancing started as soon as we arrived, all the girls from the hospital finding themselves in great demand. Several men in uniform were present, having come from an Army base some ten miles away.

One young corporal introduced himself to me as Terry Cooke.

'I haven't seen you here before. Are you at the hospital?'

'Yes, a very new recruit,' I replied, responding instinctively to the admiring gleam in his eyes. 'This is my first time at the dance.'

'I've been several times. I've been stuck here for ages. I was out at the beginning but they shipped me back with a leg wound and I spend most of my time behind a desk now.'

'Oh, poor you,' I sympathized. 'Have you asked for active service?'

'Yes, but they say I'm useful where I am.'

I danced several times with Terry but he wasn't my only partner. Eleanor's dress seemed to have worked a little magic and I didn't have to sit out one dance.

'This is fun, isn't it?' Ally said, her cheeks pink with a flush of excitement. 'I'm enjoying myself.'

She hadn't sat down all the evening either, and I noticed she also danced with Terry Cooke several times.

It was such fun that I didn't notice Tom O'Rourke arrive. I didn't even know he was there until I heard his voice speaking my name.

'You look wonderful this evening, Kathy.' I turned to face him, my heart racing. He was so attractive and he made me feel so odd – alive and excited. His eyes went over me with obvious approval. 'That dress really suits you – makes you look grown up.'

My pleasure faded as swiftly as it had flared. How dare he be so patronizing? If the dress was all that he found attractive then it wasn't me he was complimenting.

'Eleanor Ross lent it to me for the evening. I could never afford anything like this. I'm just Kathy Cole from the lanes – the scruffy kid your sister took pity on sometimes. If I look different tonight it's just an illusion.'

The tone of my voice was harsh and he looked startled, as if wondering what he'd done to annoy me. I was about to apologize, then something made me draw back.

'Excuse me. I promised this dance to someone.'

My head held high, I walked away from him. I wasn't sure why I felt so angry with him but his attitude had touched a raw spot. I didn't want to be treated as if I were still that kid from the lanes. I was training to be a nurse and people had to accept me for what I was now. No one else thought of me as a child – so why should Tom O'Rourke?

For the rest of the evening I studiously avoided looking in his direction. It was easy enough to ignore him because I never lacked for a partner and I was having a lovely time. I didn't even mind when Ally told me about the gorgeous girl he'd brought to the dance.

'She was really lovely. Not from the hospital, though. I've never seen her before anyway.'

No – nor have I,' I admitted, acknowledging that I had noticed them dancing despite my efforts not to.

'She's not from your way then?'

'No. At least I don't know her.'

She looked much too sophisticated and well dressed to be from our way, and was obviously far more Tom O'Rourke's type than I could ever be.

It shouldn't have bothered me one way or the other, but as I lay in bed that night I couldn't help wondering about the very attractive young woman Dr O'Rourke had brought with him. With someone like that as a partner it was hardly likely that he would be impressed by me, even in my borrowed dress.

Over the next days and weeks I struggled to dismiss Tom O'Rourke from my mind. It had been foolish of me to feel humiliated by a remark that was probably meant well, and there had never been a chance for me anyway. Gossip was rife in the hospital and most people said the romance between Dr O'Rourke and Barbara Retford was serious.

'Eleanor was disappointed,' Ally told me over supper one evening. 'Apparently she fancied him herself.'

'Well, she stood more of a chance than I did,' I said. 'He liked her taste in clothes better than mine.'

'Apparently Babs Retford is the daughter of a consultant he trained under. They've known each other for ages. The word is that they plan to get married in the summer.'

Ally was a mine of information. She went out most evenings when she wasn't on duty and seemed to have settled for friendship rather than romance. Mike's letters had begun to arrive regularly now and she had stopped worrying over him – at least she didn't say much these days.

Billy Ryan's mother forwarded a postcard to me from him. I'd sent him a couple of long, newsy letters but his card didn't mention them, merely saying he was all right and hoped I was. Gran had replied to my letter to her but hadn't written again, but then, I knew she wasn't good at things like that. She would probably need a little help to read the letters I sent her, and I thought she might take them to Bridget O'Rourke – which was why I always told her about all the fun I was having. Not that Bridget would tell her brother, of course.

It was silly of me to feel jealous of his lovely girlfriend, but I couldn't help it and I was relieved when he didn't bring her to the dance in the village a month later. He didn't come at all, and I heard that he had been transferred to another hospital; there was a rumour that he might have gone to France, but no one seemed to know for sure. He certainly hadn't bothered to say goodbye to me – but then, why should he? I hadn't exactly encouraged a friendship between us.

So that was the end of any hopes I might have had concerning the good-looking Dr O'Rourke. After a few weeks I discovered that I could laugh at myself. It was silly of me to have fancied him in the first place. The best thing I could do was to put him out of my mind and get on with the job I was paid for!

I had my choice of young men willing to take me out if I wanted, though more often than not I chose to stay in and read a book or talk to my friends. Quite often I lingered in the canteen in the evenings, where Eleanor Ross joined me. I had come to like her a lot, and to discover that she wasn't at all the spoiled darling of a rich father Ally thought her.

Ally still didn't like her, and I noticed that sparks flew each time they met. They didn't actually have a flaming row, but Ally was always picking at her, seeming as if she couldn't leave her alone.

Eleanor and I sat cross-legged on my bed, sharing a bottle of wine, one evening. Ally was on the night shift, and Sally had gone out for the evening. We had both agreed that we were too tired to go anywhere, and Eleanor had suggested she bring a bottle of wine up so that we could spend some time together.

'This was a good idea of yours,' I said. 'And this wine is delicious, better than anything I've had before.'

Eleanor smiled. 'I thought you would like it – it's a good medium French white, not too sweet and not too dry.'

'Well, I definitely approve.' I held my glass out for more. 'It's always port and lemon for the ladies where I come from, but from now on I'm a wine drinker.'

'And just the weeniest bit tipsy,' Eleanor said gurgling with affectionate laughter. 'Oh, it is good to unwind sometimes, isn't it, Kathy?'

'Yes. I'm enjoying myself.'

'Do you ever think what you'll do when this dreadful war is over?'

'I'm not sure. I might get married – or I might stay on in nursing. What are you going to do, Eleanor?'

'I don't think I want to marry, not for years and years anyway. I've never met a man I wanted to go to bed with for the rest of my life – although I've seen a few I wouldn't mind having the occasional romp with in the hayloft.'

I giggled. The wine was doing its work and I didn't feel in the least shocked by her revelations. 'You're wicked, do you know that?'

'Yes, of course,' she agreed, her eyes bright with mischief. 'My father was afraid I was going to disgrace the family, that's why he packed me off here, of course.'

'I'm sure it wasn't.'

'There isn't much love lost between us, Kathy.' For a moment sadness flickered in her eyes. 'I respect him, but he isn't a loveable man.'

'My father isn't easy to love either, but Gran is wonderful. She's been like a mother to me.' I looked at Eleanor as she fondled her wineglass. 'Is there anyone you really love, Eleanor?'

'Yes, there is one person,' she said and her face took on a new softness. 'My cousin Mary. If I love anyone, I love Mary. She's sweet and good and . . . well, best not to say too much. I just love her.'

'It's good to love someone.'

'And to have good friends like you, Kathy.' She touched her glass to mine. 'To love and friendship, may they continue forever . . .'

I echoed her toast and sipped my wine. Eleanor had seemed to have everything with her expensive clothes and money of her own, but I sensed that deep down she wasn't any more confident about the future than either Ally or me.

'I've been waiting for this for ages!' Ally cried, a note of excitement in her voice. 'My mother is dying to meet you, Kathy. I've told her all about you in my letters.'

'I've been looking forward to this too,' I said, smiling at her as she grabbed her case and jumped down from the bus. 'I can't believe it's more than eight months since we met.'

'That's because we don't have time to breathe let alone think,' she said and laughed. 'But now we've got four whole days to do exactly as we like.'

It was the first leave we'd been able to take together, though both of us had had a weekend in between. I'd stayed at the hospital, taking walks to the village and spending time lazing by the river, but Ally had gone home on the train.

Her mother saw us from the window and was waiting to greet us. She hugged her daughter and then turned to me. We started to shake hands politely, and then she grabbed me and hugged me to her ample bosom.

'I feel I know you, Kathy. Ally has written so much about her friend.'

'I hope it was good,' I quipped and she smiled.

'I think you've been good for her, Kathy. She says you're much better than she is at all kinds of things.'

'I'm no better than Ally, she just thinks I am, because I got good marks in the exam we took last month. We're both trying very hard to learn all they have to teach us, but it's hard to take it all in.'

'Yes, I am sure it is,' she said. 'Ally's father and I are

very proud of her and I'm sure your family must be proud of you, Kathy.'

'I haven't heard from Gran in a while,' I said. 'I think perhaps I ought to pop over one day on the Tube and see how she is . . .'

'That's a good idea,' she replied. 'But come in, my dear, sit down and have a good rest. I've got the kettle on and your dinner will be ready in a minute. From what Ally tells me you must both be starving.'

It was warm and welcoming in Ally's house. Her parents were kind, generous people and I settled in straight away.

Ally and I went shopping together, and Ally helped me choose two new dresses – one for afternoons and the other for dances and parties. The evening dress wasn't as impressive as Eleanor's, of course, but it suited me and I felt comfortable in it.

'I've never had so many new things,' I said as we went back to Ally's home our arms full of parcels. 'I feel terribly extravagant for spending all that money.'

I had bought a couple of small presents for Gran, and I intended to give her some money when I visited the next day, but I had spent most of the wages I'd been saving on my new clothes, and I was really pleased with my purchases.

I was wearing a new skirt and blouse under my jacket when I walked up the lane the following morning. It was nearly spring again – the spring of 1918 – and the weather was mild, the sun making the lanes seem less dreary than usual. I'd asked Ally to come with me but she said it might be better if I went alone, and in my heart I was relieved. I wasn't sure what kind of a reception I might get at home if my father happened to be around.

As I approached the house, I saw Bridget O'Rourke coming out of the front door. She looked surprised, then smiled and waited for me to reach her, giving me a quick kiss of greeting on the cheek.

'Your Gran will be so pleased you've come,' she said.

'She's had a bit of a chill. I wanted to write to you, but she wouldn't let me – she's all right now, though, so don't worry.'

'Was she very ill?'

'Not at all,' Gran said coming to the open door. She had heard our voices and was beaming with pleasure. 'Bridget fusses too much, lass. I'm fine and there was no need to trouble you – with you being so busy and having such a good time with all your friends.'

'Tom said they work the girls hard,' Bridget said. 'I doubt Kathy has much time to go out with friends.'

'Oh, we get out now and then,' I replied, a faint flush in my cheeks. 'I had a drink with your brother once, Bridget. How is he?'

'In high fettle. He has been in France working in a field hospital for a few months. It was what he wanted all the time, you know, but they wouldn't give him the chance, and then they happened to need a doctor with his specialist knowledge in burns and they flew him out. He's managed to stay on there until now, but he says they are sending him back soon.'

'Oh, I expect he will be disappointed.' I avoided looking at her. 'Is he coming back to our hospital?'

'Oh yes, I think so,' Bridget said. 'They've asked for him so I expect you will be seeing him soon.' She smiled at me and then Gran. 'Well, I must go or Joe will be shouting for his dinner. And my sister Lainie is coming this evening. We don't often see her so I'm looking forward to having a nice chat.'

'You don't need to worry about Joe,' Gran said. 'That husband of yours never raises his voice to you, Bridget.'

'No, he doesn't,' she admitted. 'I'm very lucky.'

'Lucky with 'er 'usband,' Gran remarked as Bridget went up the street. 'I don't know about that sister of 'er's though . . .'

'What do you mean?' I looked at her curiously. 'I thought Lainie was doing well, working as manageress at a posh dress shop in the West End?'

'Aye, she is. It were different in the old days, but never

mind that now. Lainie O'Rourke were a bit of a dark 'orse if yer ask me. Not that it matters. Water under the bridge, as they say. Come in, Kathy love,' Gran said, her eyes going over me as she closed the front door behind her visitor. 'That's a smart skirt you're wearing. You're quite the young lady now.'

'I expect it's the new clothes.'

'No, it's more than that.' She studied my face. 'You've seen and done things that have changed you, lass. You've grown up since I saw you last.'

'You do see a lot of things at the hospital,' I admitted. 'It's hard work and sometimes it's very sad.'

'Yes, of course, love,' she said and reached up to pat my face. 'But I can see it has been good for you.'

'How have you been really – and Father?'

I laid a package on the table. I had managed to buy a packet of her favourite biscuits and a bar of Fry's dark chocolate, which my elderly admirer at the village shop near the hospital had saved under the counter especially for me. Gran looked inside, shaking her head at me, but I could tell she was pleased with the small gift.

'Your da's the same as ever,' she said with a wry grimace. 'I manage well enough, Kathy. Don't you go worrying about me. I'm proud of you and you're doing something you enjoy, and that's all that matters.'

'Oh Gran, I do love you!' I put my arms about her and hugged her. 'If you are ever really ill you must let Bridget send for me, promise me you will.'

'I promise you, lass,' she said. 'If I need you I'll send for you, but not before. Now, tell me all about yourself and what it's like at that hospital of yours . . .'

The subject was changed and we spent the next hour or so talking happily. I was a bit apprehensive at first in case my father should come in and make a scene, but Gran said he was working at the brewery again and wouldn't be home until late.

When I left her waving at the door I felt a tug at my

heartstrings. There was no doubt that she was getting more frail and I felt a little guilty at leaving her alone, and yet I was already anxious to return to the hospital and my work.

Four

I had found a warm spot in the hospital gardens to sit and read my paper, which one of the patients had given me as I came off duty. It was June now and the sun was shining as I glanced at the headlines. After months of terrible news, when it seemed that everything was going wrong for the allies, the papers were talking of a counter attack.

'Hello. May I share your bench – or shall I be intruding?'

My head shot up as I heard the voice and I felt my cheeks warm to a blush. It was months since I'd last seen Tom O'Rourke and I'd almost forgotten him. At least, if I was truthful, I had succeeded in preventing him from dominating my thoughts.

'No . . . I mean of course you can sit here.'

'You won't run away?' His tone was half-serious, half-teasing. 'Only I think I must have done something to offend you the last time we met?'

'I shan't run away. I've grown up since we last met, Doctor.'

'Yes, you have.' His eyes went over me and I saw a flicker of admiration. 'But you weren't a child when we had that drink together last year, Kathy. It was just that I felt I was probably too old for you.'

'I suppose there is quite a difference in our ages, but I don't see that matters – if people like each other and want to be friends.' I blushed because that sounded as if I was asking to be his friend.

'I've thought about you while I was away, Kathy.'

I felt it safer not to answer that one, because something in the way he was looking at me was making my heart behave oddly.

'You've been in France, haven't you?'

'Yes, but Belgium mostly. It was hellish out there for a time.'

'You mean during the German offensive? They nearly broke us, didn't they?'

'The Allies lost 400,000 men in three weeks.'

I experienced coldness at the bottom of my spine. Like most people, I read the papers avidly for news and I had seen the reports saying that a lot of men had died, of course, but to hear Tom speak of the numbers like that was chilling. I tried not to think of all those wasted lives, and of all the grieving families.

'We knew how bad it was – the gas attacks and the shelling. The people of Paris were catching it too from Big Bertha.'

'Yes, I understand they had a rough time. I was due to come back home in March but things got so dire out there that I couldn't leave.'

'A lot of nurses volunteered around that time. Eleanor Ross is over there now but my application was turned down. I was told they need us here. Matron said she couldn't afford to let any more of us go . . .'

'That's perfectly true. I think they like to hang on to anyone who survives the first year, because quite a few decide it's easier to work in one of the other services.'

'Women have been doing a lot of useful things since the beginning of the war, working as mechanics as well as in offices and factories. Perhaps that's why they've promised us the vote. Ally says they will allow women to stand for Parliament after the war.'

'I think she's right. How could they refuse after what you've all done? Girls like you, Kathy, with no experience – coming to a place like this, working all hours and seeing things no young woman ought to see. You are all heroines, believe me.'

His look was making me feel odd, my stomach fluttering as if it had butterflies trapped inside.

'Well, I'd better go.' I got to my feet reluctantly. 'I'm due in a lecture in half an hour and I want a cup of tea first.'

'I'm due on duty soon,' he agreed rising with me. 'I've enjoyed our little chat. Perhaps we could go out one evening? I know a nice place where we can have a meal. They do good fish on the meatless days . . .'

Some months ago the Government had brought in rationing so that restaurants were not allowed to serve meat on two days a week. Unless you went somewhere where the meals cost one shilling and tuppence or less, of course. Now they had brought in general rationing and things were getting worse.

I hesitated for no longer than a moment but it made him frown.

'Yes, I think that would be nice.'

His frown vanished to be replaced by a smile that made my heart leap.

'Good. What about Friday?'

'Yes, I think I can manage that.'

I might have to change duty but one of the other girls would stand in for me if I asked. I had done it for them often enough in the past.

'You must be mad!' Ally said when I told her about my date later that evening. 'It took you ages to settle down after the last time he hurt you.'

'He didn't mean to,' I said defensively. 'It was mostly in my mind. Besides, I've grown up since then. I'm tougher and more aware of the ways of the world.'

'We've all grown up,' Ally replied and looked upset. 'I've just heard that Eleanor Ross has been killed. She had gone up to the front line with a medical team and a shell hit their ambulance.'

'Eleanor has been killed?' I clutched at the back of a chair as the world seemed to spin round me, cutting the ground from my feet. The shock made me feel ill and I experienced a physical pain in my chest as though someone had punched me. 'That's awful. I can't believe it. For her to die that way . . .' It was so shocking that someone on a mission of mercy should be killed by a stray shell from enemy fire.

I thought about the night we had shared that bottle of wine sitting on my bed, the night I had sensed the loneliness inside Eleanor and my heart ached for my lost friend.

'I feel terrible,' Ally said looking as sick as I felt. She sat down on the edge of the bed, and I could see she was really shaken by the news. 'I was such a pig to her, always on at her whenever we met, making her life here a misery. I think she only volunteered for duty out there to get away from me.'

'Don't be silly. That isn't true, Ally. She told me that she thought it was something really worth doing.'

Ally shrugged, remaining unconvinced. 'Well, I feel like I've committed murder at the moment. I suppose it will pass and I'll live with it, but I don't much like myself right now.'

'Eleanor chose to go. I'm sure she must have volunteered for duty at the front – and you were nowhere near her when she did that. You didn't fire the shell that killed her, Ally.'

'Thanks for trying to make me feel better. You're a good friend, Kathy. I've always been glad we met when we did. I'm not sure I could've stuck the first few months here if you hadn't been with me.'

'It was the same for me.'

'No, I don't think so. I came close to giving up and going home. You've never even thought about it, have you?'

I shook my head. 'Perhaps if I'd had a home like yours I might. But I don't get on with my father; I'm better off here, believe me.'

She nodded, giving me a sympathetic look. 'You haven't heard from your family in a while, have you?'

'Gran isn't one for writing letters, but Bridget wrote to me recently. She says Gran is fairly well at the moment. I had a letter from Billy's mother yesterday. She told me he had been wounded in the leg but that it wasn't serious enough for them to send him home.'

'Oh, poor Billy. The men say it's worth getting shot for a trip home to Blighty. It's rotten luck being patched up out there and having to go straight back to the front.'

'He hasn't had home leave in over a year . . .'

'Nor had Mike,' she said and reached into her skirt pocket for an envelope. 'Did I tell you he's coming home next week? He's got three weeks this time.'

'That's wonderful. You should ask for time off to meet him in town, Ally.'

'I already have. Matron says we're too busy for me to be away for more than three days. But she's always had it in for me. She thinks I'm a bad influence on some of the others – inciting them to rebellion.'

'It's a shame she won't give you longer, but with the new offensive they've launched we're bound to get an influx of patients, and we're always short of trained staff. Three of the latest recruits left within two weeks of starting here, went back to the munitions factory because the work was easier.'

'Yes, I know.' She sighed and I could see that she was still fretting over the news about Eleanor. I understood, because I was hurting too, but Ally felt guilty over the way she'd behaved to Eleanor. 'Besides, I'm one of the lucky ones. Sally's youngest brother was badly wounded last week. She was crying over a letter this morning so you know the news can't be good.'

'I think she should ask for compassionate leave. They would have to give it to her in the circumstances.'

'I've told her a dozen times but she refuses to go home. She says she's needed here and it will only be worse if she has to sit around and twiddle her thumbs.'

'Well, it's true we need her here.' There had been a constant flow of badly mutilated patients over the past few months, the injuries from burns and gassing were horrendous.

I saw Sally coming towards us as we made our way to the canteen a little later that evening. She was putting on a brave face but we all knew she was very upset.

'I'm going for supper,' she told us. 'What about you two?'

'On our way,' I said. 'I was looking at the roster earlier – would you swap Friday night for Saturday with me please?'

'Got a date?' She looked pleased as I nodded. 'It's about time you went out, Kathy. You haven't had a proper date for ages. Of course I'll swap. It means I might have time to pop home. I shall be free for the whole weekend then without asking for time off. Yes, it suits me very well.'

I smiled at her but didn't mention her reason for wanting to go home. We didn't mention things like that unless someone wanted to talk, and Sally seemed to prefer to keep her worries to herself.

I was thoughtful as I went to the library to study for an hour on my own after supper. My feelings of depression were not all to do with Eleanor's death, although that nagged at me like a painful tooth. From Maggie Ryan's letter I knew that she was taking it for granted that there was something between Billy and me. Perhaps I ought not to have agreed to go out with Tom O'Rourke, and yet I hadn't promised Billy I would wait.

Just because I'd written to him faithfully every week didn't mean I was going to marry him, but I'd sensed that Maggie thought it would happen when Billy came home and perhaps Billy did too.

I wore a new dress I'd bought from Eleanor before she went over to France for my date with Tom. It was a pale green wool and beautifully cut to flatter the figure with a narrow waist and flowing skirt. She had wanted to give me several of her things, but I'd persuaded her to accept a small amount of money for them.

'If it's what you want, Kathy.' She'd given me a peck on the cheek. 'I don't want to hurt your pride. You've been a good friend and I've enjoyed knowing you.'

'You can always write to me. Keep in touch, Eleanor.'

She had promised she would but there had been only one letter. I knew that she had probably been too involved in her work to think about writing to me. She had been young and full of life, and she couldn't have expected to die the way she had.

Wearing her dress made me feel sad in a way and yet I was proud too. I was proud of the friend who had given her own life to help others.

I told Tom about Eleanor, and the way she'd died, when he was driving me to the restaurant he'd told me about in his sporty little roadster.

'Yes, I remember Eleanor,' he replied, looking shocked. 'That's terrible news, Kathy. I'm so sorry she died like that. Eleanor was a thoroughly nice girl. She asked me to bring a letter and some perfume home for a friend of hers – a Miss Maitland. I think they were second cousins through their mothers' side of the family.' He frowned. 'I never met the girl. She was some years younger than Eleanor and at boarding school. I simply left the package with the headmistress. I wonder if Miss Maitland has been told?'

'I should think she's bound to know.' I glanced at him. 'So you met Eleanor when you were over there in France?'

'Yes, a couple of times. We went out as friends . . .' He smiled at the memory. 'As a matter of fact we spent most of our time talking about you that evening. Eleanor liked you a lot. She told me that your friend Ally was rather jealous of you – of your having other friends – but that you had been kind to her when she was finding it hard to settle in.'

'She was kind to me,' I replied. 'She told me she had a cousin called Mary, of whom she was very fond. Eleanor was deeper than a lot of people realized. I liked her a lot and I like to think we were friends.'

'Eleanor certainly counted you as a friend.'

'Then we were.' I smiled at him. 'You've cheered me up. I've been feeling upset over it since Ally told me the news.'

'She was very dedicated to the Service,' he said. 'She was considering staying on in nursing after the war.'

'Really? I didn't know that. She told me she didn't want to marry for a long time, but I wasn't aware that she was considering staying on as a nurse.'

'She didn't want to join, did she? She told me that herself – but in the end she loved it, said it made her feel that her life was worth something.'

'She would've made a good professional nurse. I think she was clever at the theory as well as the practical side. I have to study hard to learn things that came easily to Eleanor.' I choked back a sob. 'It's such a waste for her to die like that!'

'This whole thing is a waste, Kathy.' Tom glanced at me as he pulled into the front drive outside the hotel. 'Have you thought what you will do when it's over?'

'Is it ever going to be over?'

He chuckled huskily. 'We've all thought that at times – but yes, I think the tide is turning. The Germans had it all their own way for a while but it's a different war now. We are using more tanks and planes than before. The Air Force has downed more than four thousand of their aircraft against less than two of ours. I believe that the combined might of the Allies will triumph in the end.'

'I do hope you're right!'

'We can only pray. Anyway, let's forget about war and its consequences for a while. We came here to enjoy ourselves.'

'Yes.' I smiled at him. 'I haven't forgotten. It's nice just being with you, Dr O'Rourke.'

'It's time you called me Tom.'

'Yes, Tom.' I threw him a teasing look. 'I hope this place lives up to its reputation. I'm starving.'

For the rest of the evening we talked about music and books we'd read. The hotel owner employed a pianist and she played throughout our meal. Some of it was classical stuff that I didn't know but she also gave us a medley of the most popular songs of the war.

'"If you were the only girl in the world and I was the only boy",' Tom sang the first line of a song that had been on every soldier's lips. 'We had concerts in Belgium for the men and they all requested that one.'

'Yes, I know. It's special for a lot of people. The men remember it from taking their girlfriends to a theatre when they're home on leave. Ally's boyfriend is coming home soon. She's going to meet him in London. She has a couple of shows she wants to see lined up – something at the Comedy Theatre and a variety show with Jack Buchanan singing.'

'Do you like to go to the theatre, Kathy?'

'I've only been a few times – but yes, I do enjoy it.'

'Perhaps we might go together? If you have a free weekend?'

'Oh . . .' I was surprised as I hadn't expected an invitation of that kind. 'Yes . . . perhaps.'

'We'll fix it up,' he said. 'It won't be easy to arrange corresponding free time. We can't appeal to Matron. She doesn't approve of her nurses fraternizing with the doctors.'

'No, she doesn't.' I pulled a face. 'I used to think she disliked me, but she told me the other day that I was coming along nicely.'

'High praise indeed!' His eyes sparkled wickedly. 'So, have you decided to take it up as a career – stay on when the war is over?'

'I might. I'm not sure.'

'You would have to give up when you got married, of course.'

'That's so silly, isn't it? Why do they have rules like that?'

'Nursing and marriage don't mix; I suppose that's the

thinking. Children tend to get in the way. You do want children, don't you, Kathy?'

Something in his look made me blush and look down.

'Yes, of course – with the right man. Don't you?'

'With the right woman.' His tone of voice caused me to raise my head. 'I was interested in someone for a while but she wasn't the right one. We parted by mutual agreement.'

'Are you speaking of Miss Retford? Everyone thought you were engaged to her before you went to France.'

'It never got that far. I'm not sure why. Babs told me I wasn't in love with her – and she was right. I admired her. I didn't love her. I think the girl I might love would be very different. Someone warmer – more sincere.'

I swallowed hard as I saw the meaningful expression in his eyes, then looked away. His words seemed to convey more than I was ready to accept. He had come back into my life so suddenly and I found it hard to believe that he felt something more than liking for me. I was still Kathy Cole from the lanes, even if I had grown up.

'You think I'm just saying these things, don't you?'

'You hardly know me.'

'I threw away my chance to know you better. Will you give me another one, Kathy?'

Looking into his face I could not doubt that he was sincere.

'Yes. If you mean it.'

'I thought about you after you snubbed me at that dance. I knew I must have hurt you – and after that I found myself looking for you, waiting for a chance to ask you out again.'

'And then you went away.'

'I had no choice, Kathy. I was needed.'

'Yes, I do understand that, Tom. But I'm glad you're back.'

'So am I.' His smile seemed to caress me. 'And I'm glad that you've forgiven me.'

Tom's kiss was soft and gentle as we said goodnight later.

He drew back from me as I responded, melting into his arms, and touched my cheek with his fingertips.

'I'm not going to rush you, Kathy. We need to get to know each other, and I want you to be sure of me.'

'I know I enjoy being with you – and being kissed.'

'Then that's enough for now.' He grinned. 'Sweet dreams, Kathy – provided they're of me.'

'My dreams are my own, sir.'

'We'll do this again soon.'

'Yes, please.'

'Go in before you're reprimanded for staying out late. I'll talk to you in a day or so.'

'Goodnight, Tom.'

I was smiling as I went upstairs. Ally was alone in our room. She looked at me sharply and then pulled a wry face.

'Lover boy came through this time then?'

'We had a lovely evening. The food was nice and I enjoyed myself.'

'Are you going to see him again?' There was a faint hint of jealousy in her voice.

'Yes, I think so. He was talking of a weekend in London so that we could go to the theatre.'

'You be careful! When men suggest something like that they are usually after one thing.'

'Ally! Tom isn't like that.'

'Isn't he?' Her eyebrows shot up in disbelief. 'Believe me, they all are. Your wonderful Dr O'Rourke is no exception.'

'You don't know that. I think he's serious about us getting to know each other.'

'Like the last time?'

'That was . . . we got off on the wrong foot. It's different now. He really likes me.'

'Just be careful, Kathy, that's all.'

'You sound as if you're jealous?'

I was annoyed. It wasn't the first time she had found fault with people I liked.

'I care about you – about what happens to you,' she insisted.

Suddenly the anger evaporated. 'Yes, I know, but it's all right. I do know what I'm doing, and I trust Tom. He wouldn't do anything to hurt me.'

Ally pulled a face but didn't say any more. She had sensed that we were close to having a quarrel and neither of us wanted that.

'You could come to London with me,' she suggested. 'It would be safer if there were four of us.'

'I'm not sure. We'll see . . .'

I was making no promises. I thought it might be nice to spend a weekend alone with Tom.

Tom took me to a dance at the Military base the following week, and we went out for a drink on the Wednesday after that. Both of us were busy and it was difficult to manage more than two outings a week, but we snatched a few minutes in the garden sometimes when it was fine and drank several late-night coffees in the canteen.

No mention was made of that weekend in London and I thought he was saving it as a special treat. We were getting to know more about each other as the weeks passed and our friendship had developed into something more passionate. Once or twice we had found it difficult to stop after a heavy kissing session in Tom's car and we both wanted more.

Several times Tom had spoken of the end of the war, which looked more likely to happen as the summer wore on and the Allies began to advance. In July we heard that the Russian tsar had been murdered in a cellar with all his family, and that that country was now in turmoil, torn between the Red and White Armies.

I also read about a controversial book by Dr Marie Stopes, which discussed the importance of sex in marriage and called for contraceptive advice for women. The idea that women should enjoy sex and that it was not simply for procreation was so shocking that, before this, it would never have been discussed openly in decent homes and showed how much the world was changing, particularly for women.

'It would make such a difference,' I said to Tom one evening, 'if women could decide when they wanted to have children, they could then continue with a professional career like nursing until they were ready to stop.'

'Attitudes will have to change a great deal before that can happen,' he replied. 'Besides, most men would hate the idea. I doubt many of them would agree. Anyway, most women want children when they marry.'

'Yes, of course. I do, too. I just meant it would be helpful to be able to choose the time.'

I could see that Tom didn't really agree and I knew most men would feel the same way. I thought about some of the women I knew in the lanes who lived in dread of bearing a child almost every year, and of seeing many of their babies die because of the poverty in which they lived. If those women could limit their families to perhaps two or three? But Dr Marie Stopes was ahead of her time and her ideas had been criticized vociferously.

In August, the Allied forces were in action near Amiens and we heard that the enemy had collapsed under a sustained attack by tanks and from the air.

'It's nearly over,' Tom said the night we heard the good news. 'Oh, Kathy darling. It's only a matter of weeks, a month or two at most. As soon as it's final you can ask to be released and we can get married.'

'Tom . . . ?' I was taken by surprise. Although our embraces had become more and more intimate of late, he hadn't actually said he wanted to marry me until now. 'Are you asking me to be your wife?'

'Of course. I thought you must know how I felt, Kathy. We've discussed marriage and what it means for you often enough. Surely you understood what I was getting at?'

'I wasn't sure.'

'Do you want me to get on my knees?'

'Don't be silly. You can't in the car.'

'We can get out, spread the blanket on the grass.' His voice was suddenly husky, hoarse with desire. 'I love you . . . want you so much, Kathy. You are going to marry me, aren't you?'

'Yes, Tom. You know I am. I love you.'

He swept me into a hungry embrace, his kiss taking my breath away. His hand moved to my breast, caressing me through the fine material of my blouse, sweeping away all thought and leaving only feeling. My pulses raced, my body clamouring with a sudden urgent need to be close to him, to be one with him.

'Let's get out and lie on the blanket, Kathy. I don't see why we should wait any longer. We shall marry as soon as the war is over and that can't be long now.'

A part me was warning against agreeing to Tom's urging, but I was young and in love and the excitement was sweeping me along recklessly. I had been aware of his need and my own for a while, and the touch of his hand on my bare flesh as it slid inside my blouse sent shivers of delight running through me. He was bending his head, kissing my breasts, his tongue flicking at the nipples. I moaned softly, panting a little as I thrilled to these new sensations that were coursing through me, driving me beyond any sense of right or wrong.

'Yes, Tom,' I murmured. 'Oh yes, let's not wait any longer. Let's do it now. Let's make love now . . .'

He drew back and looked at me. 'You are sure, Kathy? I'm not forcing you?'

'No, of course not. I want it to happen.'

Our loving that first time was sweet and tender. Tom was so gentle and considerate, leading me so carefully into the pleasures of physical love that I hardly realized what was happening.

We made love and then lay talking for a long time before making love again. The first time was a little painful but the second was better for me.

'It will get much better in time,' Tom promised as he stroked my hair. 'For both of us.'

'I knew it might hurt the first time. Ally told me . . . about her and Mike. They did it on his leave for the first time. She said it got much better after a while.'

Tom leaned over me, a frown creasing his brow. 'Will you tell her about us?'

'No – no, I shan't. Ally likes to talk but I'd rather this was just between us.'

'So would I – it's our affair, Kathy. Let's keep it that way.'

'Yes, of course.' I sat up and he helped me to my feet. 'We ought to be going or I'll be late.'

'That's the last thing we want. I've got some leave due next month, Kathy. If you could get a few days off we can go somewhere – either to London or perhaps the sea?'

'I'd love to go to the sea, Tom. I've only ever been once.'

'That's what we'll do then,' he said looking pleased. 'I often go to the sea when I can get time off. I learned to love it when I was a kid. Sometimes I think I might have died if Bridget hadn't managed to get me away from the lanes when she did.'

'But you didn't have consumption, did you?'

'They thought I did at the time. I was supposed to have gone into remission, but I had a specialist look me over a couple of years back and he says there is no sign of my ever having had it. So I think I probably had a very bad chest infection, which responded to the treatment I was given. They were only just beginning to come to grips with the problem then and in the early days of X-rays I believe a lot of mistakes were made, people diagnosed wrongly. It still happens now. After all, doctors aren't infallible.'

'I suppose mistakes always will happen. Doctors are only human as you said. Very human, I'm glad to say.' I gave him a naughty look, then reached out to touch his cheek. 'I'm just glad you're well and strong, Tom.'

'Don't worry about anything,' he said and bent his head to kiss me. 'I love you, Kathy, and we're going to have a wonderful life together.'

'Yes, of course we are.'

I smiled at him as he gathered our rug. Everything was already wonderful as far as I was concerned.

I didn't tell Ally we had made love. She dropped a lot of hints when I told her Tom was taking me to the sea in early September but I ignored them. I wanted to keep my love affair private, even though I knew most of the girls discussed these matters with each other.

'Mike says the war will be over soon,' Ally told me the day before I left for my trip to the sea. 'We're going to get married when he comes home for good. He's got his eye on a pub down Bermondsey way. We're going to run it together.'

'So you won't carry on with your nursing for a while after the conflict is over?'

'I might if they would let me, but you know the rules.'

'Yes. It's a shame though. We've worked so hard.'

'Well, they won't need half of us once things settle down.' Ally shrugged. 'Besides, marriage is the only real way for girls like us.'

'Yes, I suppose so.'

Ally looked at me expectantly. She was waiting for me to respond with news of my own and looked annoyed when I didn't. I'm not sure why I was so reluctant to talk about it. Perhaps I was afraid that if I actually told anyone Tom had asked me to marry him it wouldn't happen.

Tom took me to Norfolk for our weekend by the sea. I had been to Southend on a day trip once as a child with the Sunday school, but this was entirely different.

We travelled in Tom's car, stopping to have coffee and then lunch at nice hotels along the way. The hotel he had chosen for us to stay in was at a place called Old Hunstanton and it was newly built, finished just before the war, the owner told us, and very modern. The bedroom we were given had its own bathroom en suite and was extremely comfortable.

'I've never been anywhere like this before,' I told him. 'It's really lovely, Tom.'

'This is just the beginning, my darling. I'm going to find us a nice house with a big garden for the children to play in and we'll go on seaside holidays every year.'

The picture he painted of our future was a rosy one and made me feel good inside. It was September now and for the few days we'd chosen the sun shone, making it warm despite a breeze from the sea. We breakfasted early in the mornings, then went for long walks on the beach. In the afternoons we drove for miles, visiting little villages and places of interest in the area.

We went to Wells and Brancaster and Cromer, where we had fresh crab for our tea. One night we went to the pictures to watch a new Charlie Chaplin film, but mostly we liked to walk or just sit over our dinner and talk.

'I wish this could go on forever,' I said as we enjoyed a bottle of wine sitting out in the garden on our last evening. 'I've loved being here with you, Tom.'

'I'm glad you've enjoyed yourself, Kathy.' He smiled as he took my hand and kissed it. 'Soon we shall be together all the time.'

'Yes, of course.'

My heart beat faster as he put down his wineglass and gave me that special look that I knew meant he wanted to make love to me. Our lovemaking had become much more fulfilling of late and I was as eager as he.

'Let's go up now, Kathy?'

'Oh yes . . . please.'

That night I discovered the meaning of true passion in my lover's arms. It was as if the knowledge that this was the last night of our holiday had added an urgency to our loving. I experienced a deeper climax than ever before, clinging to him as my body shook with little spasms of pleasure.

'Oh, Tom . . . Oh, Tom,' I murmured into the salty warmth of his shoulder. 'That was wonderful.'

'You are wonderful,' he responded throatily. 'I love you so much, Kathy, and I almost lost you because I was a fool.' He shuddered and clutched me to him. 'I don't think I could bear to lose you now.'

'You won't, of course you won't. I love you, Tom.'

And yet even as I lay wrapped in the warmth of his arms I shivered. An icy chill was trailing down my spine and a feeling of dread had come over me.

I smiled and waved as Tom let me get out of the car before driving away. He had dropped me just outside the hospital grounds because we didn't want everyone to know we had been away together.

My suitcase wasn't heavy and I was walking briskly in the direction of the Dower House when I heard someone speak my name. I turned to see Matron staring at me and her expression was one of displeasure.

'Yes, Matron. Did you want me?' My heart jerked with fright. Had she heard that I was seeing Dr O'Rourke? She certainly looked very stern.

'You have been away for a long weekend, Miss Cole?'

'Yes, Matron. I went to the sea with a friend.'

'It's a pity you did not leave some indication of where you would be staying. We have been trying to find you. There is an urgent message from your home. I understand that your grandmother is extremely ill. Mrs Bridget Robinson telephoned me. She is most anxious that you should go home at once.'

'Go home?' I was stunned by the news, unable to think straight. 'What is wrong with Gran?'

'I believe she has a very bad case of Influenza. We are hearing disturbing reports about a strain called Spanish flu, and I imagine Mrs Cole must be seriously ill for your friend to telephone here.'

'Yes. Bridget wouldn't have troubled you if she weren't worried,' I agreed. 'Would it be all right for me to go, Matron? I should report for duty this afternoon.'

'In the circumstances I shall release you but I expect you to return as soon as you are able. The war may be almost over, and I dare say a lot of our volunteers will leave us soon – but you would make a good nurse. Unfortunately, you will probably marry and your talents will be wasted like so many others.'

I stared at her, lost for words. She pursed her mouth, waving me away impatiently. 'Go and pack whatever you need and get off home – but do not forget what I've said.'

'Yes, Matron. Thank you, it's very kind of you to let me go home and to say I would make a good nurse.'

I felt a little guilty as I hurried away, knowing that I would be leaving shortly. I was pleased that Matron believed I would make a good nurse, but I loved Tom and I wanted to be his wife – and I couldn't do both. Even if there had been some way of bending the rules, Tom had made it clear that he expected me to give up work as soon as we married.

Ally wasn't in her room so I left her a letter explaining what had happened. I also wrote a short note to Tom and asked Ally to deliver it. Then I went downstairs and used the telephone in the hall to ring for a taxi to the railway station.

Fortunately for me 'Granddad' was at the other end of the telephone. Since the Government had permitted women to drive taxis his daughter ran the local service, and he said that she would be there to pick me up within twenty minutes.

I was anxious about Gran now and eager to get home. I knew she had to be very ill or Bridget wouldn't have telephoned the hospital and asked to speak to Matron.

Five

'It's a good thing you're home, Kathy. Your gran's proper bad, lass. Bridget has been worried to death over her.'

One of Gran's neighbours called out to me as I hurried past the corner shop but I didn't stop to answer her. I was too anxious to get home. As I approached, the front door opened and Bridget came out with the doctor.

I ran the last few yards, my heart thudding as I saw their grave faces. 'How is she?' I panted. 'I came as soon as I heard.'

'Mrs Cole is very poorly.' The doctor shook his head. 'It's as well you've come back now, Kathy. Your grandmother needs nursing and Mrs Robinson can't be here all the time.'

'I know. I'm sorry they couldn't trace me earlier, Bridget. I was away with . . . a friend for a few days.'

'You weren't to know,' she said. 'It was all very sudden. One minute she was in the shop buying cheese for your father's supper and the next thing we knew she had collapsed in the street.'

'Poor Gran,' I said, my chest going tight with fear. 'They say this Spanish flu is affecting a lot of people and it can be nasty.'

'Yes, it looks like being very nasty indeed. A lot of people are going down with it already.' The doctor nodded his agreement and went off. I followed Bridget into the house. She turned and gave me an anxious look.

'I hope it didn't make things awkward for you at the hospital, my phoning there. Your grandmother didn't want

79

us to send for you, Kathy, but I'm very worried about her.'

'I'm glad you did, Bridget. I've been given special leave and I shall stay until she's better.'

'Good.' Bridget looked at me oddly. 'We shall have to pray that she gets over it, Kathy. She's been fading recently . . .'

'Are you trying to tell me she might die?'

'Or be too frail to look after herself.'

'I see . . .' I understood what she was telling me. 'I shan't desert her if she needs me.'

'She's been like a mother to you, Kathy. She needs you now.'

'Yes, of course. I'll go up and tell her I'm home.'

'I'll get off then. You know where I am if you need me. Don't be afraid to ask for help, Kathy. I'm always ready to do what I can.'

'I know that. You've been a good friend to Gran – to us both – but you're busy and you can't be here all the time.'

'I've always had a soft spot for you, love. I expect it was being there when you were born; it was a special moment for me, the first time I'd thought of having a child of my own, and I've never forgotten it.'

Bridget smiled and left. I went upstairs to Gran's room. She was lying with her eyes closed and her breathing was laboured. My heart caught with fear as I realized for myself how very frail she was, and how much I loved her. Tears of regret stung my eyes, because I was afraid she might die and never know I was near.

'Gran,' I whispered hesitantly, not wanting to wake her if she was sleeping. 'Are you awake? It's Kathy. I've come home to look after you.'

For a moment there was no response and I was about to leave her to rest when her eyelids fluttered. She looked up at me seeming puzzled for a few seconds, and then she smiled. It was a weary smile but full of warmth and love.

'Hello, Kathy love,' she murmured. 'I'm glad you're here.'

Kathy

I sat on the edge of the bed, taking her hand in mine. It felt thin and the skin was very soft, easily bruised. 'Is there anything you need? A nice warm drink or some soup perhaps? There was a pot on the stove that Bridget brought.'

'Just you, love. I don't need anythin' more. Stay with me for a while. I shan't keep you long.'

'Oh Gran . . .' I smothered the sob that rose to my throat as I realized what she was saying. 'You'll be better soon.'

She made a negative movement of her head but was too tired and too ill to say more. As I sat holding her hand, the tears trickling down my cheeks, I knew she was right. She was gradually slipping away from us and there was nothing either the doctor or I could do about it.

At some period during the late evening I heard a noise down in the kitchen. Someone was there and by the sound of it that someone was either in a bad temper or drunk, sending things crashing to the floor and making enough noise to waken the dead. Gran was sleeping so I left her and went down to investigate.

My father was cramming a piece of bread into his mouth, which he then spat out in disgust on discovery that it was stale. He swore loudly and turned to face me standing in the doorway watching him.

'I 'eard you were home,' he muttered sourly. 'Where's my bleedin' tea then?'

'I haven't had time to think about food. I've been sitting with Gran. She's dying.'

'Bloody old witch,' he said. 'Leave 'er to get on with it and fix me something to eat.'

'Get yourself a pie from the shop – or have some of the soup Bridget brought; it's there on the stove so it will still be warm. Tomorrow I'll do some shopping for proper food but I'm not leaving Gran tonight.'

'You'll feel the back of me 'and, girl!'

'Oh no I shan't. Try it and I'll have the police on you. I'm

not your punch bag and I shall not be treated as one. You've
no right to hit me and I'm not prepared to put up with it.'

He scowled furiously. Clearly he was tempted to assert his
authority by using his strength, but he could see I wasn't going
to back down.

'Bloody bitch! You're just like your mother. I was a fool to
marry her when I did. She wasn't even carrying my child . . .
took me for a right sucker!'

His words stunned me and I felt icy cold all over.

'What do you mean, she wasn't carrying your child?'

'Work it out fer yerself since you're so bleedin' clever!'

He lurched towards the door where I was standing, aiming
a clumsy blow at me in passing. I avoided it easily but I felt
shocked and numbed by his words. If I wasn't his child then
who was I? Why had he and Gran let me believe I was his
daughter all these years?

My thoughts were abruptly suspended by a cry from
Gran's room. I ran out into the hall. My father had gone
out again, leaving the street door wide open. I pushed it to
before hurrying upstairs.

Gran was trying to get out of bed and had ended up half
in and half out; flopped over helplessly, she couldn't move
and was making pitiful whimpering sounds. I went to her,
helping to swing her legs back under the covers.

'Don't try to get up, Gran. You're too weak. If you want
the pot I'll help you to use it where you are.'

She clutched at my arm, her eyes wild and staring. I
realized that her mind was wandering and that she didn't
know me.

'I have to tell Kathy,' she muttered feverishly. 'Should've
told her the truth a long time ago. She mustn't come here.
It's not safe for her . . . not safe . . .'

'It's all right, Gran. Kathy can take care of herself. She
knows about Ernie. She will be all right.'

'He's mad and evil,' she went on without listening to
what I was saying. 'Tell 'er . . . tell 'er to be careful of

82

'im. She weren't Ernie's. He never ought ter 'ave married Grace and it's made 'im bitter and evil. 'E'll 'urt 'er one of these days . . .'

'Just rest now,' I urged. 'There's no need to fret, Gran. I'm all right. Don't worry about me.'

She lay back against the pillows with a sigh, closing her eyes. I knew her efforts to reach me had exhausted her frail strength and I wondered if she would last the night.

Sitting by her side as she gradually faded I thought about what I'd learned that night. Ernie Cole's bitter words might have been spoken out of spite but Gran's fevered ravings were obviously something that had been playing on her mind for a long time.

My mother had tricked Ernie Cole into marrying her by claiming I was his child, but that was a lie. The truth about my mother was like a nasty taste in my mouth and it left me wondering.

If I wasn't Ernie Cole's child – who was I?

Bridget came round early the next morning with some bacon she had fried for my breakfast, and Gran was still clinging precariously to life.

'You eat this bacon sandwich, lass,' Bridget said, bringing it up on a tray with a cup of tea. 'I knew you wouldn't want to leave her and you can have this sitting here.' She glanced at the bed and looked upset. 'She's fading, lass. I doubt she'll last much longer. Do you want me to stay with you?'

'No thank you, Bridget. I'm not afraid of death. I've seen it often enough at the hospital.'

'Yes, I expect you have, Kathy. Your Gran was very proud of you. She used to talk about you all the time.'

'I feel I let her down when she needed me . . .' The tears rose up to choke me. 'I should've been here sooner.'

'Ah, don't take on so, me darlin',' Bridget said, sounding more Irish than she usually did these days. 'Sure it wasn't your fault. And she wouldn't have wanted you here too soon . . .' Bridget halted, looking conscious as though aware of having said more than she ought.

'You mean because of my father?' I blinked the tears away. 'Only he isn't my father, is he? My mother was carrying me before she married him and I wasn't his, was I?'

'Who told you that, Kathy?'

'He did – last night when he came in drunk and expected me to get his supper. I wouldn't leave Gran so he told me I was like my mother and that she was a bloody bitch who had taken him for a fool.'

'He was drunk, Kathy.'

'Yes, but it was the truth, wasn't it? Gran said something in a fever last night. She was trying to warn me against him. She was afraid he might harm me.'

'Yes, she has said something like that to me in the past,' Bridget admitted. 'As for whose child you are, I've never known for sure. When your father married Grace he was convinced you were his – and you might have been. But then, later, after he had begun to regret his marriage he told me that she had lied to him at the start and . . . when they argued she taunted him by saying that you weren't his.'

'You don't know whose child I might be?'

'I'm sorry, Kathy. I've no idea. Ernie promised me he would always be your father, and Jean loved you from the start. When Grace went off and left you, she took you on and nursed you as if you were her own. As far as your gran was concerned, you were her baby and it didn't matter who your mother and father were. She just loved you for yourself.'

'I know Gran loves me. I love her.' My throat tightened. 'I'm going to miss her so much. I shouldn't have gone off to be a nurse and left her alone.'

'Of course you should,' Bridget said. 'You've been doing a worthwhile job and children always go away when they grow up. My children are no exception. My eldest son joined the Air Force as soon as he was able as a cadet, my second son is away at college training to be a doctor like his uncle, and my daughter Amy will no doubt fly the nest as soon as she's old enough. She's talking of going to an art school when she finishes at school, but what good that will do her I don't know. At least you did something to help others, Kathy.'

'I think I *have* been helping others in my own little way – but I feel bad over Gran.'

'Well, you needn't. I've done everything you could have done if you'd been here, Kathy. She was always very independent and she wouldn't let anyone do much, but I saw that she was all right.'

'I know.' I smiled at her and then blew my nose, blinking back my tears. 'I'm just being sentimental and silly because I don't want to lose her.'

'I know, love. I know – but she's ready to go. It's her time.'

'Yes, I suppose so.' I went back to the bed. Gran seemed to be sleeping but as I sat down and reached for her hand she opened her eyes and smiled at me.

'Kathy love . . .'

And then she closed her eyes again and I knew she had slipped away between breaths.

'She's gone,' Bridget said and her voice was thick with emotion. I turned to see tears trickling down her cheeks. 'God bless her. She was a good woman, Kathy.'

'Yes, she was.'

'I'll leave you to sit with her for a little,' Bridget said. 'Would you like me to arrange things for you – or will you look after her yourself?'

'I'll wash her and do what's necessary,' I said. 'But could you ask someone to call about the funeral arrangements? My father isn't likely to stir himself and she must have a decent burial.'

'My Joe will do all that for you,' Bridget said. 'And don't worry about money, Kathy. Your gran had been putting a few shillings by with Joe for this day, and he promised her he would do things just as she wanted. There will be black horses and a proper hearse, so that the whole street can show their respects.'

'Thank you.'

I wasn't sure Bridget was telling me the truth about the money. I had suspected for years that she had given Gran money to help out with the housekeeping when Ernie left her short, but Bridget and Joe Robinson were good friends of hers, and if they wanted to do this for their friend I couldn't go against them. Besides, I might soon be married to Bridget's brother so in a sense they were my family.

Maggie Ryan came to see me after Bridget left. She asked if she could do anything to help, but I told her I could manage. She seemed disappointed, looking at me expectantly as if she was waiting for me to tell her something. I wasn't in the mood for talking, and after a few minutes she got up to leave.

'You're upset, Kathy, and tired, I dare say. I'll go and leave you alone.'

'Yes, yes I am a little tired. Thank you for coming, Maggie. I just don't feel like company much at the moment.'

'Come and see me before you go back,' she said. 'We can have a nice gossip about things when you're feeling better. All this was a shock for you, you being away and not knowing how poorly she'd been.'

'Yes, all right, I'll come if I can,' I promised, wanting her to leave. I was afraid she was going to talk about Billy and I didn't know what to say to her. I had allowed Billy to think I might marry him when he came home, and somehow I had to find a way to let him down gently.

Tom managed to get time off for the funeral. He stood with me throughout, reassuring me and helping me to face it without more tears.

'I would rather you didn't tell Bridget that we're more or less engaged just yet,' I told him when he came to the house to see how I was the evening before the funeral. 'This isn't the time, Tom. I'll be back at the hospital soon, and we'll tell everyone when it's official.'

'If that's what you want, Kathy.' Tom looked at me anxiously. 'I was worried when you went off like that without a word. Why didn't you let me know?'

'But I left a letter for you with Ally. Didn't she give it to you?'

'No.' His eyes flickered with anger. 'I asked her where you were and she told me you had gone home but not why – and she certainly didn't give me a letter.'

'She must have forgotten it.'

'On purpose. I was very worried until I got your telegram telling me about your gran.'

'I'm sorry, Tom. I thought Ally would give you the note I left. I can't understand why she didn't.'

'Eleanor said she was jealous of you, and I think she was right.'

'Ally doesn't quite trust you. She thinks you are playing with my affections and will let me down.'

'You don't think that, do you?'

'Of course I don't. I know you love me, Tom – and I love you.'

'That's all right then,' he said but I could see he was a little put out. 'I would have liked to tell Bridget. She's very fond of you, Kathy. She will be thrilled when I tell her we are going to be married. She has been wanting me to settle down and have a family for ages.'

'We'll tell her soon,' I promised and reached up to kiss him. 'But let's keep it to ourselves for the moment – just in case.'

'Are you frightened of your father?' Tom looked at me oddly. 'Bridget told me he was drunk most of the time these days.'

'I haven't seen much of him. We had one confrontation but since then he's been avoiding me as much as possible. I've put his tea on the table at the right time each evening, and he eats it and then goes out to the pub. I lock my bedroom door every night, just in case, but he hasn't tried to come near me.'

Tom frowned as I finished, clearly uneasy about the situation. 'I don't like the idea of you stopping here alone, Kathy.'

'I'm not going to stay long. Don't worry, Tom. I shall leave soon after the funeral.'

'You could always stay with Bridget if you wanted a few days off before you go back to work. She would be glad to have you.'

'Yes, I know. I'll think about it and decide tomorrow.'

After Tom left that evening I went to bed and locked my door as always. It was very late when I heard a crashing sound downstairs and then the tread of heavy feet up the stairs. I lay still and tense as I heard the footsteps stop outside my door, and then the handle was rattled making me jump with fright.

'Let me in, damn yer! I want to talk to yer about the future. I hope yer know your duty to me, Kathy. I hope you're not going to go running off and leave me. I need someone to cook my tea and see to things 'ere. You owe me that after all I've done for yer. You've got to take 'er place now she's gone.'

I kept quiet and didn't answer him, hoping that he would just give up and go away. If he hadn't told me that I wasn't his child I might have done what he wanted and stayed home to look after him for a while, but he wasn't my father. He had done very little for me. It was Gran who had cared for me and fed me – and I suspected that the clothes I'd been given had been mostly provided for me by Bridget. I didn't owe him anything, and I wasn't prepared to give up my future for his sake. I was going to marry Tom and then I would probably never see Ernie Cole again.

It surprised me the next morning to see that he had washed and shaved and appeared presentable in a suit that smelled of mothballs and looked as if it had been packed away in a cupboard for years.

'Don't stare at me like that,' he muttered. 'You didn't think I'd stay away from me mother's funeral, did yer?'

'I wasn't sure,' I said. 'You've been drunk most of the time I've been home.'

'That's my business, damn you!'

'I wasn't criticizing. I don't care what you do.'

'You're a cold-hearted bitch like your mother.'

'I'm sorry if she hurt you.'

'Spare me your pity. All I want from you is that you do your duty to me like a daughter should.'

'I'm not your daughter. You told me so.'

He looked startled, then swore and spat into the fireplace. 'Makes no difference what I said. I've been a father to you and I expect you to do your duty by me now your gran's gone.'

'I have to go back to work. I was only given special leave because Gran was so ill. I have to report back tomorrow.'

'Tell the buggers you've got to look after your father.'

'That would be a lie,' I said. 'Unless you can tell me who my father was?'

'Mebbe I could if I wanted.' He looked at me craftily. 'I was good to yer as a kid, Kathy. Stay 'ere and 'elp me and I'll give yer money on the table regular.'

'I'm sorry,' I said. 'I couldn't if I wanted –'

I was saved from further argument by a knock at the door. Bridget and Joe had arrived to make sure I was ready and to go through the arrangements with me, and a few minutes later Tom arrived to tell us that the hearse had just turned into the lane.

Ernie scowled at them but didn't speak another word, just taking his place behind the hearse as the chief mourner at his mother's funeral. I followed behind with Tom, then Joe and Bridget joined us, and quite a few of Gran's neighbours tagged on behind as we walked slowly through the lanes to the church.

Joe had arranged a meal in the church hall, and since he was well known for his hospitality, there was no doubt that Gran would have a good attendance at the funeral and afterwards.

Tom and his family made things easy for me, and once the sad business of laying Gran to rest was over we went back to the church hall for the buffet meal Joe had laid on.

Since there was beer and sherry as well as tea and lemonade, the company soon became less mournful and I was overwhelmed by the kindness of people who came to tell me how much they had liked and respected my grandmother.

Ernie Cole was sitting in a corner drinking beer and watching the proceedings with a sour expression on his face. I noticed that very few people bothered to approach him and offer their condolences, and after a while he got to his feet and slouched off.

'You don't have to go back there,' Bridget said. She had come up behind me without my noticing. 'You can stay with us until you are ready to leave.'

'I think I may as well collect my things and leave this evening.'

'That's a good idea, Kathy,' Tom said. 'I can drive you back myself.'

'That *is* a good idea,' Bridget said warmly. 'You'll be safe with Tom, Kathy. I don't like to think of you staying in that house more than need be.'

'I don't suppose I shall need to come back much in future. I've already made it clear that I shan't be looking after him.'

'I should think not!' Tom said in a tone that made his sister look at him. I wondered if she suspected there was something between us but she didn't say anything, though there was a speculative expression in her eyes that seemed to say more than words.

'We need not go straight back to the hospital this evening,' Tom said when we were driving away from the lanes. 'We could stay somewhere overnight . . . ?'

'I think I should report back at once,' I replied. 'It was good of Matron to give me time off like that – and I haven't been released from duty yet. We mustn't take advantage, Tom.'

'If that's what you want.'

He kept his eyes on the road, but a nerve was flicking in his neck and I could tell that he wasn't pleased because I had turned down the chance to stay with him that night, and perhaps it had been foolish. No real purpose would be served by returning that evening. I almost changed my mind to please him but something held me back. I wasn't in the mood for making love. Perhaps I was still grieving for my grandmother or perhaps I still felt guilty because I'd been off enjoying myself with Tom when she needed me.

'It's what I think I ought to do, Tom. Matron needs every nurse she can get at the moment. You know how busy we are.'

'I hope you're not thinking about staying on at the hospital for a while after the war? I thought we had settled it that we were going to get married straight away?'

'We have – more or less. You've made it clear that's what you want, anyway.' I was horrified immediately the words were out of my mouth. Why had I said that? 'No, I didn't mean it that way, Tom. Of course I want to get married.'

I would have liked to carry on and pass all my nursing exams but I knew it was out of the question. Tom *had* made it clear that he expected me to give it up and marry him as soon as possible.

'I think you did mean it,' he said, his mouth drawn into a tight line that meant he was angry. 'If nursing means so much to you, perhaps we should think about this for a while.'

'Perhaps we should . . .'

Even as I spoke I wished the words unsaid. Of course my nursing didn't mean more to me than Tom! I wanted to apologize at once but he looked so angry that I couldn't.

We drove all the rest of the way back to the hospital in silence. Tom spoke only once as he took my case from the back of the car.

'Let me know when you've made up you mind, Kathy – but don't keep me waiting too long.'

'Is that a threat?' I was suddenly angry. He was implying that our quarrel was all my fault when that wasn't strictly true. He should have understood that I wasn't in the mood for a romantic evening. Gran's death had really upset me, and Tom should have been more sympathetic. 'If that's the way you feel, don't bother holding your breath.'

He glared at me but said nothing as he returned to the car and drove off. I felt like weeping but pride wouldn't let me. I loved Tom but I wasn't going to be dictated to by anyone.

Ally was in our room packing a case when I got in. She turned to face me, giving me a sullen stare.

'You've come back then. I was going to write to you. I'm leaving. I've had enough of being told what to do.'

'Leaving?' I was so surprised that I could only stare at her. 'But why? It can't be long now until the war is over. Surely you can wait until then?'

She bit her lip, hesitated, then said, 'I've got no choice. I've been dismissed.'

'Oh, Ally! Why?'

'Because Matron found out that I got married when Mike was home on leave – and I'm having a baby.'

'Having a baby? Congratulations!' I stared at her, torn between surprise and pleasure at her news. 'And you got married when Mike was on leave? You didn't tell me that bit.'

'I didn't tell you because you were being so close-mouthed about you and your precious Dr O'Rourke. Besides, it was necessary to keep it a secret. I should have had to leave if Matron heard, but when I realized I was pregnant I had to tell her the truth. I thought you might have guessed. I did tell you we made love.'

'I thought you'd just given in because you wanted to make Mike happy before he went back out there.'

'I'm not that much of a fool,' Ally said with a wry grimace, her normal good humour restored. 'I made sure of his ring on my finger first. It was just a civil ceremony, but it counts the same. Anyway, now I'm going home until he gets back and then we'll get that pub I was telling you about.'

'I'm so glad for you.' I hugged her. 'I shall miss you – but I hope you will be very happy.'

'Mike suits me. He's easy-going and generous. I get most of my own way. I expect things will work out OK for us.' She looked at me speculatively. 'What are you going to do now, Kathy?'

'I–I'm not sure. I shall stay on here for a while.'

'What about Tom O'Rourke? Are you going to marry him?'

'Perhaps.'

'He has asked you?'

'Yes. We've had a bit of a tiff, that's all.'

'Oh, that's nothing,' Ally scoffed. 'Mike and I have them all the time.' She looked guilty. 'I hope it wasn't over that note? I forgot all about it, Kathy. I wasn't feeling well and I was worried about telling Matron. I had thought I might manage a few more weeks, but someone noticed I was getting a bit plump round the middle and she sent for me. I had to tell her then.'

'Was she very annoyed?'

'She wasn't pleased. She said I had been wasting her time, and that I was irresponsible and deceitful.'

'That was a bit unfair!'

'Well, I suppose she had the right to be angry. I did break the rules. Anyway, I'm glad it's out in the open and I'm ready to go home. It was all more difficult than I expected – the exams and things. I wouldn't have stayed on this long if it hadn't been for you, Kathy.'

She had said as much before but I'd thought she was just having a moan when things were tough. Now I wasn't so sure. Perhaps she wasn't really cut out to be a nurse.

'I shall miss you.'

'I don't expect you'll be staying on much longer. The war will be over soon now.'

'Yes, everyone says so. I expect they will tell a lot of us that they don't need us soon anyway.'

I wondered what I should do once that happened. Either I would have to apply to go on with my training or . . . what? After my quarrel with Tom the future seemed uncertain. I didn't feel like going back to the lanes with my tail between my legs and yet I didn't see why I should be the one to apologize.

In October the Government voted to allow women to become MPs. I wished Ally was still at the hospital, because I knew she would have been thrilled. Other news was not so good. Spanish flu had taken a heavy toll in Britain and Gran wasn't the only one to die. Some schools had been forced to close temporarily because so many children were down with it, and we had our problems at the hospital. Quite a few doctors and nurses and been worryingly ill and some of the more vulnerable patients had died.

When I was sick that first morning I thought I was probably going down with it myself. It was only as the sickness was repeated for several days in a row, without any signs of the fever, that I began to suspect that it might be something very different.

I hadn't seen my monthly flow for ages – since before Tom took me to the seaside! It came to me as a blinding flash and my stomach clenched with fear as I realized that I might be pregnant.

If only Ally was here! Or Eleanor – she would have known what to do. My mind was in turmoil and I wished desperately that there was someone I could confide in. Perhaps I was imagining things – perhaps it was just overwork? I had been standing in for nurses who had gone down with influenza, doing extra shifts. Yet I didn't feel tired; I felt wonderful apart from the morning sickness.

If I hadn't quarrelled with Tom I could have told him my fears, but he hadn't been in touch since the day he brought me back to the hospital. He'd meant it when he'd told me to let him know when I'd made up my mind. I had thought he would relent and come to me, but he hadn't.

I couldn't go running to him now. It would look as if I only wanted him because I was having his child, and that wasn't so. Not a day had passed without my wanting to see him, to apologize. My stupid pride had kept me from doing so and now I was trapped.

Ally had tried to carry on for as long as she could after discovering she was pregnant, and I decided I would do the same. If I could manage a few more weeks on duty perhaps I would see Tom and things would somehow come right.

And then I fainted on the ward. There was such a commotion. Sister thought I had the flu but when I assured her I was quite well I saw suspicion in her eyes. The next day Matron sent for me. Her expression was as severe as usual and yet her tone was not harsh.

'I understand you fainted on duty, Miss Cole. Are you ill?'

'No, Matron.'

'Then perhaps you would like to explain?'

'I must have been working too hard.' I took a deep breath, knowing there was no escape. 'I think I should like to offer my resignation.'

'I see . . .' She looked at me in silent disapproval for several seconds. 'I am very disappointed. I had high hopes of you, Miss Cole.'

'I'm sorry, Matron, but I've made up my mind.'

'I imagine we both know why. Will he marry you?'

I remained silent, refusing to either confirm or deny her suspicions.

'In that case I can only wish you luck. Should your circumstances alter and you found yourself able to return, I might forget this interview ever took place.' She allowed her words to sink in before gesturing with her hand. 'Very well, you are dismissed.'

It was only as I was packing my suitcases later that I

really thought over what she'd said. Had she actually been suggesting that I should have the child adopted – or have an abortion? Such an idea was horrifying. Not only was it against the law, it was dangerous. I knew some women were driven to try it, often in dirty little back-street houses where they were given unsuitable treatment. Many suffered ill health afterwards and some of them died.

Of course, if a doctor did it, it might be different. I knew one nurse who had got a doctor friend to do it for her and she'd been back to work in days, with very few people the wiser. I could ask her if he . . . I smothered the thought immediately. There was no way I was going to get rid of my child. I must have been wrong. Matron couldn't have been hinting that I should.

Adoption was another matter. It might be a way out of my difficulty . . . yet the easiest way was to tell Tom. He would stand by me.

I decided that I ought in fairness to tell him. It was his child too. But I couldn't bring myself to face him. I would write to him, but first I would go home. Ernie Cole needed a housekeeper and I could stay there for a while if I wished. I wouldn't stay long. Just until I decided what to do for the best.

'So you've come slinking back then, 'ave yer?' Ernie glared at me as I walked in with my cases that afternoon. 'What's wrong? Been chucked out, 'ave yer, now the bleedin' war's over?'

'No. I left because I wanted to . . .' I took a deep breath. 'I shan't be staying long. I'm here while I make up my mind about something.'

'Yer should be thinkin' of yer duty ter me.'

'I'll keep house for you while I'm here – it looks as if it could do with a clean.' I glanced round in disgust. He couldn't have lifted a finger since I'd left and the sink was stacked with dirty pots, the floor filthy. 'But if you hit me, I'll leave.'

'I only 'it yer the once. I was drunk and yer cheeked me. I were a good father ter yer fer years, Kathy.' His voice was heavy with self-pity, his eyes bleary as if he might cry at any moment.

'Do it again and I'll walk straight out. I won't stand for violence.'

He eyed me thoughtfully. 'Tell me the truth, Kathy. Why did yer come back? I thought you were set on bein' a nurse.'

'I can't be a nurse and be married. It's against the rules.'

'Some bleedin' bloke's got yer in trouble, ain't he?' His eyes narrowed suspiciously. 'I'll knock 'is 'ead orf, if 'e comes 'ere!'

'Tom asked me to marry him weeks ago. I'm just making up my mind . . .'

'Tom . . . that bloody O'Rourke what come here so arrogant when Ma died? No daughter of mine is goin' ter marry in ter that family!'

'But I'm not your daughter. You told me so . . .' I blurted the words out without thinking.

'No, you ain't . . .' He hesitated, his eyes narrowed and crafty. 'And yer ain't goin' ter marry O'Rourke neither.'

'You can't stop me.'

'Can't I?' He gave me a look filled with malice. 'Well listen ter me, Kathy. Yer can't marry Tom O'Rourke because he's yer uncle. Yer father were 'is elder brother Jamie – him what went orf ter America.'

'You're lying! You made that up just to punish me.'

'I'm tellin' yer what Grace told me. She swore he were yer father and I believed 'er.'

'I don't believe you. You're a hateful, bitter man.'

I stared at him in horror for a few minutes longer then turned and ran from the house. I wouldn't believe him. I couldn't! He was just trying to hurt me because he hated my mother and he wanted to punish me for defying him and going off to be a nurse. Perhaps he thought I would stay on as his unpaid servant if I had nowhere else to go.

Tears were streaming down my cheeks. Even though Tom and I had quarrelled I had clung to the belief that we would get together again. We had to because I loved him. I was carrying his child. My thoughts were whirling in confusion, my chest so tight I could hardly breathe. It felt as if my world had tumbled into ruins around me and I did not know what to do or where to go. There was no one I could turn to . . . no one I could ask for help.

'Kathy . . . Kathy! Wait for me . . .'

I had been running blindly without knowing or caring where I was going. Now I realized that I was near Maggie Ryan's house in Farthing Lane and someone had just come out of the front door.

'Where are you going? What's wrong, Kathy. You're crying . . .'

I stood absolutely still as Billy Ryan walked up to me, my heart beating against my ribs like a trapped bird in a cage. He was looking concerned and his concern for me made me feel guilty. I couldn't tell him the truth!

'I've been having a row with my father – at least he says he isn't my father.'

'Don't you take no notice of that rotten bugger,' Billy said. 'It ain't worth cryin' over, Kathy love. Don't matter whether 'e's yer father or not. You've got me and Ma now. Come in and 'ave a cuppa with us. You can stay 'ere if yer like. Ma will be pleased ter 'ave yer. She were upset 'cos yer didn't come ter see 'er when yer gran died.'

'I didn't want to be any trouble. I was too upset to think about anything at first – and I had to get back to work as soon as it was over.'

''Ave they let yer go now? I've been sent 'ome from the army. My wound opened again so they gave me an early demob. I was due leave anyway and it's all over bar the shoutin' now.'

'Yes, thank goodness.' I noticed he was limping slightly. 'Does your leg hurt, Billy?'

'A bit,' he admitted. 'Ain't nuffin' ter worry about, Kathy love. I'll be right as rain fer the weddin' next month.'

'What wedding?' I stared at him stupidly.

'Our weddin' o'course. We might as well get on with it, Kathy. No sense in waitin'. You've got nowhere to live – nowhere decent that is – and I'm home fer good. No reason why we shouldn't get wed is there?'

There were several very good reasons why I shouldn't marry him: I was in love with Tom and I was carrying Tom's child. I ought to tell Billy straight away and put an end to his false hopes. Yet somehow I couldn't find the words.

My mind was still reeling from the shock of being told Jamie O'Rourke was my true father. Supposing it was true? How could I be certain one way or the other? If Tom were my uncle . . . a marriage between us would be a terrible sin. Tom was a Catholic and I supposed his religion meant a lot to him. We'd never discussed it but I knew Bridget and her family attended regularly at her church.

Tom would be disgusted if I told him what my father had said – it would horrify him and make him feel guilty. We had committed a deadly sin. We hadn't known what we were doing, but people would point their fingers at us if they knew. And if I defied him, Ernie Cole would make sure it was common knowledge.

It might be a lie but mud sticks. If Tom married me now his career would be ruined – and if he believed it was true . . . No, I couldn't let that happen. He must never know!

'What's wrong, Kathy?'

Billy was staring at me, waiting for my answer.

'I'll come and have a cup of tea with Maggie,' I said. 'Maybe I'll marry you in three weeks, Billy Ryan, and maybe I won't.'

'That's my Kathy,' he said and grinned. 'You haven't

changed. 'For a minute there I thought you'd gone posh on me – thought yourself above the likes o' me.'

I gave him an old-fashioned look that hid my thoughts. If only Billy knew the truth. I wasn't too good for him. It was true what they said, I was no better than my mother was and I had almost decided to do the same to him as she had to Ernie Cole.

Six

'It's what I've dreamed of for months,' Maggie declared and hugged me. 'Real good news, Kathy. The best! I'm so excited I don't know whether I'm on me head or me heels.'

Billy told his mother as soon as we went into her kitchen that afternoon that I'd agreed to marry him, and Maggie went into raptures of delight. She'd had the wedding planned for months and as she started to tell me all the things she'd put aside for us, I knew I was trapped. I couldn't hurt Maggie or Billy by drawing back now and I was still too confused and upset to think clearly.

Besides, if I couldn't have the man I really loved, why not marry a man who loved me? Billy had been after me since I was at school and he was looking as pleased as a dog with two tails. Yet my conscience told me that I was doing a terrible thing. I ought to have at least told him that I was having another man's child. If I'd done so at once he might have understood. Now, after seeing his pleasure because I'd more or less consented to marry him, I couldn't bear to see the happy glow turn to hurt and disappointment in his eyes.

There were a dozen reasons why I should have confessed the truth to him that afternoon, but a mixture of pride and fear held me silent and then it was too late. I felt as if I were caught up on a roller coaster ride and couldn't get off without falling.

'You were a bit quiet,' Billy said as he walked me home later. 'If yer want things different I'll tell Ma. We shan't live with 'er long. It's just until I get a job and earn some decent money.'

'I don't mind living with Maggie. It's better than living at home.'

'Yer don't 'ave ter go back there unless you want.'

'He may not be my father, Billy – but perhaps I do owe him something. I'm going to get things sorted between us. But if I'm worried I'll come to Maggie's later.'

'Do you want me to sort him for you?'

'No!' the last thing I wanted was for Billy and Ernie to have a row. 'I'll be all right. I promise you.'

'Well . . . if you're sure. But remember you've got me ter look out fer yer now, Kathy. If he lays a finger on yer, I'll beat his 'ead in!'

'Billy! Don't say things like that. You wouldn't be much good to me if they hung you for murder.'

'I didn't exactly mean it – but I'll make him sorry if 'e 'urts yer, love.'

'He won't. There's no need to worry. I know exactly what to do with Ernie – whether he's my father or not.'

'That's my offer,' I said facing Ernie across the kitchen table a few minutes later. 'I'm going to marry Billy Ryan, but if you keep your mouth shut about Jamie O'Rourke, I'll come every day to tidy the house and your tea will be ready when you come in.'

'So yer 'avin' a kid then.' Ernie's eyes narrowed craftily as he looked at me, and I knew my face had given me away. 'Does Billy Ryan know? I'll bet a bleedin' shillin' yer 'aven't told 'im. Yer as bad as yer mother.'

I felt my cheeks burn with shame. He was right to accuse me. It didn't matter how many excuses I made about not wanting to hurt Maggie or Billy, or that I was doing this for Tom's sake and the child. The truth lay like a stone in my breast. I was cheating Billy. I was deceiving him.

'What I do is my business. If you breathe one word of any

of this to Billy or anyone else I'll leave you to rot in your own filth.'

'I'll keep me mouth shut as long as you do your duty by me. Don't think you can come for a start and then stop. Do that and I'll tell Billy and the whole street what a dirty little slut you are.'

'Talk to me like that and I'll run off like my mother did. If I don't marry Billy you won't see me again.'

He stared at me, then scowled. 'No need for us to speak at all. Just keep your side of the bargain, that's all.'

I stood like a stone statue as he went out, slamming the street door behind him. What had I done? Could I trust him to hold his silence? And for how long? I was caught in a trap of my own making and I couldn't see a way out.

After many tears and false starts I managed to write a letter to Tom that evening. I said that I still cared for him as a friend but had decided I did not want to marry him. It was hard to write the lies that I knew would hurt him – and yet if he really loved me he would surely have tried to heal the breach between us long before this.

Perhaps Tom wasn't truly in love with me. Ally had doubted him from the beginning. She had said he would let me down. Tom said she was jealous of all my friends, but he didn't like her much. Perhaps he no longer liked me as much as he had. It might be that he had deliberately exacerbated our quarrel because he wanted to break it off with me. Or perhaps I was just telling myself that to ease my feeling of guilt.

I did not dare to think about any of it too deeply. If I had I should not have liked what I saw. I did not like what I was doing or myself very much. Deep inside myself I was ashamed.

I was ashamed and my conscience told me I should confess to Billy and then go away somewhere I was not known to have my child. I knew it was what I ought to do, but I also knew that I would not do it. I had always thought I was brave enough to do anything, but faced with the prospect of bearing an illegitimate child I discovered that I was afraid of the disgrace. Like many other girls before me, I was going to take the easy way out. I was going to marry Billy for better or worse.

Bridget insisted on coming to the house on the morning of my wedding to help me dress. We were getting married at the registry office because I wasn't a Catholic and neither of us wanted to wait until I had been accepted into the church; it just seemed easier to have a civil ceremony.

'I should've liked to see you wed in church,' Maggie Ryan had been regretful when we told her our decision. 'But you can have a blessing later if you decide you want to – and we'll have a good do afterwards just the same.'

Bridget had seemed surprised when she'd congratulated me on the news. I knew she had sensed something between her brother and me after the funeral, but she didn't mention Tom. She just insisted on buying me some lovely things for my trousseau and said she would be round on the morning of my wedding.

'I've always thought of you as almost a daughter, Kathy. You've got no mother to be with you on your special day, so I shall take that privilege for myself – if you will permit me?'

'You've always been good to me. It will be lovely to have you there, Bridget. Thank you for your kindness.'

Her kindness had brought tears to my eyes, making me even more aware of what I had done and what I had lost.

Ernie Cole had taken not the slightest interest in my wedding. He was drunk most of the time he wasn't at work and I seldom saw him. Joe Robinson was to stand up with me as my witness at the ceremony and he and Bridget had been generous in so many ways.

I had wondered if Tom might come to the lanes to try to persuade me to marry him, but I hadn't heard from him. There was no answer to my letter – no word of any kind. I wasn't sure what I would have done if he had come, but it seemed that he was no longer interested in me.

That hurt me more than I dared to acknowledge even to myself, but it was what I deserved. I had behaved badly and it was my own fault if I was unhappy. Several sleepless nights were my punishment, nights during which I alternated between running away and impossible longings that left me weeping into my pillow.

Yet come the morning I did nothing. For all my pride and determination I couldn't find the courage to walk away from a marriage I knew was wrong. Instead I comforted myself by making myself believe it would all work out for the best. Billy loved and wanted me, and I wanted to be safe from the shame of bearing a child out of wedlock.

I had made up my mind that I would be a good wife to Billy. Somehow I would make up to him for what I'd done. If I could make us both content simply by trying then I would leave nothing undone. Billy would have no reason to complain about his marriage.

'You make a lovely bride, Kathy,' Maggie said when she popped in to see me just before we were due to leave for the ceremony. 'Doesn't she, Bridget?'

'Kathy always looks lovely – and that dress she chose suits her a treat. That pale grey wouldn't be everyone's choice for a wedding dress but it looks wonderful on her.' Bridget smiled at me fondly. 'Where is Billy taking you for your honeymoon, – or hasn't he told you?'

'We're going up to the West End for a few days. The armistice is due to be signed on the 11th of the month and Billy says that's the place to be for the celebrations.'

'Yes, I agree.' Bridget looked thoughtful. 'It's to be signed on the eleventh day of the eleventh month at the eleventh hour. Joe was saying we might go up West for the celebrations.'

'I should've thought Billy would have chosen somewhere more romantic,' Maggie said with a little sniff. 'Like the seaside . . . ?'

Bridget laughed and shook her head. 'In this weather?

105

You're mad, Maggie Ryan. They would freeze at the seaside.'

Bridget and Maggie were the best of friends and Maggie smiled.

'I suppose you're right but I've always fancied a holiday in Blackpool. They say it's real lovely there.'

'Oh no,' I said. 'I didn't want to go too far away. Billy is going to take me to the theatre and the music hall, and then we'll come home after the armistice. He wants to start work as soon as possible.' And I hadn't wanted to go to the sea; the memories would have been too painful.

'Well, start as you mean to go on,' Maggie agreed. 'Billy wants to get you a home of your own, Kathy – though you know you're more than welcome to stay with me. There's only Mick and me now. Our Billy was the last at home.'

'He never would have budged if he hadn't wanted to get married,' Bridget teased. 'You've spoiled him, Maggie.'

'Things have been so much better for us since your Joe gave me that nice little job in the store, and we don't have to worry about the rent these days. Besides, you should talk, Bridget Robinson! You spoil that girl of yours something rotten.'

'Well, I am soft over our Amy.' Bridget laughed. 'The pair of us are as bad as one another, so we are.' She glanced at the pretty silver wristwatch Joe had given her recently for a present. 'We'd best get moving, Kathy love. If I'm not mistaken, Joe has just arrived with the cars.'

They had made such a fuss of me between the two of them, making me laugh with their banter and teasing. The time had slipped by and I hadn't thought much about what I was doing.

I thought about it in the wedding car with Joe Robinson, and I was terrified. What on earth was I doing? Why was I marrying a man I wasn't in love with?

'Don't look so scared, Kathy.' Joe reached for my hand and gave it a squeeze. 'Everyone is nervous on their wedding day. Billy is a decent lad. He loves you and he'll do his best to look after you.'

I smiled my thanks at Joe. He was being kind but he didn't

know what I was doing. All my generous friends would be horrified if they knew the truth.

As the car slowed and I saw Billy outside the registry office waiting for me with all his family, I knew I was making a terrible mistake. Had I been braver I would have changed my mind then, but I was afraid – afraid of the disgust that would replace the smiles on their faces.

And so I allowed myself to be carried along by the momentum. We all trooped into the office, me hardly looking at Billy in his smart suit and polished black shoes. He was a good-looking man and seemed so happy it hurt. I was trying to tell myself everything was going to be fine and that marriage to one man was very like marriage to any other; trying to convince myself that it didn't matter that I wasn't in love with him, but of course it did. It ought to have been Tom standing beside me. Oh, why wasn't it Tom?

My throat was tight with emotion but somehow I kept it inside. I answered the questions I was asked, felt Billy slip the ring on my finger and then we were back outside being showered with dried rose petals.

'Well, Mrs Ryan, how do you feel now?' Billy asked, grinning.

'Bewildered,' I answered truthfully. 'That was so quick.'

'Short and sweet – but now the fun begins.'

He looked so pleased with himself that I began to feel better. I hadn't begun to show any signs of my pregnancy yet and the morning sickness had stopped. Perhaps everything would be all right after all. Perhaps Billy need never know the truth.

The reception was fun with all our friends laughing and joking, teasing Billy and making a big fuss of me. I had begun to feel much more relaxed now that the ceremony was over. It was done and there was no going back so I might as well make the best of things.

People kept giving me drinks and I drank them, knowing full well that I was getting a little bit tiddly. Since most of it was port and lemon I didn't have enough to make me drunk, but it certainly took the tension out of me.

By the time Billy and I left for our hotel up west I was feeling fine. He kissed me in the car and I responded enthusiastically. Billy had always been a good kisser and I'd made up my mind not to cheat him in that way. The least I could do was to be a loving wife.

I knew he was pleased by my response. He had bought me a string of seed pearls as a wedding gift and in the car he gave me five pounds.

'That's to buy yourself something nice from the shops, Kathy.'

'You shouldn't,' I said. 'It's a lot of money, Billy, and I know you haven't got the job you want yet.'

'It's the last of my army wages,' he said. 'I've enough to pay for the hotel and things but I'll need to earn some pretty sharpish when we get 'ome. I've been savin' fer this, Kathy, and Ma 'elped me. You take it and spend it on what yer like.'

'Thanks, Billy.'

I tucked it safely inside my purse. I would spend a little of the money to please him, but I would save most of it for the future. With a baby on the way we were going to need more money than Billy yet realized.

He had booked us into a pleasant but inexpensive hotel near the tube in Oxford Street – so that we were nice and central, he told me. The room was a bit noisy and we had to go down the hall to a shared bathroom. It wasn't as nice a hotel as the one Tom had taken me to that time, but I tried not to think about that.

Billy had gone for the best he could afford, and a lot of girls from the lanes would have thought themselves in paradise to be taken up to the West End for a few days. It was now the end of the first week in November and we were booked in until the twelfth – five whole days to enjoy ourselves.

I wanted it to be a good time for both of us, and when Billy made love to me later that night I returned his kisses warmly.

There was no need to fake my responses, because Billy was sure and certain in his loving and I obviously wasn't the first girl he'd been to bed with. It was easy enough to close my eyes and let myself dream.

I wept a little afterwards against his shoulder and he stroked my hair but didn't say anything. I wondered if he knew it wasn't my first time but my fears receded when he didn't jump out of bed and accuse me of not being a virgin.

Billy made love to me again the next morning when he woke, but this time he wasn't quite so bothered about pleasing me, merely taking his own pleasure. He was a bit rough and if I hadn't been aware of guilt I might have complained. As it was, I accepted his behaviour without comment.

He was quiet during breakfast but then he suggested we go to the waxworks before having a meal out somewhere.

'We could go shopping if you'd rather?' he said when I didn't answer immediately.

'No – let's go to the waxworks. It's your holiday as well as mine.'

'Honeymoon,' he said and for a moment there was a steely glint in his eyes.

I didn't answer. My heart was beating fast. I was almost sure that he knew the truth now and I felt sick inside. What was I going to say to him if he demanded to be told the name of my lover? I couldn't tell him the truth, I just couldn't! That would make nonsense of what I'd done to protect Tom's good name and my child.

Billy was a bit moody as we left the hotel but at the waxworks he relaxed and really got into the spirit of things, lingering over the figures of some famous boxing heroes he admired. By the time we left he seemed more like his old self. We went to a nice little café for our lunch and then to an afternoon matinée at the pictures.

That evening Billy took me to the pub. We both had several drinks and when he made love to me later it was good between us.

'Kathy . . . ?'

I tensed myself in the darkness as I waited for the accusations.

'Yes, Billy?'

'I love yer, Kathy. No matter what, I love yer.'

'I love you, Billy.'

I hid my face against his shoulder, my heart aching. I was so desperately sorry for what I'd done and wished that I could go back to the moment I met Billy after the quarrel with my father. If only I'd told him I was having a child then! I could've made up some story.

As Billy slept and I lay wakeful, the lie came to my mind. If my husband ever realized that the child I was carrying wasn't his I would be ready with my story.

Billy's moods alternated between cheerful and sullen over the next few days, his lovemaking either tender or selfishly urgent. When he was gentle with me I responded, clinging to him and telling him how good it was, but when he hurt me I turned away from him and said nothing.

Armistice Day started quietly. We were out early, mingling with the people who had come prepared to celebrate. There was an air of anticipation but it was as if everyone was holding their breath; then, at the appointed time, church bells started to ring out all over London and suddenly the streets were full of cheering people. Boys rode their bikes hooting horns and ringing bells, flags were waved and everyone who could crowded into the square in front of the palace to cheer the royal family.

The war was now officially over and the country went mad with joy. People were dancing in the streets, parties springing up all over the place. Children ran wild, shouting that the Kaiser was beat and shooting imaginary Germans.

Billy hugged me, grinning in the way I had always liked. When he was happy like this he was a very attractive man, and I thought that perhaps we might be happy together after all.

'It's all over, Kathy love. It's all over.'

'Yes, I know. I'm so happy, Billy. I'm glad you won't have to go away again.'

'Are yer?' He looked at me hard.

'You know I wouldn't have married you if I hadn't cared about you, would I?'

'I don't know.' He frowned. 'But you're me wife, Kathy, and there ain't no changin' it.'

'I don't want to change it, Billy. You've been good to me – and I'll be a good wife to you. I want us to be happy together.'

He nodded but didn't say anything. That night he was gentle and tender as he took me, and I slept in his arms.

It was our last night at the hotel and I prayed that we would be like this when we got home. And yet at the back of my mind lurked a nagging fear of what might happen when Billy discovered I was pregnant. Would he instantly suspect that the child wasn't his?

Billy found a job on the docks almost as soon as we got back. It wasn't just luck as Maggie told me, though Billy didn't know he'd had help behind the scenes.

'Don't tell him, Kathy,' Maggie warned as we sat over a cup of tea one morning when the men had gone to work. Billy and I had been home a couple of days and this was the first chance we'd had for a sit down and a chat. 'But Joe Robinson got Billy that job. It wasn't his company but he's got influence with the boss, if you know what I mean?'

'Yes, I do, Maggie, but I shan't say a word to Billy. He's very proud of getting that job with more than twenty others after it.'

'He would never have asked Joe for help himself. I had a word with Bridget. She only has to drop a hint to Joe and he does the rest. Worships the ground she walks on, that man does.'

'He is a good man. Bridget is lucky.'

'She nearly married Ernie, you know. At least she might have done if he hadn't got in with Grace when he did. It was Bridget he wanted but he did what he thought was right.

Besides, she wouldn't have had him if she believed he'd got another girl in trouble. We all thought you were Ernie's at the start – except for your gran. She never did believe it.'

'You don't know who my real father might have been?' I took a deep breath as I waited for her answer.

'No idea, love. It might have been one of several. Only your mother could tell you that for sure, if she knew herself.' Maggie shook her head as she saw my expression. 'It might have been Ernie. He certainly thought it at the time.' She pulled a wry face. 'You don't owe him much, Kathy. There's no need for you to go there unless you like?'

I had been keeping my promise to clean and cook since my return from honeymoon. So far I'd only seen Ernie for a moment as he left the house one morning, and we hadn't spoken to each other.

'I've said I'll do a bit for him, Maggie. You keep this house as neat as a pin, and I've plenty of time after I've done the washing and ironing.'

We had agreed that I would do the laundry, making things easier for Maggie. She was teaching me to cook dishes I'd never attempted before and I made the bed in Billy's and my room each morning, but Maggie had her own way of cleaning and there was no point in my getting under her feet all the time.

'You know your own business best,' she said. 'You may change your mind when the babies start to come, but that's up to you, love.'

A chill ran down my spine as I wondered if she had guessed my secret, but she was smiling at me and I realized that it was just my guilty conscience punishing me again. My guilty secret hung over me like some mythical sword of ancient lore, waiting to fall.

I knew that it was only a matter of time until I began to show my condition. How long would it be before Billy or Maggie became suspicious?

* * *

Kathy

We had been married for exactly a month when it happened. I was undressing for bed and Billy came into the room as I stood there in my shift. I knew that the swell of my belly must be noticeable. In the dark in bed I'd thought he hadn't noticed but now he was staring at me and there was an angry glint in his eyes.

'How far gone are you – two months?'

His tone was so cold that a shiver ran through me. I knew that I could not avoid the inevitable confrontation any longer.

'Billy . . . I wanted to tell you when I was sure.'

'Don't try to lie, Kathy. I knew you'd been with someone else on our wedding night. Yer knew yer were 'avin' a kid when yer married me.'

I was trembling as I turned to face him. 'Yes, I did. I'm sorry, Billy. I should've told you straight away – when you spoke about us getting married. I did try later but you and Maggie were so pleased over the wedding I couldn't bring myself to hurt you.'

'Don't give me any rubbish! Yer thought I were a mug and wouldn't know any better.'

'It wasn't like that . . .'

He crossed the room and grabbed my wrist, twisting my arm behind my back and holding it tight as he glared down at me. I caught a faint whiff of strong drink on his breath.

'Don't lie or you'll be sorry, Kathy. Who was it – and how many times did it happen?'

'I–I don't know how many times. I'd had too much to drink and – and they raped me. I think there were two or perhaps three of them. It was at a dance . . . they were soldiers.' My eyes filled with tears as he jerked my arm up. 'That hurts, Billy. Please don't hurt me. I'm sorry I didn't tell you. I was ashamed.'

That much at least was true. I had been ashamed to tell the truth – and I was even more ashamed now.

'They raped you – three of them?' Billy stared down at

113

me, letting go of my arm abruptly. I turned away from him, covering my face with my hands as I wept. I didn't need to pretend. I was desperately ashamed of what I'd done and of my lies. Billy hadn't deserved this! I ought to have told him the truth even now, but I was caught in a web and the more I struggled the more enmeshed I became. 'I'll kill the buggers. Tell me their names and I'll kill them all.'

'I don't know.' I was scared now. Billy was furious, his eyes glittering. I remembered the night he had fought Sam Cotton in the dance hall and I knew he might be capable of anything. 'I told you. I'd had a few drinks. It was hot and I went outside. They grabbed me and . . . I don't remember what happened next.'

'You're tellin' me the truth?'

I looked up then, believing that my marriage depended on what happened next.

'I'm so ashamed, Billy. I wanted to tell you, really I did. I know I've done wrong by you. If you want me to I'll leave – go away and have the baby. You can just forget me.'

'No! I just want the truth.' He studied my face. 'You were so ready for me that first night. I knew I wasn't the first with you, but if you were raped . . . ?'

'I don't remember it, Billy. I was unconscious most of the time. I'd had a lot to drink on our wedding night. I thought it was going to hurt like the first time. When it didn't I was so grateful to you.'

He was obviously suspicious. I could see he wasn't sure whether to believe me or not. I was ashamed of lying to him, but I couldn't tell him about Tom, I just couldn't.

'You've hurt me, Kathy. I loved yer.'

'Don't hate me, Billy. I'll be a good wife to you – or I'll go away.'

'I don't want yer ter leave. I'd look a bloody fool in front of me mates then – can't keep a wife five minutes. No, you stay 'ere and I'll live with it, but if I ever catch yer makin' eyes at another bloke I'll kill yer both.'

'You won't, Billy. I promise you. I'll never let you down.'

'You hadn't better,' he warned and I went cold all over as I saw the expression in his eyes. 'If I ever find out you've lied to me about this you'll wish you'd never been born.'

I sat down on the edge of the bed as Billy went out. My knees had turned to jelly and I was terrified. I *had* lied to him and I knew he would never forgive me.

The scalding tears burst from me as I lay on the bed and gave vent to my misery. What a fool I had been! I had made one terrible mistake after the other, compounding my sins.

I should never have agreed to marry Billy. Once that was done I was trapped. My shaming lies had piled one on the other burying me under a mountain of deceit.

I could never have told Billy the truth, that was impossible – but instead of marrying him and being forced into that wicked lie I should have gone off somewhere to have my child. There were places that would have taken me in and then adopted the baby – or I might have tried to pass myself off as a widow and kept my child. The choice would have been entirely mine.

I knew now what I ought to have done but it was too late. Far too late.

It was three days before Billy touched me again, and when he did he hurt me deliberately. I turned away from him afterwards, crying silently into my pillow after he had fallen asleep.

He'd had too much to drink that night. In fact he'd come home drunk for two nights in a row, causing Maggie to berate him for it the next day.

'That's no behaviour for a man just married,' she told him. 'If you're not careful Kathy will go off and leave you.'

'I don't think she'll do that,' Billy said bitterly. 'She knows where she's well off.'

After that he flung out of the house, leaving a silence between Maggie and me. I had no alternative but to tell her the same lies I'd told Billy. By the time I finished I was weeping from shame – the shame of being a cheat and a liar.

Maggie gathered me into her arms, holding me until I was quiet. 'You should have told him, Kathy. I know my Billy. He worships you. He would have stood by you, but he had the right to know first.'

'I'm so ashamed, Maggie. If I could go back . . .'

She would never know how desperately I wished I could go back to the beginning. If I had only walked away that day. If I had said no when Billy asked me to marry him, but of course he hadn't asked. He had told me I was going to marry him, and I had let him lead me further into the trap that my marriage had become.

'If I could put things right, I would. Believe me, Maggie. I regret what I've done so much.'

'We all think that when we make mistakes – and we none of us can.' She handed me a handkerchief from the pile of clean washing. 'Dry your eyes, lass. There's no point in cryin' over spilt milk. What's done is done. Billy will learn to live with it and so must you.'

'I want to make it up to him. What can I do, Maggie? I'm so sorry for hurting him – for hurting both of you.' I was hurting inside myself, but at that moment the guilt was uppermost – the guilt and the shame of what I had done.

'It doesn't matter about me. Billy is badly hurt. There's no denyin' it – but if you care for him you'll accept his mistakes. He'll lash out at you when he feels pain, but then he'll be sorry. You'll either have to live with him the way he is or leave him.'

As I looked into Maggie's eyes I knew she thought I'd lied but she was still prepared to be my friend. If I went away I should miss her, miss the companionship and the friendship.

'I want to stay here, Maggie. I've nowhere else to go . . . no one I can talk to the way I talk to you.'

She looked at me in silence for what seemed several minutes, and then she nodded her head as if making up her mind.

'Then you know what you have to do, Kathy.'

Seven

'You look tired, Kathy – aren't you sleeping well?' Bridget looked at me in concern as I entered the corner shop that Friday afternoon. She often helped with the orders at the end of the week and was standing behind the counter checking through the tins of biscuits and Coleman's mustard stacked on the shelves at the back. 'You're like me, love. I got really big with both my boys, though Amy was no trouble, bless her.'

'I'll have a half a pound of those cream biscuits while you're there, please Bridget. Billy likes those.' I checked my purse to see whether I would have enough for all my purchases. 'I want cheese, eggs and bacon too, please. How is Amy anyway? Will she be home from school soon?'

'She's got another year to go before she's back for good, and then she might go on to that fancy art school I was telling you about, but she'll come for the holidays.' Bridget weighed the cheese, giving me an extra bit for my money as she always did. 'I had a letter from Tom this morning. He's been in Paris for some months but he says he's coming back soon – and he'll be flying. Courtesy of the Military, of course.'

In February passengers had flown to London from Paris, but because of a ban on civilians flying they had all been Military personnel. There was talk of a civilian service in the near future, but I thought it must be dangerous and my heart caught with fright for Tom.

'Is that safe – flying all that way?'

'Tom says it is. He flew during the war, of course. He has

118

been working out there . . .' She hesitated for a moment. 'I think he went out there to see a specialist last winter. His chest was bad and he was worried that his old trouble might have returned.'

'Tom was ill?' My throat felt tight and for a moment as the room seemed to spin, I thought I might faint. I clutched at the counter to steady myself and Bridget looked alarmed. 'Please, you must tell me. Has he been very ill?'

'Tom?' She seemed surprised by the question. 'He wasn't at all well, Kathy. He had influenza just after he went back to the hospital – after your gran's funeral – and he was admitted to a special unit somewhere in the country. They were a bit worried about him. If you recall there were a lot of people dying with it back then, and Tom having had a weak chest when he was young . . . Well, it did go to his chest and he was unwell for several weeks. I had no idea, of course. Tom never tells anyone that he isn't well. It's silly but I think it's because he had to go away when he was a lad. Anyway, he had a persistent cough afterwards so he went to see a friend of his in France and he told him there was nothing to worry about.'

Tom had been ill for several weeks and I hadn't even known. I was feeling sick inside, my eyes burning with the tears I could not shed in front of Tom's sister. No one must know how the news of his illness had affected me.

Somehow I took a grip on myself, changing the subject.

'Did your Joe get to watch the football match the other day? Billy was pleased that Chelsea managed to beat Fulham 3–0 and win the London Victory Cup.'

'No, he was busy,' Bridget replied, giving me an odd look. 'You know what Joe is – always doing something.'

She must be wondering why I had changed the subject so abruptly, but I couldn't bear to hear her talking about Tom being ill, and I had been close to giving myself away.

I paid for my purchases and escaped into the lane, walking blindly, my eyes stinging with tears. Tom had been ill . . .

119

I had thought he wasn't interested in making up our quarrel and he had been ill. So ill that he had been taken to a special unit for patients suffering the worst effects of the flu. Why hadn't anyone at the hospital mentioned it to me? But we had gone to great pains to keep our affair a secret and Ally hadn't been there to tell me all the news. Probably no one had thought I would be interested in Dr O'Rourke's bout of influenza. That still didn't explain why Tom hadn't let me know – but perhaps he had thought I didn't care anymore?

The regrets filled my mind. Why hadn't I tried to see him? Why hadn't I written to him sooner? My stupid pride had come between us, and all the time he had been so ill. He might have died and I wouldn't even have known.

'Oh, Tom . . . Tom . . .' I whispered. 'Tom, I love you so.'

I was overwhelmed by unhappiness. It felt as if someone had taken a knife and plunged it deep into my heart. What must Tom be thinking, feeling? My letter coming on top of his illness must have made him angry, bitter. If I'd been able to talk to him, to tell him that I still loved him. And yet if his elder brother was my father . . . ?

My thoughts turned full circle as they always did when I allowed myself to remember and regret. How could I ever have told Tom that his brother might possibly be my father? No, no, it was better as it was . . . better that he should never know. He would be upset but he would also feel ashamed, guilty. No, I could never force him to carry that shame.

Yet I knew that if I could go back I would not make the same mistakes again. I would not marry Billy Ryan. I had learned the bitterness of my folly.

Billy's temper had become increasingly worse as the months passed and the evidence of my pregnancy became more noticeable. He hadn't been near me in bed for months, lying as far away from my side as he possibly could, his back towards me.

Sometimes when he looked at me I thought I could see

hatred in his eyes, and yet at others he would laugh and tease me almost in his old way. But he was never that way when we were alone. Most nights he had been drinking heavily when he came to bed, and he never spent an evening at home if he could help it. There was no more talk of finding us a home of our own and Billy gave me only a few shillings out of his wages to buy our food.

Maggie remonstrated with him sometimes.

'How do you think Kathy can buy things for the baby if you put all your money across the pub counter?' she demanded. 'And she needs a decent dress or two now that she's nearing the last stages of child bearin'.'

'She'll manage,' he'd replied looking at me angrily. 'If she really needs money she can ask for herself.'

I hadn't needed to ask because I still had a few shillings put by from the money Billy had given me on honeymoon – and I had good friends. Bridget had given me lots of baby clothes she'd had for her children, which she said she would never need again, and Maggie had knitted little bootees and coats in fine wool for me. She had also given me one of her dresses, which would normally have been too big for me, and we had shaped it to make it fit my bulk.

The hurtful thoughts went round and round in my head, taunting me, making me suffer the bitterness of regret. It was a moment or two before I realized that someone was calling my name.

'Miss Cole . . . Please wait!' I heard the voice call to me again and turned my head as I saw a young woman running after me. She couldn't have been more than seventeen or so and to my knowledge I had never seen her before. 'Oh, do forgive me,' she said breathlessly as she caught up. 'I know you're married. The woman in the corner shop just told me – but I couldn't remember your married name. I thought it must be you when she said you had just left and that you were wearing a grey dress.' She glanced down at my swollen belly, a faint flush in her cheeks. 'You were Kathy Cole – the Kathy

Cole who worked with my cousin. I mean Eleanor Ross. She was a nurse . . .' She floundered to a halt, her pretty face flushed with embarrassment.

'Of course I knew Eleanor,' I said, looking at her curiously. She was an attractive young woman, well dressed and well spoken with soft fair hair and blue eyes. 'She was a friend of mine. I was so sorry when I heard that she had been killed like that.'

'Yes – we all were,' she said and looked upset. 'Eleanor meant a lot to me. I shall miss her dreadfully. She was the only one I could talk to after my mother died . . .' She blushed again and looked self-conscious. 'You must think I'm absolutely mad chasing after you in the street like that, but I wanted to be sure of catching you . . .'

'No, I don't think you're mad. I'm just a little curious why you should, that's all.'

'I came here today to find you,' she explained and blushed again. She was clearly a shy girl, a little uncertain of herself and frightened of giving offence. 'It has taken quite a while to trace you. I've only just discovered where you lived. Eleanor left you something in her will – and I've brought it for you. My father doesn't know I'm here, of course. He told me to leave it to the solicitors. He wouldn't approve of my being in . . . this part of London alone. He's a bit old-fashioned about what a young lady should and shouldn't do, that's why I wanted to catch you. I have to get home again before he knows I've been out.'

'Perhaps you ought not to have come. Your father is obviously very protective towards you, Miss . . . ?'

'Maitland. Mary Maitland. I don't know if Eleanor ever mentioned my name to you?'

'No, I don't think so, not exactly. I have heard of you, though. Eleanor told me she had a cousin called Mary and I think she asked Dr O'Rourke to bring you a present from France from her?'

'Yes, yes, she did. 'Mary smiled sadly. 'It was the last

thing she gave me. Eleanor was so generous. She was always giving me things – and she thought about you too, because you were her friend.' She put her hand into her smart coat pocket and produced a small leather box, which she handed to me. 'She wanted you to have this, Miss Cole.'

I took the tiny leather box, opening the brass catch to reveal the dress ring inside. It was a circle of large white diamonds surrounding a ruby, the colour of which was so deep that it took my breath away. I had seen things like this in the shop windows up west but never been close to such a fabulous jewel before.

'But this must be worth a lot of money. I can't possibly take it.'

'But you must,' she said. 'Really, it is yours. Eleanor left it to you. She made a will when she went over to France just in case something happened to her. Most of her things came to me, but she particularly wanted you to have this.'

'I'm not sure what to say . . .' I hesitated, feeling that I did not deserve such a gift. 'Are you certain this is the right ring? Perhaps something less valuable as a keepsake.'

'No, this is the one Eleanor wanted you to have.' Mary's rather fragile looks were lit by a brilliant smile. 'My cousin never did things by halves, Miss Cole. She liked you a lot and she specified exactly which ring you should have. That's why I wanted to give it to you myself – to make sure you got the right one. I don't trust lawyers . . . at least my father's lawyers.' Her cheeks went bright red as she realized what she'd said. 'No, I shouldn't have said that. Please forgive me.'

I had the feeling that she was a little afraid of her father, and I understood. 'There is nothing to forgive, Mary. I am very grateful to you for bringing this to me and I shall treasure it always.'

'I'm so glad, Kathy,' she said, blushing furiously. 'I hope you don't mind me calling you that?'

'I should like it. I feel privileged to have been Eleanor's friend. She was very brave, very dedicated to her work.'

'Yes, she was, wasn't she?' Mary gave a little giggle.

'She didn't want to do it at first, but then she found that she loved being a nurse. I think she would have been a good one, don't you?'

'I am quite sure she would,' I agreed. 'It was a sad waste of a life for her to die like that, but you should always be proud of her.'

'I am. I always shall be. I wish I had the courage to be just like her.' A wistful sadness touched her pretty face. 'It was nice to meet you, Kathy. I should go now. My father will be home soon and he will expect me to be waiting for him.'

'I thought you were still at boarding school?'

'I am – but I came home for a while because I haven't been well.'

'Not the influenza I hope?'

'Yes, I did have it but not as badly as some of my friends did. My father makes too much fuss. He insisted I came home to be looked after properly. So I had better get back before he sends people to look for me.'

'You'd best get off then.'

I stopped to watch her as she ran back down the lane and disappeared round the corner, then I looked at the ring she had given me again. It was a beautiful thing, but I should never be able to wear it, of course. Billy would want to know where it came from, and he was so jealous and so unreasonable these days that he might suspect it had been given to me by a lover. Besides, he might say I should sell it and I wanted to keep it, even if I never wore it. Eleanor had wanted me to have this ring and I felt rather sentimental over her gift.

I decided that I would put it away and say nothing. Perhaps one day when Billy was in a good mood I would show him, but as things stood at the moment it was unlikely that that day would ever come.

'There's been trouble on the docks again this weekend,' Maggie said to me that morning. 'Mick says there was an attack on the warehouse he walks past every day on his way to work, and the nightwatchman was hurt. They hit him several times over the head – nasty it was.'

'That's terrible, Maggie,' I said, looking at her in concern. 'Is he in hospital?'

'He was – they took him to the Infirmary, but he died on Sunday night. He's left a widow and three children, too.'

'Oh, Maggie!' I was distressed by the shocking news. 'Can't we do something to help her – raise some money or something?'

'That's a grand idea,' Maggie said. 'Mick was saying the lads at his firm were getting together to put a few bob in the hat, and if we could think of a way of raising a bit that would help.'

'Well, I'll put in two shillings,' I said. 'And we could have a cake stall at the church hall and raise some more that way – if you think that's a good idea.'

'I think it's a lovely idea,' she said. 'I'll have a word with a few of the neighbours and see what else we can come up with.'

Billy was in a bad mood when he came in that evening. I tried to talk to him about the attack on the warehouse and the watchman who had been killed, but he wasn't interested.

'Do as you please,' he muttered when I told him I was going to help with the collection for the widow. 'But don't ask me for more money. I've got better things to do with my money than give it to strangers.'

'I wasn't going to ask,' I said and turned away feeling hurt. It didn't seem to matter what I said or did there was no pleasing him these days.

Amy Robinson was home from school for the holidays. I saw her walking down the lane, arm in arm with a woman in a very smart fine tweed costume and a red hat. They were laughing and talking as they turned the corner and disappeared from view.

'That was my sister Lainie,' Bridget said when I spoke to

her in the shop later. 'She is taking Amy away for a few days. They are going down to Bournemouth . . .'

'Aren't you going with them?'

'I really couldn't spare the time,' Bridget said with a little frown. 'We're looking for someone to help out here at the moment, and there's my flower stall. Besides, Amy is going to look over that art school and Lainie is better at things like that than I am.'

'Oh, well, I suppose she's had some experience, working up west the way she does.'

'I think Lainie likes going to art exhibitions,' Bridget said. 'I never would have thought it once, but she's quite the lady these days.'

I noticed an odd inflection in Bridget's voice, and I wondered why she hadn't taken the time off to go to Bournemouth with her sister and Amy. But she changed the subject then, going on to tell me about the new gramophone Joe had bought her, and the records of Enrico Caruso that she had bought for herself.

'He sings so lovely, Kathy,' she told me. 'I could listen to his voice forever. Joe takes me to shows up west sometimes, but it's nice to be able to listen to music like that in your own house. Amy can play the piano, of course. They taught her a lot of things at the school she went to, things I can't see she'll ever need.'

I was thoughtful as I walked home afterwards, wondering if perhaps Amy preferred to be with her aunt, who was the manageress of a fashionable dress shop in the West End to staying in the lanes with her mother.

I'd thought Bridget seemed a bit upset, even hurt, but if she was she had quickly hidden it behind her usual smile.

I glanced at the dog searching the gutters as I made my way home from Ernie Cole's house that morning. It was not wearing a muzzle and after the recent rabies scare in Surrey I felt suspicious of any stray dog in the street; it was the law that all dogs go muzzled for the moment while the scare was on, and I stayed well away as I passed by.

It was May now and my back was aching and I had been feeling out of sorts all day. I hadn't felt like doing much for Ernie, though I had taken him some food for his supper, leaving it on the kitchen table where he would find it when he came in. I thought it might be a while before I managed to go there again. The time for my child to be born was getting very near now, and I felt huge and ungainly.

I was almost past the dog when a child came running down the street kicking a ball and yelling at the top of his voice. His noisy arrival seemed to startle the dog; it put its head up and started to bark ferociously. Without thinking what I was doing, I ran across the street, snatching the child and pushing him behind me as the dog snarled, baring its teeth and appearing ready to bite.

The child screamed and so did I as the dog tensed, seeming about to fly at us and then someone threw a heavy object at it and it turned and fled down the lane. I saw that the object was a book, which I bent to retrieve as its owner came walking up to us. As I turned to hand it back to the man who had come to our rescue, my heart began to beat wildly and I felt as if I was short of breath.

'Kathy . . .' Tom's eyes went over me, taking in the advanced stage of my pregnancy. He frowned and I knew I was not looking my best. The dress I was wearing was an old one of Maggie's and stained on the skirt, and my hair was limp with grease because I hadn't felt like washing it for a few days. 'That was a stupid thing to do.'

'I couldn't let it bite the child.' I had let go of the boy and he was staring at me resentfully as he rubbed his arm where I had gripped it. 'I'm sorry if I hurt you. I thought the dog might bite you.'

'Nah . . .' he said. 'It don't bite, I've seen it afore. You want ter watch what yer doin' missus.'

I watched as he ran off down the lane, fighting for control before I looked at Tom again.

'Well, that's told me, hasn't it?'

'He doesn't understand,' Tom said. 'But you knew the risks. It was foolish and irresponsible in your condition.'

'Yes, I suppose so.' I handed him his book. 'It was fortunate that you happened to be here.'

'I came to see Bridget and Joe.' He was still frowning. 'You might have told me, Kathy, instead of letting me find out from Bridget.'

'Find out what?' My heart raced as I looked into his angry eyes. What did he think I should have told him? Had he guessed the child was his?

'That you were going to marry Billy. Bridget said Maggie had been expecting it for months . . . all the time we were together.'

'No! That's not how it was,' I said quickly. 'Billy asked me to marry him before he went back out there, before we met at the hospital. I didn't say I would – only that I would think about it. I never promised him anything.' I broke off as his gaze narrowed. 'Don't look at me like that, Tom. You don't understand.'

'No, I don't.' He was clearly very angry, his expression cold as he stared at me. 'I thought it was me you were going to marry, if you married anyone.'

'I–I thought so too.' As I saw the expression of disbelief and disgust on his face I knew that I had to lie. 'But we quarrelled and you didn't bother to write or make an effort to see me and then I came back here and met Billy again. He wanted us to get married and . . .'

'You decided you liked him best?' There was bitterness in his voice. 'You never really loved me at all, did you, Kathy?'

My throat was tight with emotion. It hurt me that he should say these things, that he should believe I was so careless of his feelings – so callous. I couldn't answer him, couldn't say

128

the things I wanted to tell him, because they were forbidden
– and it was too late.

'I'm sorry,' I said and turned away. 'Billy will be home
for his tea soon. I have to go.'

'Kathy . . . ?' There was a new note in his voice now, a
note of despair that tugged at my heart strings, but I dared
not wait or look back. 'Kathy, I'm sorry.'

I blinked hard to stop the tears falling. It was too late. I
was Billy's wife and I could never be Tom's.

'Tom's back fer a couple of days,' Billy said when I put
his tea in front of him that evening. 'I saw him fer a minute
when I came back from work. He's asked us both out for a
drink this evenin', Kathy.'

'You go, Billy. I feel too tired.'

'You're always bloody tired these days,' Billy muttered
and grabbed my wrist as I made to turn away. 'You'll bleedin'
well come and do as yer told fer once, do yer 'ear? And yer
can smarten yerself up a bit. I'm sick of seein' yer like that
– you look like somethin' picked up from down the docks.
A bleedin' doxy, that's what I've got fer a wife.'

'That's enough of that!' Mick Ryan surprised me by
coming to my defence. 'I won't stand for that sort o' talk
in my house. Kathy's havin' a hard time with the baby, and
you haven't helped her – out to all hours and never but a few
shillin's on the table for her. I doubt she's got anythin' decent
to put on the way you've been drinkin' your money away.'

It was the first time Mick had ever spoken out, though
Maggie had done so on many occasions. Billy's face went
white and then red, and then he glared at me. He was angry
that his father had taken my side, but perhaps he was also
ashamed.

'I'll give yer some money this weekend. I hadn't thought
about it – yer will need some for the baby an' all.'

'Thanks, Billy. I can find a dress to wear if you really want
me to come.'

'I want ter show orf me wife ter Tom,' he said. 'Yer were always the prettiest girl in the lanes, Kathy – until recently.'

'I've not been feeling well,' I said. 'But I can make myself look better, if you want?'

'Right then,' he said and seemed pleased. 'Get off upstairs and tart yerself up.'

'You can borrow my best dress,' Maggie offered. 'If you pin the back and wear a jacket over it no one will know it doesn't quite fit you, love.'

'Thanks, Maggie, but I let something of my own out this afternoon. I think I can manage.'

After my meeting with Tom I had given myself a long hard look in the mirror in my bedroom and I hadn't liked what I'd seen. While Maggie prepared supper I'd sorted out one of the dresses Eleanor had given me and let out the seams. With a jacket over it and my hair tied back with a ribbon I would look more presentable than I had that afternoon.

Billy nodded his approval when I went back downstairs. Maggie gave me an encouraging smile and told me to enjoy myself.

As we walked to the pub, Billy offered me his arm. He was clearly in a better frame of mind than he had been in a long time and I thought it must have something to do with Tom being home. I knew the two of them had once been good friends and I imagined Billy was pleased to have been invited out.

Tom was waiting for us. He had reserved a table by the window and he stood up as we approached, setting a chair for me. Billy gave him a sharp look, then made a fuss of making sure I was comfortable.

'Kathy hasn't been too well lately, have you, love?'

'I suffer with the backache and other things. I expect most women do at certain times.'

'Backache is a common complaint in advanced pregnancy,' Tom agreed, his eyes going over me thoughtfully.

I avoided his gaze, praying desperately that he hadn't

130

guessed the truth. I didn't want him to know that the baby I was carrying was his, because it could only hurt him more.

'You should tell that good fer nuthin' Ernie Cole to get lost,' Billy said. 'She's always down there doin' things fer 'im. I don't know why. She ain't even sure 'e's 'er father.'

'Billy . . . don't,' I said not daring to look at Tom. 'He brought me up, gave me his name whether I'm his daughter or not. Goodness knows what might have happened if he hadn't.'

'I expect Kathy thinks it's her duty,' Tom said. 'What will you have to drink – Kathy? Billy?'

'I'll get them in,' Billy said. 'You have a chat to Kathy, Tom, Tell 'er what you've been doin' . . . flyin' an' that.'

We were silent for a moment as he walked away, then both of us spoke at once.

'Tom, I have to tell you –'

'Billy doesn't know about us?' Tom said.

'No, he doesn't, but it wasn't that. I didn't know you were ill – after Gran's funeral.'

'Would it have made a difference?'

'You don't understand.'

'You've said that twice now. What don't I understand, Kathy? I got your letter when I came back from the infectious diseases unit. I suppose Bridget told you?' I nodded. 'You said you didn't want to get married. I thought that meant you wanted to go on with your nursing.'

'You didn't reply.'

'I was upset and angry – and then Bridget wrote to tell me you were married. I couldn't believe what you'd done.'

'I'm sorry. I wish I could explain.'

'Why can't you?'

Tom's expression was an odd mixture of pain and anger.

'If I could I would . . .'

It was all I could manage before Billy returned with a tray of drinks, which he placed on the table.

'Port and lemon for you, Kathy love. Beer for you, Tom. I'll get you a whisky chaser later, if you like?'

'Beer is fine for me.'

Tom glanced at my glass as I sipped it. When I was out with him I'd always chosen a glass of white wine. I would have preferred it now but Billy hadn't asked. He never asked me what I wanted these days.

Tom seemed puzzled as Billy started to talk about sport, telling Tom about a boxing match he'd seen and totally ignoring me. I glanced down at the table, afraid of revealing my desperate unhappiness to Tom's searching gaze. Once, when I looked up, I saw him watching me with an odd expression in his eyes. My heart felt as if it was being squeezed and I looked away quickly. Was that pity in his eyes? Did he feel sorry for me because my husband did not treat me with affection and respect?

Tom went to buy the next round of drinks, asking me my preference before he left the table.

'What would you like, Kathy?'

'Kathy always has port and lemon,' Billy said. 'She likes it.'

'I wouldn't mind a glass of ginger beer.'

'You always have port and lemon.' Billy glared at me.

'I'm not sure it's good for the baby.' I'd hardly touched the drink he'd bought me. 'I don't really need one at all.'

'I'll bring a fruit juice if they have it,' Tom said. 'That will do you more good, Kathy.'

Billy scowled at me as Tom went off. 'Were yer tryin' ter make me look a fool in front of me pal?'

'No, of course not. It's just that port is a little strong for me just now.'

'Why didn't yer tell me?'

'You didn't ask . . .'

Billy's look was so full of menace that I felt cold all over. If we had been alone I thought he might have hit me. It was no good, I couldn't stay here any longer. I stood up before Tom could return with the drinks.

'Where do you think you're goin'?'

'Home. I don't feel well.'

'Sit down and I'll take yer 'ome when I'm ready.'

'I'm going now.' I felt the pain strike at my back and gasped, 'I think . . . I think it's the baby.'

'It's too soon,' Billy growled.

'No, I think it's coming.' I took a step forward just as Tom arrived with the drinks. 'I'm sorry. I have to go . . .'

'Is it the baby?' Tom asked, grasping the situation immediately. 'Kathy needs to go home now, Billy – this minute!'

There was such authority in his voice that Billy got to his feet. He was still resentful and reluctant but something made him obey.

'Come on then,' he muttered. 'It's a waste of good drinks though. I should've thought yer could wait fer a bit.'

Tom gave him a withering look, which shut him up instantly. I sensed the simmering anger in him as he grabbed my arm and hurried me out of the pub.

'I don't know why yer 'ad ter come if yer were feelin' bad.'

I was there at his express wish, but then, Billy hadn't known how close I was to my time. I refrained from answering him back, partly because I was in too much pain and partly because Tom was walking with us. He had obviously decided that Billy wasn't fit to be left in charge of a woman who was about to give birth. If there were other reasons for his decision to accompany us I dare not let myself consider what they might be.

Tom walked beside me. Although he made no attempt to touch or assist me, I was comforted by his presence. I knew that I was safe while he was there.

Billy scowled and muttered to himself but Tom's presence restrained his tongue. Had we been alone I knew I should not have escaped so lightly.

When we reached the house, Maggie came bustling into the hall to greet us. She took one look at my face and shook her head.

133

'You'd best leave me to look after her now. Can you walk upstairs if I help you, Kathy?'

'Yes, I think so.' I glanced at Tom. 'Thank you for bringing me home. There's no need for you or Billy to stay. Maggie will look after me.'

'Yeah. Ma will see to 'er,' Billy agreed quickly. 'We can go back and finish them drinks – unless some bugger 'as swiped 'em.'

'You can't think of drink at a time like this!' Tom said incredulously.

'He will be out of the way,' Maggie said, struck by the sharp note in Tom's voice. 'Kathy will be all right with me. I'll let the doctor know. He might pop in later to see as she's doin' all right.'

'I'm a doctor – and I'll be at Bridget's house if she needs me. If you are in doubt, Mrs Ryan – any doubt at all – send for me.'

'If that's what Kathy wants,' Maggie said. 'But men are best out of it when a baby's coming. Isn't that right, Kathy love?'

I nodded at Tom. The pains were coming so fast and I was terrified my waters would break and shame me in front of them all.

'Get me upstairs, Maggie.'

'Come on, love. You lean on me. You'll be all right.'

It was all I could do to climb the stairs. I did not dare to look at Tom, but I heard Billy's raised voice trying to persuade him to return to the pub as they went back outside. I was glad they had both gone. I did not want either of them to hear my screams or witness my pain.

The screams began soon after they left. I was in such terrible pain and Maggie urged me not to hold back.

'It hurts, Maggie . . . it hurts so bad.'

'I know, love. I know. Just be a brave girl and it will all be over soon,' she comforted.

She meant to make things easier for me, but I was torn by

the agony that gripped my tortured body and the guilt that nagged at my conscience. This was surely my punishment for deceiving Billy at the start – and for hurting Tom. It would be better for everyone if both my bastard and I were to die.

The pain seemed to go on endlessly. Maggie had tied a knotted sheet to the bedpost. She told me to pull on it and push when the pains came, but it didn't seem to do any good. The baby just wouldn't come.

After what seemed an eternity, I no longer cared. Why should I try? What reason was there for me to live? Billy hated me because I had lied to him and cheated him, and Tom despised me for what I had become. I might as well let go.

'You're not tryin', Kathy. You have to try . . . Tell her, Bridget. I can't seem to get through to her. She doesn't seem to care.'

Someone bent over me. I had not been aware that Bridget was there, but she stroked my forehead gently, smoothing back the damp hair.

'This isn't like you, Kathy. I know it's hard but you have to keep on pushing.'

'I can't . . . leave me alone. It doesn't matter if I die.'

'I'm going for help,' Bridget said. 'If we don't so something she will die.'

'Your brother said he would come. Mick couldn't find Dr Brownlow.'

'Tom is a better doctor than Brownlow any day!'

'No,' I whispered weakly. 'Don't bother Tom, please. He mustn't come . . . not Tom . . .'

'Ignore her,' Bridget said firmly. 'She doesn't know what she's saying.'

I was aware of Maggie bathing my face with cold water after Bridget left.

'There's no shame in givin' birth,' she said. 'Tom's a doctor. He's seen it all before. Just don't give up, Kathy love.'

Tears were streaming down my face. They didn't understand. How could they know why I didn't want Tom to come?

He ought not to see his child born. He would know the baby hadn't come too soon. Would he also guess that it was his?

I prayed that God would let me die before Tom came, but then he was in the room with us. I felt the touch of his cool, sure hands examining me and I opened my eyes as he bent over me.

'It's a breach birth, Kathy. I'm going to turn the baby and I shall have to cut you a little. I'm going to give you something so that your pain is eased.'

'No, Tom, let me die. It's what I deserve . . .'

'Don't be a fool, Kathy. You're not going to die. I'm here now and I shan't let you die. You and your baby are going to live. Just trust me and believe that it will be all right.'

I sighed and closed my eyes. I was only just conscious and I hardly knew what he did, but I was aware, through the mist in my mind, that the pain had eased a little.

'Forgive me,' I whispered hoarsely as he worked over my tortured body. 'Loved you . . . always loved you . . .'

'Billy knows that,' I heard Maggie say. 'He will be out of his mind when he knows how you're sufferin', Kathy. Mick has gone to fetch him home.'

'No . . .' I muttered but my lips wouldn't work properly. 'Not . . .'

Perhaps it was as well that I could say no more. I was too exhausted and the wail of a new-born baby cried out as if from a long way off. They may have laid the child in my arms for a moment, but I was lost in the mists of pain and the drug Tom had given me.

'It's a boy.' Maggie's voice came to me. 'You've got a lovely son, Kathy.'

'He almost killed her,' Tom said harshly. 'He's very big. Are big babies a family trait, Mrs Ryan?'

'Oh yes, one of my own lads was huge.'

'Well, it was lucky I was nearby. She should rest now. I'll pop in to see how she is tomorrow, but if anything happens that worries you call me at once. It doesn't matter what time it is, fetch me!'

'You've been wonderful, Tom. Billy will be so grateful to you for savin' his wife and child. Worships the ground she walks on, Billy does.'

Why was Maggie lying? She knew our marriage was far from happy. Why was she doing her best to convince Tom otherwise?

I wanted to thank Tom for taking the pain away, but I was too tired. I felt the touch of his hand briefly against my cheek and then he was gone.

A dreadful emptiness swept over me as I drifted away into a blessed sleep. Tom had come to me when I needed him so badly, but now I had to live without him.

The sun was shining when I opened my eyes and I knew I must have slept late into the day. Someone was sitting by the bed, his head bent as though dozing in the chair. In my first conscious thoughts I believed it might be Tom and I tried to speak his name, then the man lifted his head and looked at me.

'I'm 'ere, Kathy love,' Billy said and his voice was a cracked whisper of emotion. 'God forgive me for not bein' 'ere when you nearly died. I never shall—'

'Billy?'

'Don't say anythin', Kathy. I know yer must 'ate me after the way I've treated yer. I was so eaten up by my jealousy and hatred of those bastards what 'urt yer, but I was the one what near killed yer. Ma told me yer gave up, and that's my fault. I've made yer so miserable yer didn't want ter live.'

'It's not your fault, Billy. I cheated you . . .'

'You 'ad no choice,' he said. 'You were ashamed and desperate and yer came to me fer 'elp. I've let yer down, Kathy, but I'll be a better 'usband in future. I give yer me word.'

'I'm sorry I hurt you so badly Billy. Forgive me.'

'I'm the one what needs to be forgiven . . .' Billy broke

off as a knock came at the door and then Tom came in. As soon as he saw him, Billy burst into noisy sobs, jumped up and rushed to capture him in a fiercely emotional hug. 'Tom, can't thank yer enough fer what yer did. If yer hadn't been 'ere I'd have lost my Kathy . . . lost my lovely wife. I were a right swine to 'er and I 'ate myself fer what I done.'

'It's all right, Billy,' I said. 'I understand. There's no need to weep all over poor Tom just because we had a quarrel.'

Billy broke away, wiping his sleeve across his face.

'Will yer listen ter 'er, Tom,' he said looking sheepish. 'Barely back from the dead she is and bossin' me about already.'

'I'm pleased to see you looking so much better, Kathy.' Tom came to the bedside. His manner was detached, professional, as he took my pulse. 'How are you feeling?'

'A little sore but much better.'

'Thanks to you,' Billy said. 'You've always been me best mate, Tom. I don't know what ter say . . .' He broke off, visibly overcome.

'Billy is trying to say thank you for saving my life and that of our son – aren't you, Billy?'

Billy looked at me oddly, then nodded. 'That's about the long and short of it, Tom. I'm grateful fer what you done.'

'I'm grateful too. The child and I would both have died if you hadn't come.'

Tom's expression gave nothing away as he turned from me to Billy. 'I'm a doctor. Saving life is what I do whenever I can. I am glad I was able to help Kathy. You will need to take care of her for a while – no more children for at least two years. Another child too soon could kill her.'

'I understand.' Billy glanced at me. 'I'll take care of yer, Kathy. I promise yer. I've learned me lesson.'

'Well, I must go,' Tom said without glancing at me. 'I just popped in to see Kathy was all right. If there are any complications send for your own doctor and make sure he comes. Kathy should stay in bed for at least two weeks.'

'She won't move from that bed until she's ready.'

'Goodbye, then.' Tom offered his hand and they shook hands. 'Take care of your wife, Billy. You are a lucky man to have her – and that beautiful boy. He is a son any man would be proud of.'

'I'll come down with you,' Billy said. 'Ma will come up in a minute to see if yer need anythin', Kathy.'

I lay back and closed my eyes as they went out together. I was almost certain that Tom suspected the child might be his, and he had found a way of telling me how proud he was of the boy and of me. I had done my best to convince him that the child was Billy's, but there had been something in his eyes that made me believe he knew the truth.

Tears trickled down my cheeks. I had wanted so much to tell Tom he was the father of the baby he had brought into the world, but I knew it was a secret that I must never reveal.

'How are you feelin', Kathy love? Could you fancy a cup of tea and maybe a bite to eat – somethin' light and tasty?'

I opened my eyes and smiled at Maggie. I had wondered in my confused state the previous night why she'd done her best to convince Tom that Billy loved me, but now I understood. Maggie was my friend. She knew that I had married Billy for reasons I did not want to discuss and she had tried to protect me from my own weakness. I could never be Tom's wife and perhaps in his own way Billy did still care for me. I had to make the most of my situation.

'I should love a cup of tea, Maggie. I'll try to eat something if I can manage it.'

'Bridget brought a nice chicken for you. Roasted to perfection it is, all golden brown and succulent. A nice little bit of breast and some bread and butter would go down a treat.'

'You and Bridget are determined to spoil me.'

'We care about you, Kathy – and so does Billy in his way. He was out of his mind with worry after his father sobered him up last night. Mick gave him a right talkin' to – slapped him around a bit – and Billy took it all.

I've never seen him so down before. I think he had a real fright.'

'Yes, I know. He says everything will be different now.'

I sighed and closed my eyes for a moment. Could things ever really be different for Billy and me?

'Let's hope he means it. I'll get that cuppa for you, love.'

I sat up against the pillows as Maggie went out, telling myself to be strong. I had to think of the future, not the past. It was wrong of me to be thinking of Tom when I could hear my son crying in the next room. They had taken him away so that I could sleep but now I wanted to hold him.

As suddenly as the crying had started it stopped and then Billy came in carrying the baby and looking the part of a proud father. He looked at me, seeming oddly shy as if he didn't quite know how to behave.

'I think he wants feedin' – if you're up to it?'

'I'll try,' I said, holding out my arms.

Billy watched as I opened my nightgown and held the child to my breast. He latched on to the nipple immediately, sucking strongly.

'He knows how, if I don't!' I smiled at Billy in amusement and saw that he was also watching the child feed with a silly tender expression on his face.

'He's a fighter,' Billy said and I saw something like hunger in his eyes. I realized that the child had somehow tugged at Billy's heartstrings in a way I would not have thought possible, given the circumstances. 'Thank you for lettin' Tom think he was ours . . .'

Something in his tone touched my heart, and I began to remember that it had been good between us at the beginning. Perhaps if we both tried it could be again.

'He is ours – if you want him to be, Billy?'

He came over to the bed and sat on the edge, reaching out to touch the child's head. There was quite a bit of dark hair, which he smoothed back with his finger.

'Do yer mean that, Kathy? Can yer forgive the way I've been with yer recently?'

'Can you forgive *me*, Billy? Can you forget that I cheated you?'

'I'll try. I'll really try this time. I want us ter be a family, and I'd like a child of me own when you're well again, Kathy.'

'We'll have more than one,' I promised, feeling the sting of tears. It was my fault Billy had been so bad tempered for the past few months. Almost any man would have felt the same if they'd had to watch their wife carrying another man's child. 'Give me time to get my strength back and it can all be as you hoped before we were married. I want us to be happy, too.'

I vowed to myself that I would be a good wife to Billy. I would forget that I loved someone else, forget that look in Tom's eyes when he had placed our child in my arms.

'Yeah.' Billy grinned at me. 'You're still the best lookin' woman in the lanes, Kathy. I'll work 'ard fer yer. Ma says yer need new clothes, and I'm goin' ter get 'em fer yer – pretty things what you'll be proud to wear. And our kid's goin' ter 'ave the best an' all. I'll find us a house of our own and we'll be great together.'

I hadn't seen a light in Billy's eyes like this for months, and I knew he really meant to try this time.

'What shall we call him?'

Billy thought for a moment. 'What about Tommy? You'd both be dead if it weren't for Tom O'Rourke.'

'We could make that his second name if you like. I thought we might call him Michael, after your father.'

'That would please me da,' Billy said. 'Yeah, you're right, Kathy. We'll have him christened Michael Thomas Ryan.'

I smiled and looked down at the child contentedly suckling at my breast. It was a good name – Michael Thomas Ryan, but it wasn't the name he ought to have had.

Eight

'He's lovely, Kathy,' Bridget said as she stopped to look in the pram at Mickey. 'And you keep him so beautifully, too.'

'It's Billy,' I said and chuckled as I bent to tuck the new lace covers about my sleeping child. 'He's always coming home with something for one of us these days. And if I spent all the money he tells me to, Mickey would never get through all the toys and clothes.'

'Yes, I've noticed your Billy is doing well these days,' Bridget said. 'He must work all hours to be able to buy the things he does for you – these prams cost a fortune in the big stores up west. It's new, isn't it?'

'I saw one advertised second-hand and I asked Billy if we could afford it. He came home with this – said he wasn't going to put his son in someone else's cast-offs.'

'Yes, I thought it looked new.' Bridget looked thoughtful. 'I'm so pleased everything is going well for you, Kathy. You seemed a bit down before the baby came, but you're certainly blooming now.'

'I feel marvellous,' I told her. 'Billy is so good to me these days – and all my friends have sent presents. Billy asked Tom to be Mickey's godfather, you know. He wrote and said he wouldn't be able to come but he sent us a silver teething ring. It's a lovely thing, Bridget, and must have been very expensive.'

'Well, he did bring Mickey into the world,' Bridget said. 'I would be surprised if he'd said he would come to the

142

christening, because he's so busy and he seems to spend most of his time abroad these days. He's had offers of good jobs here in London at three of the big hospitals, but he says he likes being in France, though he pops back every now and then. He went down to Bournemouth and took Amy out to lunch on her birthday. Fancy, all that way just for lunch.'

'He came right from France to take her out? But I suppose he comes over by aeroplane. They've started a regular passenger service between London and Paris now, haven't they?'

'Tom says it's safer than crossing the roads up west,' Bridget said and laughed. 'He's a world traveller these days, Kathy. He was talking of spending some time in Italy and Spain, and they are after him in America. Apparently, he's one of the leading experts in the treatment of burns.'

'Yes, I know. Everyone said he was marvellous and his patients thought the world of him. The hospital where we both worked was sorry to lose him.'

'Tom said you were good friends while you were nursing . . . went out together a few times.'

'Yes, we did,' I said, bending down to fuss with the pram covers unnecessarily. 'Well, I had better go, Bridget. I've got a lot of washing and ironing to do before Billy gets home. We're all going to Blackpool for a few days, you know. Maggie has always wanted a holiday there and Billy is going to treat his parents as well as us.'

'That will be nice for you all,' Bridget said. 'Maggie told me yesterday. She's very excited about it.'

'Yes, she is.' I laughed. 'She's been going round the house like a blue-tailed fly all week. I asked her why she had to clean everything when we were going away, and she said she couldn't leave the house dirty.'

'As if there was a speck of dust anywhere in the first place,' Bridget said and shook her head. 'Well, I shan't keep you – enjoy your holiday, love.'

'We shall, thank you.'

I began to wheel the pram towards the house. Michael

Thomas had been born at the end of May 1919 and it was now the end of April 1920. He was a healthy, thriving boy with a good appetite and long weaned. I was sure that he would start to walk any day now. He was already crawling all over the place and could shoot across the room the moment your back was turned and be in the coal bucket before you knew where you were. And Billy swore blind that he had called him Dadda when he picked him up from his cot a few days previously.

The first thing Billy did when he came home in the evenings was to go up and look at Mickey, and if he cried when he was at home, he would have him out of the cot and nurse him until he slept. However, Mickey was a contented baby and hardly ever disturbed our sleep these days, and Billy seemed able to make him chuckle when he was out of sorts.

I could hardly believe how my life had changed since Mickey was born. Billy seemed as if he couldn't do enough to please me, and he was more than generous – too generous. I tried to save a little when I could, because Billy threw his money around as if it grew on trees.

'There's plenty more where that came from,' he'd said once when I questioned him. 'Don't you worry your pretty head about money, Kathy. I told you I would give you everything you wanted, and I shall. All I want is for you to look pretty and be happy.'

'But I don't need all you give me. Save a little in case you should find yourself out of work, Billy. Not everyone is doing as well as you, you know. I hear lots of hard luck stories when I go down the market – men looking for work and their families near starving.'

'Mugs, the lot of 'em,' Billy said with a grin. 'I work 'ard, Kathy. I ain't goin' ter lose me job, don't yer worry.'

I knew better than to argue with him. Billy's temper was much better these days, but it could still erupt if he was pushed, and I had learned not to dent his pride. It meant a lot to him to provide for his family, and he wasn't content to provide food and a roof over our heads like most of the men in the lanes. We had to have the best, because it suited Billy's image of himself. I hadn't realized before how proud he was, but now I was beginning to understand the man I had married.

He was even talking of buying us a house of our own, which was why we hadn't yet moved from Maggie's house.

'I don't see why we should pay rent to someone else when we can buy a house fer ourselves,' he'd said when I'd told him there was a house to rent in Brewery Lane. 'We'll wait a bit longer, Kathy – and then I'll give yer the biggest surprise of yer life.'

Sometimes I worried about where all the money was coming from. I knew he was the foreman at the warehouse where he worked and that his bosses thought well of him, but could he earn all the money he spent at his daytime job?

Billy often went out in the evenings, and it wasn't to the pub these days. He hadn't come home drunk once since Mickey was born, and he'd hinted that he had another job in the evenings. I wondered what sort of a job would pay him the kind of money that allowed him to be so generous to his family, but I hadn't dared to ask. Things were good between us at the moment and I didn't want to spoil them.

'Look at that, she's a real beauty.' Billy tugged at my arm, pulling me in the direction of a smart roadster parked at the edge of the kerb. 'How would you like to go for a spin in one like that, Kathy?'

We were walking along the promenade at Blackpool, on our way to an early evening show. Maggie was looking after the baby so that we could have some time together.

It had been a mild spring day and the evening – the last of our holiday – was pleasant. I laughed as Billy enthused over the sporty little car with its big shiny wheels, huge headlamps and leather upholstery.

'I'll bet that cost an arm and a leg to buy,' I said. 'We couldn't afford something like that, Billy.'

'Maybe not exactly like this one – it's a Bentley – but we will soon.' The cocky grin on his face alarmed me. 'It won't be long before I can afford something very like this, Kathy. Once we get all the expenses of the move settled.'

'What move?' I grabbed at his arm. 'What are you talking about?'

He grinned and tapped the side of his nose in an irritating way. 'It's a secret – a surprise fer yer, Kathy.'

'You just tell me right now, Billy Ryan or I'll . . .' I pulled at the revers of his jacket as he tipped his head on one side. 'Don't you dare look at me like that. I want to know. Have you found us a house – where is it?'

'It's in Brewery Lane. I've bought that house you wanted us to rent and had it done up a bit.'

'Billy! You haven't!' I looked at him excitedly. I'd been afraid he might get something away from the lanes and all our friends, and I wanted to stay close to Maggie and Bridget. 'Oh, Billy, a house of our very own!' I hugged him right there in the street, kissing the side of his face. 'I can't believe it – it's so wonderful.'

'Well, don't drown me,' he said. 'What yer cryin' fer? I thought you'd be 'appy?'

'I am. You know I am. I'm crying because I'm so excited.'

'That's all right then,' he said. 'We'll go and 'ave a drink to celebrate before the show.'

Somehow we never did get to see that show. Billy was full of himself as he told me how he'd planned the surprise for me, swearing his parents to secrecy while the house was being decorated and furnished.

I was a little disappointed when Billy said that the curtains and furniture were already in place. It was my first home and I'd looked forward to choosing the things myself, but I couldn't tell him because it would have spoiled his pleasure in the surprise.

The time had slipped by as we talked and then we realized we had missed the start of the show.

'I wasn't bothered much anyway,' Billy said. 'We can see better shows up west any day, Kathy. We'll 'ave a few more drinks, then get an early night.'

That look in his eyes meant he wanted to make love to me. Billy had been very considerate towards me in bed since Mickey was born. At first he'd been afraid to touch me.

'I shan't break,' I'd promised once I was sure my body was healed sufficiently. 'We've just got to be careful we don't have a baby too soon.'

Billy had been careful most of the time. Once or twice when he'd had a few drinks he'd forgotten, but I hadn't fallen and I wondered if perhaps nature had its own way of arranging things.

Billy was very affectionate as we walked back to our hotel later. He had his arm about my waist and kept nuzzling at my neck.

'People are looking, Billy.'

'Let them. I don't care.'

Billy wasn't drunk but he'd had more than he usually did these days and his hand moved up to caress my breast through the material of my clothes. I tried to move away from him, but he clasped me firmly to his side and I saw a couple of men grin at each other as we passed them by.

'Just wait until we get home, Billy Ryan!'

'I'm burstin' out o' me breeches with the thought of it!'

I gave him a reproving look but I couldn't be cross with him for long. He had tried so hard to please me, and I knew I was very lucky. Few girls who married lads from the lanes could look forward to the kind of life I'd been leading these past months.

Billy started to undress me the minute our door was closed. Our son was staying in Maggie's room for the night, because he'd been sleeping and we hadn't wanted to disturb him.

'You've got lovely tits,' Billy said, bending his head to

suck at the nipples, catching them with his teeth and tugging gently. 'And real slim hips. Most women get fat after a baby, but not you, Kathy.'

'I'm just lucky.'

I smiled up at him as we lay down together and he began to caress my body, taking his time to arouse me and seeming to draw pleasure from just looking at me.

'Basher said you 'ad the looks of a film star. I told 'im to keep his bleedin' thoughts and eyes to 'imself or I'd black 'em fer 'im.'

'Who is Basher? I haven't heard you mention him before.'

'Just someone I work with sometimes.'

Billy slid his hand between my legs, his body covering mine as he thrust deep inside me. Any further questions I might have asked were lost beneath his hungry assault on my body and senses. I was relaxed and content to let him have his way, responding as I always did whether I wanted to make love or not.

It was usually good between us. I did not always reach the ultimate climax of love, but that night my body throbbed with pleasure and I gasped his name as we clung together at the last.

'You're mine,' Billy breathed against my ear as I was drifting off to sleep. 'I'd kill any bugger what touched yer.'

'Oh, Billy, don't be daft.'

He had made threats so often that I no longer felt alarmed by them. It was just Billy talking. He always had to be the dominant one. However, I did wonder what kind of a man went by the name of *Basher* – and exactly what kind of work did he and Billy do together?

We moved to our new house a few days after our return from Blackpool. The curtains were a pretty blue and white flower pattern, which went with the blue carpet square in the front parlour. It looked better than I had expected and I was excited by our new home.

'Oh, it's lovely, Billy,' I said as he took me round. 'And I like the furniture.'

There was a sideboard made of a pale wood with a stringing of ebony, an oak gateleg table with four chairs in the same style of barley sugar twist legs, a sofa covered in a dark blue upholstery and two elbow chairs by the fireplace.

'This is just fer a start,' Billy said preening. He was obviously very proud of the house and what he'd bought for us. 'When yer ready yer can get more bits and pieces. I wanted somethin' we could move into as soon as the house was finished, but yer can change things as we go along.'

'You spoil me, Billy.'

'You're worth it.' He smiled. 'Come on, I'll show yer the bedrooms.'

I knew that look in his eyes. He pounced on me as soon as we were in our bedroom, and we had to try out the new bed. When he was in this kind of mood Billy was fun to be with, and I went along with him, kissing him and responding freely to his loving.

It was only later, when I had started to unpack some of our things, that I realized it was the second time recently that we had forgotten to be careful.

I came from the toilet three weeks later having been violently sick. It was a Sunday morning and Billy had been having a bit of a lie-in for a change. He looked at me expectantly as I sat on the padded stool in front of the dressing table, feeling drained and unwell.

'What's wrong, love? I 'eard yer bein' sick. Did yer eat somethin' what disagreed with yer?'

'I think it means I'm pregnant, Billy.'

He pushed himself up in bed, his gaze narrowing thoughtfully as he looked at me. 'Are yer sure?'

'I'm not certain yet, but I think the signs are there. My breasts feel a bit different – and morning sickness is one of the surest signs.'

'Are yer mad at me, Kathy? Fer not bein' more careful?'

Something about the way he was looking at me told me that he wasn't really surprised. He had deliberately neglected to be careful that night on holiday, and again when he was showing me over the house that first day. Billy had wanted me to get pregnant. He meant to put his mark on me, because I was his wife – his possession.

This past year, he'd accepted Mickey as his son, but now he was impatient for a child of his own. As usual he hadn't consulted my wishes, he'd just gone ahead and done what suited him.

A part of me was angry over the way he'd behaved. I would have liked a little more time between babies, but I wasn't going to risk everything we had built together by quarrelling over something that couldn't be changed.

'No, I'm not mad at you, Billy. What do you want – a boy or a girl?'

'A boy,' he said and then a shadow passed across his face. 'I don't really care – as long as you're all right, Kathy. I know Tom said we should wait two years . . .'

'Tom O'Rourke isn't my husband, you are. I want more children, Billy. By the time the baby comes it won't be far off the two years. I'm sure I shan't have any trouble this time. A lot of women have it hard with their first child.'

'You take care of yerself. Yer can stop that cleanin' fer that Ernie Cole fer a start. You've got enough ter do with the 'ouse and Mickey. Now the baby's comin' you've got ter take more care.'

'I'll cook something for him here and take it along, but I won't do any cleaning. I can't just desert him, Billy. He can't manage to cook for himself.'

'I'd let the bugger starve. If I think yer doin' too much I shall put me foot down. If yer afraid ter tell 'im, I'll do it fer yer!'

'Please don't. I promise I won't do too much.'

The last thing I wanted was for Billy to have a row with

Ernie Cole! We had been contented enough in our own way these past months, but I knew that it could change at any time. If Billy discovered that I had lied again – it didn't bear thinking about!

I had stopped to buy flowers at a stall on the market, and was holding a bunch of sweet-smelling pinks to my nose when I noticed a woman staring at me. She was sort of hovering near the stall, waiting until I moved away, and then she came up to me.

'You're Mrs Billy Ryan, aren't you?'

'Yes?' I stared at her in surprise, not recognizing her. 'I'm sorry, do I know you?'

'No, we've never met, but I heard you was the one what 'elped to raise money fer me and the kids when me 'usband were killed in that raid down the warehouse.'

'Mrs Branning,' I said and smiled at her. 'I'm sorry I didn't recognize you. How are you getting on?'

'We're doing all right,' she said. 'Managin' anyways. I wanted to tell you . . . to say thank you to your 'usband fer what he done fer us. We were turned out of our 'ouse when we couldn't pay the rent, but he found us another place to stay, and he put in a good word fer me in the right place. I've got a decent little job now.'

'Billy did that for you?' I was surprised because at the time he hadn't wanted to know.

'He was real good to me, Mrs Ryan. He's a good man your 'usband, and don't yer let no one tell yer no different.'

'Thank you, I won't.'

She nodded and smiled, then walked off. I stared after her, wondering why she had seemed to think that someone might tell me Billy was not a good man. I knew only too well that he could be generous, but he was also a man of moods.

For a while, I was sick every morning, but then the sickness stopped and I began to feel really well. There was none of the dragging tiredness I had felt with my first baby, and I didn't neglect my appearance as I had during the later months of that pregnancy.

Billy was working hard. He gave me more money every week than I needed, and I saved a little just in case things went wrong and we needed it one day. Not that it seemed likely at the moment. Billy had money to burn.

He had bought himself a smart suit, which he put on when he went out three nights a week. I was curious about where he went, and if I hadn't been sure he was as jealous of me as ever, I might have thought he had another woman.

I teased him one night when he came downstairs with his hair slicked down flat and smelling of fancy oil.

'Are you off to see a woman, Billy?'

'Yer know I wouldn't do that, Kathy. I've not laid a finger on another woman since we wed – not even when I was mad at yer.'

'Where are you going, then? It's a funny sort of work if you need a smart suit. Are you working in a bank?'

Billy chuckled, seeming highly amused. 'Some people reckon Mr Maitland's got more money stashed away than most banks, but 'e don't lend none of it out as fer as I know.' His gaze narrowed as he regarded me thoughtfully. 'Can yer keep a secret?'

'If you ask me to.'

'I work at a kind of club three nights a week. I'm a sort of . . . well, I protect the boss, see. There are people he don't want ter see, what try ter come in and I keep 'em out.'

'Does that mean you have to use violence?'

'Nah . . .' Billy preened and gave me a cocky grin. 'When they see me and Basher they behave respectful. I've only 'ad ter use force a few times. Maitland's a good boss, Kathy. Some nights I drive 'im places instead of workin' at the club.'

'What kind of places?'

'Never you mind that. I've told yer more than I should now.'

'Is that where the money comes from? It's not from your job at the factory, is it?'

'You don't buy houses on wages from the factory, Kathy. A man 'as to 'ave a bit o' ambition if 'e wants ter get on. I'm looking ter be rich one day. Richer than Tom O'Rourke will ever be despite his doctorin'.'

I heard a slight note of jealousy in Billy's voice. Was he jealous of Tom? I hadn't realized it before. I'd thought Billy respected and liked his friend, but now as I looked at him I knew that he was harbouring resentment deep down. Tom had been born in the lanes the same as Billy, but he'd gone to better schools and then to college – he'd made something of his life.

Billy needed to be better than his friend. I understood now why he had wanted me to look pretty the night we went for a drink with Tom. He'd wanted Tom to envy him his wife – he'd wanted to show me off as if I were a trophy. Since the night Tom had saved my life, and then told Billy he was a lucky man, Billy had made sure I had everything I needed to look my best.

Was that why he'd bought us a house, why he was talking of buying a similar car to the one Tom had been driving at that time? Because he had to compete with his friend – to be bigger than Tom?

A chill ran through me as I understood my husband's motivation as never before. What would Billy do if he ever discovered that Tom O'Rourke was Mickey's father?

In the November of 1919 Nancy Astor had been elected as the first woman MP. I'd received a letter from Ally at that time; she told me that she was just about to give birth to her second child. Her first had been a boy, and she had brought him to visit once just after Mickey was born, but I hadn't seen her since, until she turned up on her own one morning out of the blue.

She told me she'd had to get out of the pub or she would have gone mad.

'Mike is a lazy so and so sometimes,' she complained. 'I have to keep on at him all the time or he would leave everything to me. I've got the child to look after as well as the cooking and cleaning, but he expects me to serve behind the bar as well. This morning I just walked out and left him to it. He can see how he likes it for once.'

'Maggie says all men are lazy if you let them be, but Billy is always at work these days.'

'I always thought you would marry Billy,' she told me with a satisfied look. 'It's far better than trying to go above your station.'

I hadn't argued with her. Besides, I had warned her not to mention Tom in front of Billy, and she'd been very careful when he was around.

'We're friends, Kathy,' she told me. 'We might not have been friends now if you had married the other one.'

Ally said we were friends, and we were – but I knew Tom was right when he said she was jealous of me. She had found running a pub much harder than she'd thought it would be, and she told me she wished now that she hadn't got married for a while.

'I wish I'd waited,' she said pulling a face. 'Do you ever think about the time we were nursing, Kathy? It was fun, wasn't it?

I agreed that it was fun, but hard work.

'Not as hard as looking after a pub and a kid,' she said. 'You're lucky, Kathy. Billy gives you everything you want.'

'Yes, he does,' I said. 'I know I'm lucky.'

I was lucky but if I could have gone back to the time when we were nursing together I would.

It was in December 1920 that Billy took me to hear the Dixieland Jazz Band from America at the London Palladium, and then the following January we heard that alcohol had been banned in America.

'We shall have all the Yankees comin' over now if they can't get a drink,' Billy quipped. 'Don't bleedin' blame 'em neither!'

Our daughter was born at the beginning of February 1921. This time I gave birth easily and Billy fetched the doctor to me himself. He waited downstairs and came into the room soon after Sarah made her entrance.

'I'm sorry, Billy,' I said as he bent over the child that laid in my arms. 'I know you wanted a boy. I'll try to do better next time.'

'She's beautiful,' he said and bent to kiss me on the mouth. 'I don't care that she's a girl, love. You're both well and that's all that matters.'

Billy had bought me a little seed pearl necklace, which he gave me as a thank-you gift for giving him his daughter.

'You're spoiling me again, Billy.'

'I've always said yer were worth it.' He gave me an odd glance. 'Did Bridget tell yer that Tom's back from America? He's comin' on a visit next month.'

'That will be nice. We haven't seen him since Mickey was born.'

We hadn't seen him, but not a day had passed that I hadn't thought about him, hadn't wondered where he was and what he'd been doing. Despite things being so much better for Billy and me, I could never quite forget the man I still loved. I supposed I never would.

'He's been travellin',' Billy said. 'We'll 'ave 'im ter dinner, Kathy. You'll be feelin' better by then. Yer can get a new dress and spend a bit on things fer the 'ouse, if yer like.'

'I'll make everything look nice, Billy. If I'm lucky, I'll have my figure almost back by then.'

'I've got another surprise fer yer,' he said and looked pleased with himself. 'As soon as yer up and about again I'll take yer for a spin in me car.'

'You've bought a car? Oh, Billy!' I could see he was excited but there was a cold feeling at the back of my neck. How could he afford a car? Surely he didn't earn enough from just throwing people out of a nightclub? It wasn't as if he'd been mean with his money lately. 'Can . . . can you afford it?'

'Don't start naggin', Kathy. I'll make the decisions about what I can and can't afford.'

There was a flush of annoyance on his face. Billy did not like to be questioned about money or where it came from, and I knew better than to push the point. My husband's temper could flare up without warning and I didn't want to quarrel with him.

The news that Tom was coming on a visit made my heart race. It seemed so long since I'd seen him, though he'd sent the occasional postcard addressed to Mr and Mrs Billy Ryan. He wrote longer letters to Bridget and she told me what he was doing and where he was whenever I saw her.

Bridget was aware of something between her brother and me. She had never said so in as many words, but there was an odd note in her voice when she gave me news of him that told me she knew. She didn't understand why things had worked out the way they had, and I couldn't tell her the truth. But I think she sensed that my life wasn't as good or as happy as I pretended.

It wasn't that I was desperately unhappy. Billy was good to me in many ways, and as long as I didn't question him or go against his wishes he was good humoured and loving. Sometimes I hated myself for having married him. I hated what I had become.

My life with Billy was comfortable, but I sometimes felt I was living in a gilded cage. I was Billy's wife, a possession he guarded jealously, something to be shown off rather like his new car, but I wasn't a person in my own right. We didn't share things. Billy gave and I was expected to take whatever he handed out and smile.

At other times, when I saw friends that I'd known at school

struggling to make ends meet, I knew I was lucky. They had no more freedom than I, and some of them had violent husbands who beat them on a Saturday night or whenever they'd had a few drinks.

Billy wasn't often violent. He had been rough with me a few times, but he hadn't beaten me the way some men beat their wives, and for that I was thankful. Yes, Ally was right when she told me I was lucky. I ought to put Tom right out of my mind and stop wishing for the moon.

'What do yer call this bleedin' pap?' Ernie Cole glared at me as I set a rice pudding down on the kitchen table. 'Don't give me rubbish like that. I want a good meat pudding.'

'You were sick yesterday and you didn't eat the stew I brought you. I thought you might like something light for your stomach.'

'Well, don't bleedin' think,' he muttered and knocked the dish on to the floor. 'Get me some bread and cheese.'

'You can get it yourself,' I said. 'I don't have to put up with this and I'm not going to.'

He glared at me as I walked out, but I'd had enough of his grumbling for one day. Billy got annoyed with me for coming here at all, and there were times when I almost made up my mind that I wouldn't come again. Yet the threat of what Ernie might do if I ignored what he thought of as my duty hung over me and so I continued to visit now and then, despite my husband's and Ernie's continual complaints.

I saw Tom as I was returning from the market that afternoon. Mickey was in his pushchair. He could walk quite well now, but it was too far to the market and back, so I usually took the chair that Billy had bought for me. It was, of course, brand new.

'Kathy . . .' Tom's eyes went over me and I was glad that I was wearing a dress that suited me and was one of the new shorter-length dresses that were beginning to become so fashionable. It wasn't as daring as some young women wore, but flirted above my ankles and had a flattering tunic style. 'How well you look . . . lovely. I think motherhood suits you. Bridget told me you have a little girl now.'

'Sarah is with Maggie. I can't manage them both when I go to the market. Mickey doesn't like being in the pram with his sister and he makes a fuss if I try to take him like that. So I usually bring him on his own at the moment. Sarah sleeps most of the time in the afternoon and is no trouble for Maggie to look after.'

Tom looked at the boy and I caught a wistful expression in his eyes. 'He's getting a big lad now. I think he will be tall when he grows up, Kathy.'

'Yes, I think so too. Sarah is much smaller. She's like a little doll, but very pretty.'

'Her mother was always pretty.' Tom's gaze reflected a hungry yearning. 'Have you got time to stop for a drink somewhere? We could put the pushchair in the back of my car. I've got a Daimler Phaeton now, which has a lot more room than my old roadster.'

'I don't think I should.' I saw the disappointment in his eyes and relented. 'But as it's a nice day we could walk as far as the river and back. I sometimes take Mickey to see the boats going by to the docks. He loves them, especially when they blow their hooters.'

'That would be pleasant.' Tom fell into step beside me. We walked in silence for a few minutes, then: 'Are you happy, Kathy?'

'I . . . I'm content most of the time.' His question had surprised me into the truth. 'Billy is good to us. He bought a house and he's got a car now – but happiness is something that doesn't come easily, I've found.'

'I knew Billy had bought a car. Bridget told me it's similar to the one I had during the war. I drive something more sensible now.'

'Perhaps Billy will change his for an Austin saloon. It would be better for the children when we want to take them out, but he was set on that roadster.'

'Because I had one?' Tom raised his eyebrows. 'Bridget always said he was jealous of me when I went away to school. I've tried to be the same with him as I was when we were lads, but it doesn't quite work. I'm not sure why.'

'Billy is very proud. He likes to be the best – to have the best.'

'Why did you marry him? You're not in love with him.'

His last words were a statement, not a question.

'I can't answer that question, Tom. It wouldn't be fair to you – or Billy.'

'Not answering isn't fair to me, Kathy. Surely I have a right to know why you chose him! What did I do wrong?'

'We had quarrelled. You didn't try to contact me . . .' I faltered as I saw his look. 'I should have apologized, Tom. You were angry because I didn't want to stop with you that night, but I was upset over Gran. Afterwards I wished I had said yes. I missed you so much, but I was proud and foolish – and then . . .' My breath trailed away as I realized how fruitless this was. I couldn't tell him the truth so why go on?

'And then?' Tom took hold of my arm, turning me to face him. 'That doesn't explain why you married Billy. Unless, you were having my child.' His face was grey and twisted with grief. 'I've agonized over this for months, Kathy. Mickey wasn't born too soon the way Maggie Ryan pretended. He was far too big. He couldn't have been Billy's. He was still in France in September.'

'Of course he isn't,' I said my heart contracting with fear. 'But Billy doesn't know Mickey is yours and you mustn't let him guess, Tom. He would go mad with jealousy. I didn't realize how much he envied you until recently, but now I know that he feels it deep down. He thinks that you've done so much better than he has and he wants to be as good or better than you. If he knew the truth he might harm Mickey or me.'

'I shall never tell him.' Glancing at Tom I saw the sparkle of tears in his eyes and understood how much this hurt him, knowing that he had a son he could never claim or acknowledge as his own. 'But thank you for telling me. So it was my fault. I didn't make up our quarrel and you thought I'd abandoned you – that's why you married Billy.'

'Something like that.' I couldn't look at Tom as I went on. 'I was ashamed, and frightened of having an illegitimate child, and Billy had always wanted me. He said he was going to marry me and I –'

'What did you tell him? He must know Mickey isn't his?'

'He knows. He was furious when he found out so I . . . I lied to him. I told him three soldiers raped me and I didn't know who they were.' My cheeks were flaming as I met Tom's look of disbelief. 'I know . . . I know it was a terrible thing to do. I've been ashamed of myself ever since. I shouldn't have married him and I shouldn't have lied. It would have been better if I'd had put Mickey into care.'

'Is that what you really wanted?'

'No! No, I love Mickey – but what I did was unfair to Billy.'

'Is that why you let him treat you like a doormat?'

'I don't! He doesn't.' I smiled wryly. 'He's much better since you told him he was lucky to have me for a wife. I'm his prized possession along with the house and the car.'

'Are you very unhappy?' Tom's eyes seem to probe deep into my mind.

'No, no, of course not. I told you, Billy is very generous with his money.'

'But it's not what you want from life – is it?' Tom looked thoughtful as I remained silent. 'I'm to blame. I was in too much of a hurry, Kathy. I shouldn't have pushed you into making love when I did. You wanted to go on with your nursing.'

'It wasn't your fault, Tom. That time you took me to the sea – I was never happier. Nursing meant a lot to me, but I know now that being your wife was what I really wanted.'

'Why didn't you come to me? If you'd only told me . . .'

My throat was tight and the tears were very close.

'I couldn't, Tom. You don't understand.'

'Then tell me, Kathy. Make me understand.'

'No. I can't, it's too late.' Tears were blinding me. 'I'm going home, Tom. Please don't try to stop me. Don't follow me. I'm going home to my husband.'

'You could leave him. We could go to America . . .'

'No!' I held out my hand to ward him off. 'I can't leave Billy. I won't leave him. I loved you, Tom, but it's over. It's over!'

I turned Mickey's pushchair and walked quickly away from him. My heart felt as if it were being torn in two. I wanted so desperately to tell Tom the truth, to make him understand why I'd had no choice, but I knew I mustn't. It was too late. Far too late.

The night Tom came to dinner I had the house polished from top to bottom and smelling of lavender. There were lace cloths on the table and flowers everywhere.

'It looks really posh,' Billy said when he saw what I'd done. 'You've made it a real home and you didn't spend a lot of money either.'

'I did buy those cushions and that pretty wine table,' I said. 'But it's the small things that make the difference.'

'It's the way you look after the place,' Billy said. 'I always knew you were different from the other girls, Kathy. I reckon I got myself a winner.'

The meal I produced was as good as you could buy in any fancy restaurant according to Billy, and Tom seemed to enjoy it. He had bought a bottle of my favourite wine to go with the meal and some special chocolates to enjoy with our coffee.

'I never realized that Kathy was such a good cook,' he told Billy after the meal. His eyes were warm with approval as he looked at me and I was afraid that Billy would notice but he seemed to take the compliment for himself. 'Where did you learn to make puddings like that, Kathy?'

'Ma taught her,' Billy said. 'She taught Kathy to cook, didn't she, love?'

'Yes, Maggie taught me most things, but I found the recipe for the pudding we had tonight in Mrs Beeton's cookery book.'

'Ah yes, Mrs Beeton – the housewife's trusty friend.'

'Yes. I bought it some time ago when we were in Hunstanton at that little bookshop near the front.'

I saw something flash in Tom's eyes and realized too late that I had made a mistake.

Billy was looking at me oddly, his eyes narrowed to suspicious slits. 'I didn't know yer 'ad been ter Hunstanton, Kathy. When were that?'

'Oh, it was when I was working at the hospital. I went away with a friend – a few days before my grandmother was taken ill.'

'Did yer go with Ally? You've never mentioned it.'

'There were several of us. No, Ally didn't come that time. I often spent weekends with my friends, Billy. Sometimes we came up to town and sometimes we went to the sea.'

'Yer ain't ever said nuthin' before.'

'It wasn't important. It was just that I remembered where I bought the book.'

'I like your car,' Tom said as he sensed the tension between us and sought to change the subject to less dangerous ground. 'It's like one I had some years back, but in much better condition than mine was.'

Billy turned to look at him. He was still frowning but his attention was diverted. They talked about cars and the various merits of different marques for a long time, but after Tom had gone Billy followed me upstairs to our room.

'What were that all about then?' he asked. 'I thought yer couldn't cook until Ma taught yer?'

'I couldn't cook very much, Billy, not the kind of things Maggie does, just bits and pieces that Gran had taught me. That's why I bought the book when I saw it.'

'Thinking about when yer got married, were yer?'

'Yes, I suppose so. I was just interested when I saw the book and so I bought it.'

His hand shot out, gripping my wrist.

'Don't lie ter me, Kathy. If I catch yer flirtin' with a bloke – any bloke – I'll make yer sorry.'

'I don't know what you mean.' I pulled away from him, rubbing at my wrist. 'You hurt me, Billy. I don't like it when you're rough with me.'

'I'll be more than rough with you if you make eyes at me mate.'

'What do you mean? I wasn't making eyes at Tom, if that's what you are insinuating.'

'And don't give me them long words neither. I saw yer smilin' at 'im and tellin' him yer liked that wine – tasted like vinegar to me. Don't think I'm blind or soft in the 'ead, Kathy. I see the way yer looked at 'im all soppy and puttin' on airs.'

'I thought you wanted to make an impression on him? I went to so much trouble for your sake, Billy.'

'That's what you say. It ain't the first time I've noticed somethin', Kathy. I'm warnin' yer. If I ever find out there's somethin' goin on between yer . . .'

'Of course, there isn't! How could there be? I haven't seen Tom for ages. Not since the night Mickey was born. You know he couldn't come for the christening.'

'Yer were talkin' in the street with 'im the other day, so don't say yer weren't. Someone saw yer and I 'eard about it.'

'We were just talking, Billy. Tom O'Rourke is your friend. Surely I can talk to him without you thinking I'm having some sort of an affair with him?'

'You just better hadn't,' he said. 'I forgave yer once, Kathy – next time I'll beat the livin' daylights out o' yer!'

Nine

B illy's outburst really frightened me. I knew I'd made a slip of the tongue when I spoke of buying the cookery book in Hunstanton, but I must also have given myself away in other ways. Billy had certainly noticed something between Tom and I, which meant I had to be very careful in future.

Although a part of me wished Tom would stay on at Bridget's for a while, the sensible half of my mind was relieved when he left almost at once. Billy's suspicions were aroused now, and I couldn't be sure I wouldn't betray my thoughts again. Being near Tom, talking to him, just seeing him, affected me so powerfully that perhaps I wasn't able to behave as I normally did.

Tom didn't attempt to see me alone again. I wasn't sure if he was angry with me for refusing to explain why I'd married Billy instead of him, or if he was simply being careful for my sake.

'He had thought of returning to America,' Bridget told me when I met her in the street a few days later. 'But he's been offered a job that interests him here in London and he has decided to take it.'

'Tom is staying in London?'

Why did my heart gladden at the news? It was foolish of me to feel pleased because Tom had decided to stay nearby. Nothing had changed for me, and it would be dangerous to let myself hope that I might see him sometimes. We could never be together in the way we wanted and it would just make Billy jealous if Tom came to visit us.

164

Kathy

'He said it was only for a year or two – just until he makes up his mind what he wants to do next.'

Surely he wasn't hoping that I would change my mind and leave Billy? Sometimes I wished desperately that I could just walk away, but since I couldn't be with Tom, there was no point in leaving my husband and breaking up a home that could still be happy on occasion.

Billy's moods had got worse again recently. He was seldom in the house and when he came to bed late I caught the stink of strong drink on his breath.

He didn't often make love to me now, but when he did he was rough, taking what he wanted without bothering if I felt any pleasure, carelessly inflicting bruises and pain. I retaliated in the only way I could by pretending to be asleep; refusing to be roused whatever he did. My passive resistance did nothing to improve his temper and he was forever complaining about something.

Maggie noticed how things were going when she came round one Saturday morning to bring the children some fruit she had bought for them in the market. She said nothing during Billy's outburst, but turned to me in concern after he had gone out.

'You don't have to put up with that, Kathy. If Mick spoke to me so rudely I'd take the rolling pin to him, so I would!'

'If I say anything it only makes him worse. You told me once that I had to take him as he was or leave him, Maggie.'

She looked at me thoughtfully for a moment. 'If this continues you might be better to take the children away rather than let him treat you like that.'

'You don't mean that, Maggie. Not a good Catholic wife like you. What would Father O'Brien say if I did?'

'He'd tell you it was your duty to stay no matter what – that's if you'd been married in the church, but you weren't. There's a case for a divorce with it bein' a civil service.' Maggie shivered suddenly. 'Mercy on me, it's a mortal sin

I'm tellin' yer to commit, lass. O' course I don't want yer to leave him, Kathy. He's my son, whatever he is, but I think you should stand up for yourself more. Billy will have no respect for you otherwise. You were always willing to give back as good as you got in the old days.'

I smiled but didn't answer. Her words had gone home, though. Tom had implied that I was letting Billy walk all over me, and now Maggie was saying the same thing. I had simply taken the easy path to keep the peace, but Maggie was right. My guilt had made me accept Billy's moods at the start, but I'd paid for my mistakes. I'd been a good wife to him and there was no reason why I should put up with his temper.

Bridget was reading a letter when I popped into the shop to buy some boiling bacon to make a pudding for Billy's supper. She was frowning over it and for a moment my heart stood still.

'Not bad news?' I said, wondering immediately if the letter was from Tom.

'No, not bad news; it's good news actually, for my sister. Lainie's boss has just died and left her quite a bit of property. There's the dress shop and a flat up west – and a house in Cornwall.'

'That must amount to quite a bit of money, Bridget. I'll bet Lainie is excited?'

'Yes. She isn't quite sure what to do at the moment. She says she wants to keep the shop and the flat – but she might sell the house in Cornwall. She doesn't think she'll use that much. She was always a town person. And she's needed at the shop, because she doesn't trust the girls she's got to look after it for her.'

'Still, the money it brings in will be nice.'

'Yes, it will. I'm pleased for her.'

Bridget was still frowning and I sensed there was something more on her mind, but I didn't press her. She told me most things, and if this was something she needed to keep to herself, it wasn't my business to pry.

I told Billy I'd had enough of his moods when he came home for his supper that evening.

'I don't deserve this, Billy, and I'm not going to stand for it any longer. If you don't treat me with more respect I shall leave you.'

'And where do yer think yer goin'?'

'I don't know. I'll find a job – anything would be better than putting up with the way things have been between us lately.'

Billy glared at me and for a moment I thought he would fly into another rage. His fists balled at his sides as though he wanted to strike out, but then he sat down at the kitchen table and I saw something like fear in his eyes.

'I've lost me job, Kathy. I did somethin' stupid and Mr Maitland told me I was through. There'll be no more extra money comin' in for a while.'

'Is that why you've been in such a mood lately?'

'I reckon I've taken it out on you.' Billy looked oddly ashamed. 'I've got ter let the car go. I never finished payin' fer it . . . only a deposit and so much every week. Without that extra money I can't afford to keep it.'

'Oh, Billy . . .' I felt sympathy for him as I saw how much it had cost him to tell me that. 'It doesn't matter. I didn't want a car anyway.'

'Yer would if it was one like Tom's – comfortable for takin' the children out now and then.'

'Maybe you'll be able to get another car one day. You might find another job in the evenings, Billy.'

'Not like the one I 'ad. I were a fool.'

'What did you do that upset your boss?'

His eyes slid away from mine. 'Some things are better left untold, Kathy. I knew the rules and I broke 'em. I'm lucky ter be let orf as easy as I were.'

'What do you mean?' Again I saw that flash of fear in his eyes. 'Are you afraid of Mr Maitland?'

'Anyone with any sense is afraid of crossin' 'im.'

'Who is he, Billy?' I wondered about the man who could instil such respect and fear into my husband.

'You just forget I ever mentioned 'is name. I'm warnin' yer fer yer own sake, Kathy. Don't poke yer nose in me business. I've been let go from me job, but there's a chance he might offer me other work if I keep me mouth shut and do as I'm told.'

'I think you should forget about him and look after your job at the factory. I don't need all the money you've been giving me. We can manage on what you earn from your proper job.'

'I gave that up months ago. I was makin' so much money, but I got greedy, thought I could make more on my own account. I tried to take advantage of somethin' I 'eard and I got caught.'

'Perhaps if you apologized?'

Billy gave me what was a shadow of his old cocky grin.

'Yer don't know 'im, Kathy. I've been told 'e's considerin' me case. If I behave 'e might give me another chance. If I don't . . .' Billy made a chopping gesture across his throat. 'Curtains.'

'Billy! You can't mean that? He wouldn't . . . ?' A cold shiver ran down my spine as I saw the fear in his face – fear he was trying unsuccessfully to hide. 'He wouldn't harm you?'

'Nah.' Billy shrugged his shoulders in an attempt at bravado, but I sensed that he was far from confident. He really was afraid of this man he called Mr Maitland. 'It just means I'll 'ave ter find other work, and that ain't easy the way things are. There are plenty of blokes lookin' fer a job – and I walked out of me last one.'

That meant he had no references to offer a new employer. There were jobs that would not require references, but they were often unskilled labour that paid badly. Billy would find it difficult to get as good a job as he'd had before without help.

'I can't ask Bridget to put a word in for him this time,'

168

Maggie said when I spoke to her the next day. 'She doesn't approve of the way Billy has been carryin' on. He gave up a good job without even working his notice – and there's the way he's been splashing money about. People think it wasn't earned honestly.' She stopped as if feeling that she had already said too much. 'But that's nonsense.'

'Billy didn't steal the money, Maggie. He was working for someone.' Maggie looked curious as I stopped abruptly. 'I can't tell you his name. It might get Billy into worse trouble.'

'I knew he was up to no good!' Maggie's mouth thinned with disapproval. 'I told Mick you don't get money like that doin' honest work.'

'I'm not sure what kind of work he was doing. I don't think he was breaking the law.'

'If he wasn't, he was pretty near to it, I'll be bound. I've been bothered over it for a while now, but I didn't want to upset you, Kathy.' Now that Maggie had started, the words came pouring out. 'Stands to reason most folk can't earn that kind of money.'

'Well, whatever it was that he's been doing, he upset the man he was working for and he's lost his job. He says there's no chance of him getting it back.'

'It's probably a good thing if he has lost that job if what I've been hearing is right. He's been hanging out with people I wouldn't care to know, Kathy. Maybe he'll straighten himself out now.'

'Let's hope he finds something else and settles down.'

I was thoughtful after Maggie left. Could the Mr Maitland Billy had been working for be the father of Miss Mary Maitland – the young girl who had brought me Eleanor's ring?

I'd considered the possibility a couple of times since Billy had told me the name of his employer but not pursued it further. Mary had seemed nervous of her father's disapproval, and Billy was obviously worried about something.

This mysterious Mr Maitland was clearly a dangerous man to know.

I had been shopping in the market one morning when I heard the voice calling to me. I stopped and looked round. For a moment I didn't recognize the woman coming towards me, and then I realized it was Valerie Green. I hadn't seen her for ages – since the night Billy had got into a fight at the dancehall.

Her hair was a lighter colour than before and I thought she must have used some kind of bleach on it, because it looked a bit dry and frizzy. She was wearing a shorter skirt than most people I knew would think decent, and a lot of red lipstick.

'I thought it was you,' she said. 'I hope you didn't mind me calling out to you like that?'

'No, of course not. Why should I?'

'Some people round here would rather not know me these days – not since I started working at that club as a hostess. They think I'm a prostitute, but I'm not. I just talk to men and get them to buy drinks. Some of the men ask me to go with them, but I don't. The boss doesn't approve of girls working a sideline.'

'Oh?' I was surprised by her confession. Why was she telling me? It was as if she thought I knew where she worked. 'What made you give up nursing?'

'The same as you, I expect, but he wouldn't marry me so I got rid of the kid. You were lucky, Kathy. Billy's all right.'

'I thought you didn't like him?'

'I didn't – but he's been nice to me recently. Helped me out with money a couple of times. Nothing wrong – nothing you wouldn't like, Kathy. He thinks the world of you. Never looks at any of the girls at the club.'

'You've seen Billy, at the club?' Now I understood. Valerie must work at the club where Billy had been a bouncer.

'Yes. I thought he must have told you?'

'He didn't tell me much about it at all – he said it was better that way.'

'He's got sense . . . or I thought he had.' She looked at me doubtfully. 'I heard somethin' I wasn't supposed to the other day. Tell Billy to be careful. I don't know much, but he wants to be real careful.'

'Of Mr Maitland?'

She nodded, looking over her shoulder uneasily. 'He doesn't forgive lightly, Kathy. Tell Billy not to trust anythin' he says in future. It would be better for all of you if you went somewhere right away from London.'

'What did you hear? It must have been bad?'

I felt cold shivers run down my spine as I saw her expression.

'I can't say any more or I'll be in trouble too. I have to go now. Just tell Billy what I said.'

I watched as she walked quickly away. I would tell my husband about my meeting with Valerie, but I doubted if he would take much notice. Billy did things his own way. I worried about Valerie Green's warning, but there was nothing very much I could do. Billy never listened to me.

My anxiety for Billy's safety receded to the backwaters of my mind when he found a job at a factory. He was the nightwatchman, which meant that he came home and went to bed when I got up and started my day. The work didn't pay very well, but at least there was some money coming in and we managed. I still had a few pounds I'd put by when Billy was giving me far more than I needed, and that helped out with the bills.

And then I started to be sick in the mornings again. Billy looked at me as I came back from the toilet on the third morning in a row. He had just gone to bed and I knew he must have heard me being ill. The look in his eyes was wary, showing none of the delight there had been the last time I was pregnant.

'You're 'avin' another kid,' he said accusingly.

'It looks that way.'

'We can't afford it. Can't yer get rid of it? Drink some hot gin sittin' in the bath, or somethin'.'

'Billy! You can't mean that?' I stared at him in horror.

'We can barely keep the two we've got. I've 'eard there are ways ter get rid of a kid yer don't want.'

'Well, I'm not going to so don't say another word! Most of the remedies don't work – and those that do are dangerous.'

'You'll 'ave ter manage with less then. Yer could go ter work fer a couple of hours, or get that bleedin Ernie Cole ter pay yer fer what yer do fer 'im.'

'I shan't have the time or the energy to go to work with another baby on the way. Couldn't we sell the house and move into a rented place?'

'I still owe fifty quid on it. I was buyin' it in instalments. We may 'ave ter let it go fer what we can get and move back in with Ma.'

Billy glared at me angrily, as though blaming me for the reversal in his fortunes.

'That wouldn't matter. I'm sure Maggie wouldn't mind for a while. I'm not sure she'd want us there for long, though. It wasn't so bad when we just had Mickey . . .'

Three children to shatter the peace of her home was rather a lot to ask of Maggie. She would do it if she were forced, but it wouldn't be easy. It would be better if we moved into a rented house. Billy could surely sell ours and pay off his debt – unless there were more debts that he hadn't told me about?

Billy had clearly been spending far more than he ought for a long time. Where had that money come from? Was it just from the job he'd told me about, or was there more that he was hiding from me? I felt the coldness spread through me as I realized the obvious source of the loan for the house. If my husband owned money to the dangerous Mr Maitland, what was he going to demand in return?

'I'm sorry to be the one to tell you,' Bridget said. 'I heard it this morning, Kathy, and thought you would rather hear it from me than someone else.'

'Is it something about Billy?' My heart beat wildly as I saw the anxious look in her eyes. 'Is he in some kind of trouble?'

'No, not Billy, it's Ernie Cole,' Bridget said. 'He has finally lost his job for good. Apparently there was a huge row at the brewery and Mr Dawson told him not to go back there again. And then last night he got drunk and smashed up the pub where he was drinking. The police took him away and they say he'll go to prison for at least a couple of months; malicious damage and disrupting the peace.'

'He gets worse,' I said and sighed. 'Oh, well, at least I shan't have to bother about getting him a meal this evening, shall I?'

'You look tired, Kathy,' Bridget said, her eyes going over me anxiously. 'Is there anything wrong – anything I can do to help?'

'No, it's just that I'm feeling a bit down,' I said and smiled at her. 'Problems, you know what it's like. I'll be fine again soon.'

'Yes, I did hear Billy had some problems,' Bridget said. 'If you need money, Kathy . . .'

'No, we're fine,' I lied. 'Honestly, Bridget we're fine.'

We might have problems but I wasn't so desperate yet that I needed to beg from friends. I still had my pride.

One of Billy's problems was solved when I fell down the stairs a few days later. Mickey had left a toy train on the third stair from the top and somehow I didn't see it. I caught my heel on it, tripped and tumbled all the way down.

My scream brought Billy from his bed. He bent over me anxiously as I tried to get up and couldn't.

'What's wrong, Kathy? Oh, God! Yer ain't broke yer back? Not in a little fall like that?'

'It wasn't a little fall,' I snapped. 'I could easily have broken my neck, Billy, but I think it's just my ankle. It hurts a lot.'

'I'll carry yer up ter bed.'

'Just leave me alone!'

Despite my protests, he picked me up, took me to the bedroom, then pulled his outdoor clothes on and went rushing off to fetch Maggie.

'It looks like a bad sprain,' she said after she'd bathed my ankle with cold water. 'You were right, Kathy, there's no bones broken. Not that I can feel anyway.'

'It still means I shall be laid up for . . .' I gasped as I felt the new pain in my belly. 'Oh no! Maggie, I think I'm having a miscarriage. The fall must have brought it on.'

I could feel the warm trickle between my thighs and I knew I was bleeding. The baby Billy hadn't wanted wouldn't be born after all.

Maggie insisted on calling out the doctor, even though I told her we couldn't afford it.

'Be damned to the money,' she said fiercely. 'You need a doctor, Kathy, and if Billy won't pay for his visit I will.'

There wasn't much anyone could do. The doctor advised rest and a nourishing diet to build me up again, but it was a common enough occurrence for women to miscarry in the early stages of pregnancy. For women who lived in our area it was often a blessing, and falls like mine were not always accidental.

I grieved for the child that had not been given the chance to grow in my womb for its full term, but Billy made no secret of the fact that he was relieved.

'As long as yer weren't 'urt bad it don't matter,' was all the comment he made when told of the miscarriage. 'Yer can 'ave another baby when I get on me feet again.'

'And when will that be?'

There was a note of bitterness in my voice I could not control. Billy might not have been aware of it. He seemed more cheerful again, as if he had hopes of something that might restore his fortunes.

I didn't ask. The loss of my baby had left me feeling

numb. I wasn't very interested in Billy or his schemes at the moment.

At first the pain and shock of losing my baby had driven everything else from my mind, but then I began to think and remember.

I had remembered that Mickey's toy hadn't been on the stairs when I went up the previous night. It was his favourite and it had been beside his bed where it always was while he slept. My son was still fast asleep when I fell, so who had put the train on the stairs and why?

The only answer I could think of was one so chilling that I was afraid to face it even in my own mind. I was just aware of a dull ache about my heart and a feeling of being alone.

I had done wrong by Billy when I married him without telling him I was carrying a child, but I was certainly paying for it now.

A month had passed since my fall. It was early summer but a chilly day and I had been to the corner shop to buy some eggs and cheese to make an omelette for the children. About to let myself into the house I heard someone call my name and I paused on the step. My heart did a rapid somersault and I turned as Tom came up to me. He was carrying flowers and parcels, and he smiled as he reached me.

'May I come in, Kathy? Bridget told me what happened. I'm so sorry about the baby. I would've come sooner but I was away at an important conference and I only got her letter when I returned.'

I hesitated for a moment, remembering Billy's angry outburst after his last visit, but the sight of Tom's eager face was more than I could resist. I had been feeling so empty – so hopeless – and I wanted to be with him, if only for a short time.

'Yes, come in, Tom.'

He studied my face as I led him into the house and then turned to look at him. The parlour was clean but I hadn't polished the furniture for a while and it looked dull.

'I'm sorry the place isn't right. I've been feeling a bit low and everything seems too much bother.'

'That's natural enough after what happened. A miscarriage is one of the worst things a woman can suffer – and I know you've had other troubles.'

'Billy, well, I expect Bridget has told you.'

'Bridget tells me everything about you,' Tom said as he laid his parcels on the table. 'She knows I love you, Kathy. I always shall.'

'Oh, Tom . . .' A sob broke from me as I gazed up at him and saw the tenderness in his eyes. 'Oh, Tom, I love you. I've always loved you.'

He reached for me then, drawing me into his arms. As his mouth came down to touch mine in a sweet, lingering kiss I shivered with pleasure and melted against him, the longing I had suppressed all this time sweeping over me in great waves. I felt weak and dependent and I needed to be held, to be loved – and God forgive me, I needed Tom.

Tom's kiss deepened, his tongue exploring the inner softness of my mouth, arousing sensations I had believed long dead, forgotten in the numbing deadness of marital duty. I responded eagerly, matching his hunger with a hunger of my own. I was trembling, meltingly ready for love. Oh, how I wanted to lie with him, to forget everything in his arms, to leave all the pain and disappointment of the past years behind and glory in his loving.

'I want you, Kathy.'

'Oh, Tom. I want you, too, but we mustn't. We mustn't . . .'

'Because of Billy? Tom looked down into my face. 'No, it isn't just because you're married to him, is it? There's something more – the reason you married him in the first place.'

'Yes.' I broke away from him, turning my back, my arms folded across myself to stop the shaking that swept over me. 'I can't tell you, Tom. It would hurt you . . . shame us both.'

I felt him come to me, encircle me from behind with his arms, his breath warm on my neck and my body went weak with desire. He turned me, kissing me again until I was almost ready to promise him anything – but I knew it could not be.

'It isn't because you don't love me?' I shook my head as his eyes searched my face, probing my mind for answers. 'You feel as I do – and you never loved Billy.'

'Billy was there and I couldn't have you, but if I could go back I would not have married him.'

'Then tell me why, Kathy. Don't you think I have a right to know? Or are you going to condemn me to purgatory for the rest of my life, never knowing why you turned to him?'

'Because . . . because we couldn't marry.'

'Why? I don't understand. We were neither of us married then. Explain why we couldn't marry each other.'

I took a deep breath. I had tried so hard to protect Tom from the knowledge that would hurt and shame him, but perhaps it was best that he should know.

'Because an uncle cannot marry his niece.'

'What are you talking about?' Tom stared at me in bewilderment. 'I don't know what you mean, Kathy.'

'I was told that your brother Jamie O'Rourke was my father.' I gasped as I saw the anger flare in his eyes. 'Ernie Cole told me, Tom. I was going to write to you about the baby. I hesitated for a while, because I didn't want it to look as though I was running back to you just because I was pregnant, but I thought if I wrote, you could come to me or not as you liked.'

'You know I would have come, Kathy. It was what I wanted – to be married to the woman I loved and have a family. I thought you had decided you would rather pursue a career, and then you married Billy. I nearly went out of my mind with anger and pain.'

'But, don't you see, Tom?' I looked at him in a desperate appeal. 'I couldn't tell anyone. I was afraid you would hate me . . . would be disgusted by what we had done without knowing. If you are my uncle, it's incest!'

'I don't believe it, Kathy. Ernie Cole was lying.'

'I thought that at first,' I said. 'But don't you see – it doesn't really matter if it's true. If I had defied him and married you he would have told everyone that you were my uncle. It would have ruined us both – ruined your career. You might even have been arrested. Incest is a sin and a crime. The gossip and scandal would have made it impossible for us to live together as man and wife.'

'But he is a liar. He has to be!' For the first time I saw a flicker of doubt in Tom's eyes and I knew that he had begun to wonder. 'We must be able to prove it is a lie.'

'Only my mother – or your brother – could do that.'

'Jamie went off years ago. Neither Bridget nor I have heard from him in a long time. I think she may have had one or two letters at the start, but nothing since. He may be dead for all I know.'

'And my mother disappeared soon after I was born. Ernie swears that she told him Jamie O'Rourke was the father of her child.' I gave a little sob. 'I had to promise to cook and clean for Ernie or he would have told Billy. He knows Mickey is yours and you know what that would do to Billy. It's my fault. I did something wrong and I've paid for my mistake. I should never have married him.'

'Leave him, Kathy. Come away with me. I'll look after you and the children. We'll go to America where no one knows us. It doesn't matter, I know it's a lie! Ernie made it up for some twisted reason of his own.'

I could see by the look in his eyes that despite his words he was not sure, and I knew he was beginning to realize what the truth might mean.

'Mickey is fine,' I said. 'Perfectly normal . . .'

'Then that points to it probably being a lie. You know the dangers of children between close relatives.'

'It might just be luck?' I saw the pain and indecision in his eyes. 'I love you, Tom, but now you understand why I did what I did.'

'Yes, I can understand, but you were wrong, Kathy. You

should have come to me, let me help you – let me try to discover the truth. It was cruel and thoughtless to act as you did – cruel to both Billy and me.'

'Yes, I know, but at the time it seemed the only way.'

'You should have given me the chance to discover the truth.'

He was angry and hurt that I had not gone to him in my distress, and I could not find it in me to blame him.

'How can you? How can anyone ever be sure?'

'I can try to trace Jamie, for one thing.' Tom frowned as he looked at me, his eyes meeting mine in a demanding gaze. 'If I can prove that Jamie isn't your father, would you come away with me then?'

'I . . . I don't know,' I faltered as I saw the blaze of anger in his eyes. 'I want to, Tom. You must know I want to leave him . . .' I was prevented from saying more as the front door opened and Maggie came in. 'Billy will be so sorry to have missed you, Tom. It was so lovely of you to bring those flowers.'

'The parcels are for the children,' Tom said and I could see the frustration in his eyes. 'Just a few things they might need. I ought to go now. Give my regards to Billy.' He nodded to Maggie as she stood there with Sarah in her arms and Mickey struggling to get out of the pushchair.

'Mamma! Let me out . . . let me out . . .'

'Yes, darling. I'm coming now.' I smiled at him as I went to unbuckle the straps that held him in. He was such an impatient, restless child, so full of energy. 'Have they been good, Maggie?'

'Yes, very good,' she said. Her expression was stony as Tom went out but she said nothing before the door had closed behind him and Mickey had escaped into the kitchen in search of a biscuit from the jar on the table. 'That was a bit foolish, wasn't it? Supposing Billy had come in then instead of me.'

'We were just talking.' I reached out to take Sarah from her arms. 'She's getting so heavy.'

'Don't try to change the subject, Kathy. You know what I mean. It was obvious that something was going on between you.'

'Nothing was going on,' I lied but my cheeks flamed. Maggie always knew when I wasn't telling her the truth. 'All right – Tom wants me to leave Billy.'

'Are you going to?'

'No. I'm not sure.' I faced her defiantly. 'Billy isn't easy to live with these days, Maggie.'

'You married him for better or worse remember.'

'The other week you told me I should think about leaving him.'

'I didn't like the way he was treating you, but you said he'd been better.'

'He had – until he knew I was pregnant again.' I hesitated, then: 'I think Billy put the toy on the stairs, Maggie. I think he wanted me to fall so that I lost the baby.'

Her face went white and then red.

'That's a wicked lie! You've made it up just so you can leave him.'

'No, that's not true, Maggie. I wouldn't do that – you know I wouldn't.'

'I'm not sure anymore what you might do,' she muttered, giving me a resentful look. 'You tell lies, Kathy. And I know Tom O'Rourke means more to you than Billy ever has.'

'Yes, he does,' I admitted. 'I love him.'

'Then why . . . ?' She stared at me, two spots of angry colour in her cheeks. 'Mickey is his, isn't he? Oh, don't bother to answer. I've known ever since he was born. I just hope Billy doesn't ever find out.'

'Find out what?' Billy stood in the open door glaring at us both. 'I could hear you from outside. What are you arguing about? It isn't like you two to have a row.'

'Nothing. It was just a tiff over a recipe Maggie gave me,' I replied. 'We weren't really quarrelling – were we, Maggie?'

She looked at me oddly, and for a moment I thought she was about to betray me. 'No, not arguing – just exchanging an opinion. But I'm sure I'm right, Kathy. If you do it your way you'll be sorry.'

'Perhaps.'

'I'm off,' she said and gave me what was clearly a warning look. 'I've got Mick's tea to get ready, that's why I brought the kids back.'

Billy was looking at the flowers and parcels on the table. He swung round to face me as his mother went out and closed the door behind her.

'You were both lying,' he said and his eyes narrowed in a menacing gaze. 'I knew yer were 'avin' a row. Where did these things come from? Who brought you flowers?'

'Tom – it was Tom,' I said, realizing that there was no point in trying to conceal it now. 'Maggie thought I shouldn't have taken them, but Tom said the things were for the children.'

Billy crossed the floor in two strides. He was furious and as he raised his hand to strike me, I stepped back trying to avoid the blow, but he reached out and grabbed me, then he hit me across the face three times, making my lip bleed.

'That's just for lyin',' he said. 'If I find out you've been doing more than lyin', I'll beat you until you scream for mercy.'

'It was just a kind thought on Tom's part.'

Billy gathered the parcels and flowers up, crushing the petals as he tucked them under his arm. 'I don't want charity. My kids will have what I give them or go without. Do yer 'ear me, Kathy?'

'I hear you but I don't have to do everything you say.'

'You'd better believe it. Next time I'll bloody kill yer!'

'Where are you going?' I cried as he turned towards the door. 'Come back, Billy. I haven't done anything wrong. I promise you there's no reason for you to be angry.'

'But you tell lies, Kathy. You and me bleedin' ma both. I'm goin' ter see Tom and I'll knock the truth out o' 'im.'

'No, Billy! Please don't. Come back . . .'

Sarah had started to scream in my arms and Mickey was staring at us from the kitchen doorway with a worried look in his eyes. I was terrified of what Billy might do to Tom but I couldn't leave my children. I had to stay with them and pray that Billy wouldn't find Tom at Bridget's.

'Don't be there, Tom,' I whispered in silent prayer. 'Please don't be there when Billy comes looking.'

I took Sarah upstairs and changed her, then put her in her cot. Mickey had followed me up and he stood looking at me, his eyes wide and frightened.

'Daddy's cross,' he said and began to suck his thumb. 'He hit you, Mamma.'

I left Sarah, who was already half asleep, and went to pick my son up, hugging him gently to comfort him. My face hurt where Billy had hit me, but I didn't realize my lip was still bleeding until Mickey touched it with his fingers and showed me.

'Daddy didn't mean to hurt me, darling. It was an accident.'

I could see the disbelief in his face and for the first time I realized that my son was aware of his father's temper. Billy was usually good with the children, taking his bad temper out on me when they weren't around, but this time he hadn't bothered to wait.

'Let's leave Sarah to have her nap, shall we? I might find a nice egg for your tea, if you're good.'

'Granny made me an egg,' Mickey said. 'Biscuit please, Mamma.'

'And some milk,' I said as I carried him downstairs. He struggled to get free at the bottom. Mickey was far too independent to want to be carried about like a baby. He went running into the kitchen and I followed, pouring some milk into a mug and getting out the fresh biscuits I had made earlier.

I was thoughtful as I watched my son eat and drink. Mickey

was growing up fast. If he was already aware of Billy's temper it might make life difficult for him in the future.

Would I be justified in taking the children away from Billy? Tom had promised to look after us even if he was never able to be my husband. I had hesitated when Tom asked me, my old guilt raising its head to make me feel that I owed some loyalty to Billy. Yet perhaps I had paid my debt to him.

I couldn't let his increasing bad temper and violence affect my children – and I didn't want to live with a man who hit me when he felt like it.

Yet still my conscience nagged at me. Was I using this incident to gain what I really wanted? I had been secretly hankering to leave Billy for a long time.

Billy didn't come home for hours. When he did, I heard him stumbling about the kitchen, knocking into things, and I knew he'd been drinking. I wondered whether to try to ignore him; then I got up, pulled on a dressing robe and went down to face him. If there was going to be another row, we might as well get it over with now.

He was at the kitchen sink, pouring water into a bowl, and he turned as I spoke his name. I gasped as I saw his face. It was badly bruised, his nose was bleeding and his lip was cut open.

'You've been fighting!'

'I gave that bleedin' Tom O'Rourke a hidin'!'

'You look as if you've had one yourself.'

'It's nothin' ter what he looks like by now,' Billy muttered. 'He didn't do all this ter me – someone else finished it orf fer 'im.'

I thought he might be lying out of bravado, but when I went closer I saw that some of the cuts were fresh and still bleeding profusely, while others were turning purple as if they had been inflicted earlier.

'Who was it – the second time?' I reached for the cloth and began to wipe the blood away. Billy groaned and pulled his shirt up to reveal a deep laceration on his chest. It looked as if it might have been made with a chain. 'That's nasty.'

'It were meant to be,' he said ruefully. 'It was ter teach me a lesson and to warn me what will 'appen if I go wrong again.'

'What do you mean?' I stared at him in horror. 'Was this done to you by Mr Maitland's men?'

'Yeah – but don't say nothin' or we'll all end up as dead meat. I 'ad ter be taught me lesson, Kathy, but it was worth it now 'e's goin' ter give me another chance. I've been told 'e's got a job fer me next week.'

'What kind of a job?' I looked at him anxiously. No matter how badly he had behaved to me earlier, he was still my husband – and Sarah's father. Remembering Valerie Green's warning I was uneasy. 'Be careful, Billy. I don't think you should have anything to do with that man – for your own sake.'

'I don't 'ave a choice,' he replied and smothered a groan. 'He owns me, Kathy.'

'Oh, Billy.'

'Don't yer worry, love,' he said. 'I'll keep me nose clean this time. It won't 'appen again. I'll earn a bit o' money and pay me debts – and things will be good fer us again.'

I took the cold cloth from the bruise I'd been bathing. 'Not if you hit me and shout at me in front of the children. Sarah screamed her head off until I got her to sleep, and Mickey was frightened.'

'I lost me temper,' Billy said, looking contrite. 'I'm sorry, Kathy. It were Tom bringin' them things 'ere. I've got me pride.'

'But I told you they were for the children.'

'I know yer did – but I thought yer were sweet on 'im.' He pulled a face. 'After we'd 'ad a fight, he told me it wasn't never that way between yer, Kathy. Said 'e's probably goin' back ter America soon.'

I moved away from Billy to rinse the cloth under the tap,

taking a deep breath before I turned to look at him. I felt sick
and uneasy. Had Tom really lied about our relationship – or
was Billy lying to me?

'Well, that's all right then, isn't it?'

'Yeah, sorry, Kathy. Are yer mad at me fer what I done?'

'Yes, I am, Billy. I won't put up with violence – and I
won't have the children upset.'

'It won't 'appen no more,' he promised. 'I'll be on me feet
again soon and then I'll make it up ter yer.'

Ten

I met Bridget as I was on my way to the corner shop the next morning. She hurried up to me, her eyes going over me searchingly and resting for a moment on the bruise to my lip.

'You look better than Tom anyway.'

'How is he? I'm so sorry for what Billy did.' A sob caught in my throat. 'It's all my fault.'

'That's nonsense, Kathy. Billy has been spoiling for a fight with Tom for years. It was bound to happen one of these days. Besides, Tom can stand up for himself. He knocked Billy down in the end, you know, then he helped him up and they talked for a while. Tom did his best to settle him down.'

'Do you know what Tom said to him?'

Billy had lied about his fight with Tom, implying that he'd won easily. It probably followed that he'd also lied about what Tom had said to him.

'No, Kathy. I thought it best to stay clear and let them get on with it. Especially once they had stopped hitting one another.'

'Did . . . did Tom tell you anything afterwards?'

'About Jamie being your father?' Bridget nodded and looked thoughtful. 'I can't be sure whether it's the truth or not, Kathy, because Jamie was a bit of a lad for the girls at one time, but I think it must be a lie. Jamie went away from the lanes at about that time. He worked for Joe and he was very much in love with Mary Robinson. I can't think he went with anyone else after he met Mary, but I couldn't swear to it.'

'There's no way any of us can be sure. It's hopeless.'

'I wouldn't say that.' Bridget took a sealed envelope from her pocket and gave it to me. 'That's from Tom. He's gone for the moment, Kathy, but the letter will explain.'

'Thanks, Bridget.'

I ripped the envelope open, reading the brief message inside. Tom had written to say he was going to try to trace his brother through friends in America.

> I'm leaving for the moment because I don't want to cause more trouble for you, Kathy. You have to make up your own mind whether or not you are prepared to leave Billy. You know I love you and whatever the truth about your father, I shall always care for you and the children. I'll be in touch soon, and in the meantime go to Bridget if you need help. Tom.

I slipped the letter into my pocket, making a mental note to destroy it when I got home. Billy would go mad if he found it.

'Is it all right, Kathy?' Bridget was looking at me anxiously. 'You know I'm there if you need me?'

'Yes, thank you, but I'm all right. Billy isn't often violent with me. He was in such a temper . . .'

'Once they start hittin' you . . .' Bridget pulled a face. 'I don't want to interfere, Kathy, but Maggie's told me she doesn't like the way he treats you sometimes.'

'Billy has been through a bad patch,' I said, excusing him as I usually did. 'But I shan't put up with violence. If he hits me again I shall walk out on him.'

'Good for you.' Bridget smiled at me. 'Are you going to bring the children to the party at the church hall this Saturday? Joe is organizing it and it's for all the kids in the lanes, not just the Catholic children.'

'I didn't know it was on,' I said, 'but yes, I should love to come, Bridget. What time?'

'It starts at half past two. We shall be having a few games and prizes, and then a good tea at half past three. It will be nice to see you there, Kathy. You don't get out much these days.'

'I've been busy,' I said, 'and I didn't feel like talking to anyone for a while after I lost the baby.'

'It pulled you down,' Bridget said giving me a sympathetic look. 'But you mustn't let this get you down, love. I dare say there will be other babies.'

I nodded, but didn't answer her. Billy hadn't touched me in that way since my fall and I hadn't encouraged him. The thought that he might have deliberately left Mickey's toy on the stairs, in the hope that I might fall and lose the baby, had killed any warmer feelings I might still have had for him. If he tried to make love to me now my body would reject his touch.

If I stayed with him in the future it would be out of a sense of duty, because women like me didn't just walk out on their husbands without good cause. But there were times when I wanted to leave. Oh, yes, I wanted to leave.

I hardly saw Billy to speak to that week. When he came home from his job at the factory he went straight to bed; he got up at about two in the afternoons and went out somewhere, returning only to put on his working clothes before he went off to the night shift at the factory.

On the Friday afternoon he put thirty shillings on the table for me.

'What's this, Billy? I thought you didn't get paid until tomorrow?'

'It's extra,' he said. 'I told yer I was getting' another chance with Mr Maitland. I'm not earnin' much yet because I've got ter pay orf what I owe – but there's somethin' special comin' up soon and then I'll 'ave some real money again.'

'Oh, Billy.' I looked at him anxiously. 'You won't do anything silly, will you?'

'You mind yer own business,' he muttered. 'And don't try to tell me how to do mine.'

'Maybe I shan't be around much longer to tell you any-thing!' I snapped at him without thinking.

His eyes narrowed, fists balling at his sides. 'If yer want a cut lip, yer goin' the right way ter get one!'

'Do that and I shall walk out on you!'

'Maybe I'd better take that back then.' He scooped up the money he had put on the table. 'I'll pay the bills in future.'

'That won't stop me if I want to go!'

'Don't threaten me, Kathy.' He came round the table and gripped my arm, his fingers digging deep into my flesh, hurting me. 'I've warned yer – don't push me too far. Or I might really do something you wouldn't like.'

I wrenched away from him, rubbing at my arm. Billy was the one who was pushing things too far. I had nearly had enough of his moods.

Billy and his moods were left behind as I set out for the church hall that Saturday. I was looking forward to the children's party and to meeting the other mothers. I knew most of them by sight and often stopped in the street for a few words with girls I had known at school, but I hadn't really made friends with anyone in particular since my marriage.

I thought it was probably because Billy had flashed his money about while he had it, and I knew that a lot of people had questioned where that money came from. One or two of the women I knew had hinted that he was doing something slightly shady, but no one had come right out and said it to my face – not until later that afternoon at the church hall.

I spent the first few minutes chatting to Bridget and Mag-gie, who were helping to organize the party games. Once the children were settled, Mickey as noisy and boisterous as usual as he joined in the games, doing his best to win everything, and Sarah was sitting quietly in her chair sucking a lollipop Bridget had given her, I became conscious of whispering behind me.

'She'll be in for a rude awakenin' one of these times.'

'Serves 'er bleedin' right! She always were a toffy-nosed

bitch – and no better than her whore of a mother. They said 'er kid was born early, but I reckon she'd been 'avin' it orf with some other feller afore she married 'im.'

I turned to look at the two women who were so obviously discussing me. One of them was someone I had often passed in the lane called Susie Bricker and the other was unknown to me. The second woman leered at me triumphantly as though she knew I'd heard and was pleased. She had wanted to upset me.

'Yeah, we're talkin' about you,' she jeered. 'And that bleedin' thief what yer married.'

'Billy isn't a thief. He earned his money honestly, working – doing two jobs.'

Her eyes sparkled with malice as she grinned her disbelief.

'Pull the other one it's got bleedin' bells on. If yer believe 'im yer a bigger mug than I took yer for. Me 'usband knows what your bloke's been up ter and 'e'll be getting' his comeuppance sooner than yer think.'

'What are you talking about? What is Billy supposed to have done?'

'You'll find out soon enough, I reckon.'

Coldness was spreading down my spine as I saw her expression. I turned away, pretending to ignore her as I went over to join Bridget, who was overseeing a rowdy game of musical chairs.

Bridget glanced at my face. 'Something wrong, Kathy love?'

'No, nothing,' I said. 'I just thought I'd help out with the children.'

Was there some truth behind the woman's spiteful remarks? I couldn't know for sure, but something deep inside me was telling me that Billy was getting into bad ways. I had known for months that there was something dangerous about the man who had employed him, and I had been afraid of what might happen.

Maggie had suspected that Billy was involved in something dishonest, too. I dared not think what she might say if she had heard the kind of spiteful gossip that had been meant for me that afternoon.

It was nearly five o'clock when I eventually took the children home. Maggie had asked me to go home with her first, because she had been making a dress for Sarah and she wanted to try it on her before she completed the final touches.

It was just as I got to our house that I caught sight of Ernie Cole slouching down the road a few steps ahead of me. He'd obviously come out of prison sooner that I'd expected. I would have to go down there one day soon and take him some food, because I knew he wouldn't look after himself. No matter how much I disliked him, I couldn't let him starve.

Billy wasn't in the kitchen when I got in. I had left some cold ham for his tea but it hadn't been touched, though it looked as if he had been in because there was a bottle of beer half drunk on the table.

'Billy?' I went out into the hall as I heard something upstairs. 'Billy, are you there?'

There was no reply but it sounded as if something had been knocked over. Was there an intruder up there? I turned to Mickey as he tugged at my skirt, his face anxious.

'Stay here and look after Sarah for me, darling. I shan't be a moment.'

I went upstairs to the bedroom, my heart racing as I wondered what I might find, stopping on the threshold in horror as I saw that every drawer had been pulled out of the dressing and bedside chests, the contents strewn either on the bed or the floor. Billy was standing in the middle of the mess, glaring at me as I faced him across the room. I looked into his eyes and sensed his fury.

'Where 'ave yer been all this time? I thought yer 'ad bleedin' run orf and took the kids.'

'I'll tell you if I decide to go,' I said. 'What made you do all this, Billy? Look at the mess. It will take me ages to get it tidy again.'

'What I want ter know is where yer got this!' Billy moved towards me, thrusting his hand under my nose. 'I knew yer were bloody cheatin' on me, yer bitch! Yer don't get somethin' like this fer nothin'!'

I looked at what he was holding and felt a sinking sensation inside. It was the ring Mary Maitland had given me. 'That was given to me by a friend.'

'Yeah, I know. By a bleedin' man!' Billy grabbed my arm. 'I warned yer what I'd do to yer, Kathy. Who was it – the one what give yer the kid? Tellin' me lies about bein' raped and all the time yer were goin' with a man. Filthy little whore!'

'The ring came from a girl that I knew when I was nursing. She was killed in France, Billy. Her father had money and she was very generous to me. We were good friends and she left the ring to me in her will.'

'That's a likely tale an' all,' he said glaring at me. 'Why didn't yer never tell me then? I ain't seen yer wear it.'

'I thought—' my breath caught in my throat. 'I knew you would be like this, Billy. You were so jealous and I . . . I didn't want us to have a quarrel over it.'

'Well, you're bleedin' well goin' ter get one because I don't believe yer! Yer a liar and a cheat and I've 'ad enough of yer lies. I'll teach yer to respect me, yer bitch!'

He brought his arm back and hit me across the face. I gave a cry of fear and stumbled back but he grabbed me and then hit me again several times, then he threw me across the bed and stood looking down at me, his eyes blazing with fury.

'I ain't got time ter teach yer a proper lesson right now, Kathy – I've got ter meet someone. We've got a big job on. Somethin' important – but I'll finish what I started later.'

'I hate you, Billy Ryan,' I said as I sat up and looked at him. 'I hate you and I wish I'd never married you. That's the last time you hit me. I shall leave you after this.'

'Do that and I'll come after yer. No matter where yer

go I'll find yer. And then I'll kill yer and yer bleedin' lover.'

'I don't have a lover. Don't look at me like that, Billy. I know I wasn't fair to you at the start, but I've been a good wife to you since we were married.'

'Can yer swear on your kid's life that yer ain't thought about doin' it with another man, that yer ain't wanted no one else?' Billy's eyes narrowed as I hesitated. 'That's what I bleedin' knew, and I reckon we both know who an' all, don't we? It's Tom O'Rourke you're sweet on, ain't it! Mickey's 'is bleedin kid, ain't he?'

'Don't be silly!' My breath caught as I saw the rage in his eyes. He took a step towards me and I shrank away from him. 'Don't you dare touch me, Billy Ryan. If you do I shan't be here when you get back. I mean it!'

He hesitated, then raised his hand in a threatening gesture, holding it over me as if to warn me of what was coming. 'I've told yer what I'll do if yer try ter leave me. I'm goin' now, Kathy, but I'll deal with yer when I get back.'

I stayed where I was while he went out, listening to the tread of his feet down the stairs and then the door slamming behind him. For a moment I was overwhelmed by the hopelessness of my situation and I had to fight against the tears of self-pity.

But this was taking me nowhere! I had my children to think of, and I had to plan what I was going to do in the future. Getting up when I was certain he had gone, I went to the mirror and looked at myself. There was a cut on my cheek and the bruises were already beginning to form.

I bathed them with cold water before going downstairs, calling for Mickey. There was no answer and no sign of either Sarah or Mickey as I went through to the kitchen to look for them.

'Mickey? Where are you?'

'I'm here, Mamma.' I turned to look at my son, who was clutching his sister in a manful attempt to carry her, but had only succeeded in half-dragging her along the floor on her bottom. She was sucking her thumb, looking puzzled but not protesting, eyes wide as if wondering what was going on. 'I took Sarah in the cupboard under the stairs.'

My heart caught as I saw the distress on my son's face.

'Why did you do that, darling?'

'So that Daddy wouldn't hit us like he hits you.'

'Has he ever tried to hit you?'

Mickey shook his head, but he was still looking scared and I wondered if Billy had begun to give him the odd slap when I wasn't around to see.

A dreadful coldness was creeping over me. I had always sworn that I wouldn't allow a man to beat me the way so many women almost routinely were in the lanes. I had been willing to put up with Billy's temper and the cruel things he said to me sometimes, because I knew I had behaved badly at the start of our marriage, but I couldn't allow my children to live in fear of their father.

He had left me no choice. I had to leave him. Billy had forfeited the right to my loyalty. When Tom had asked me to leave Billy and go away with him, I had hesitated because I'd felt it was selfish of me to take the children away from their father for my own happiness. Now I saw that it was for the best for them as well.

If I was going to leave it might be better to do it now, while Billy was out. The only problem was, where should we go? Bridget would offer me a refuge, but it was the first place Billy would look. I couldn't stay there, because he would cause terrible trouble for them, but Bridget would help me with money, at least until I got on my feet.

I wasn't sure about the future yet. Tom had offered to look after us, but that was asking a lot if we could never marry.

Billy had taken the ring Eleanor had given me with him, slipping it into his pocket. Even if I waited until he came back, I would never see it again. I had very little of value, but I did need to take the children's clothes and toys – and that would take time to pack.

'Come on, Mickey darling,' I said. 'I'm going to take you to Bridget's house for a little while.'

'Where are you going, Mamma?' Mickey looked at me anxiously.

'I'm going to pack all your favourite things, and then you, Sarah and Mamma are going on a nice holiday.'

'Is *he* coming with us?'

It hurt to hear Mickey say *he* in that scared voice. Billy had been a good father to my son for the first couple of years or so, and it brought home to me how bad things had become these past months without my realizing it. Tom was right, I had let Billy walk right over me.

But it wasn't going to happen again. He had gone too far this time.

Bridget took one look at my face and drew me into the house. She took Sarah from my arms, holding her in the crook of her elbow and taking charge of Mickey with her free hand.

'Uncle Joe is in the parlour,' she told him. 'Why don't we go and see what he's got? There might be some barley sugar.'

'I have to go home and pack their things,' I said. 'Would Joe take me to the train in his car, Bridget? I can't stay here.'

'No, that wouldn't be a good idea,' she said and looked thoughtful. 'I've been talking to Joe about what to do if you decided to leave Billy. Go and pack what you want, Kathy. Joe will come along in a little while and load things into the car for you. Don't worry, love. We can work something out between us. I'm glad you've finally made up your mind to leave. It's what you should have done a long time ago. I'll always help you, you know that.'

'Thanks, Bridget. I didn't want to worry you, but I can't manage alone. Billy didn't leave me any money.'

'That's the least of your problems, Kathy. Tom will take care of everything when he comes back. You knew he's still in America, of course?'

'Still in America?' I stared at her in dismay. 'No, I didn't think . . . How long will he be away?'

'Not long.'

'Oh . . . ?' I swallowed back my fear as I left Bridget's house and began to walk home. I had counted on Tom being around, because I knew Billy would come after me. He would try to take me back.

Perhaps I should have waited until Tom could fetch me himself? Yet Billy had threatened more violence when he returned and I was afraid of what he might do. If I didn't make the break now I might never find the courage again.

If I'd had the courage to go away by myself at the beginning none of this would have happened. I had to be prepared to stand on my own feet and not to rely on anyone else. If I went far enough away Billy might never find me.

I packed the children's clothes into bags and tied the toys in a sack I found out in the back yard, taking them through into the hall ready for Joe Robinson to collect. Then I went back upstairs to start packing my own clothes. I had almost finished when I heard someone knock at the door, and then it opened and Maggie's voice called to me.

'Kathy, are you there?'

I went to the top of the stairs, looking down at her.

'Maggie . . . ?' I didn't know what to say to her. 'I was going to tell you before –'

'What's going on, Kathy – what's all this stuff?' Her eyes narrowed suspiciously as I walked down the stairs towards her. 'Are you goin' somewhere? You're leavin' Billy . . . he hit you again, didn't he?' She had seen the bruises on my face and was frowning over them. 'He shouldn't have done that.'

'He hurt me, Maggie. He was really nasty – and he says he's going to teach me a proper lesson when he gets back.'

'Well, he won't be doin' much of that for a while,' she said. 'I came to tell you that Billy's been in some sort of a fight and he's hurt – but perhaps you don't care?'

'What do you mean – what kind of a fight?' I felt chilled as I saw the anger in her eyes. 'Don't look at me like that, Maggie. Mickey is frightened of him. He dragged Sarah into the cupboard under the stairs when Billy was yelling and hitting me. I'm not prepared to risk the children.'

'Billy would never hit him, you know he wouldn't, Kathy.'

'He wouldn't have once, but he's changed, Maggie. He's not the same as he was.' I took a deep breath. 'But you said he was hurt – what happened?'

'I don't know exactly. We had someone at the door – a bloke I've never seen before. He said Billy had been in a fight and was hurt bad. It seems they took him to the Infirmary.'

I stared at her in silence for a moment, knowing what she was asking me to do. 'You want me to go and see him, don't you?'

'You're his wife, Kathy. He loves you.'

'If he loved me he wouldn't do this to me.' I touched my cheek, wincing as I felt the soreness. 'Billy doesn't love me, he just wants to own me.'

'A lot of men are that way, possessive.' Her eyes were cold with dislike. 'I never thought you would be like this, Kathy. I knew you didn't love him, but I thought you had some decency in you.'

'I've been a good wife to him.' Her words stung me raw and I felt my cheeks go hot as I met her scornful gaze.

'You must do as you please,' she said, 'but I'm going down there myself just as soon as I've told Mick.'

'What is it, Kathy?' Joe Robinson was in the open doorway. 'Are you ready to leave?'

'I'm not sure.'

'I might have known,' Maggie said bitterly. 'You're all in this together. It just shows who your friends are. I thought I could trust Bridget Robinson, but blood's thicker than water.

197

Go with him then, Kathy, run off with your fancy man and leave your husband to die alone.'

She turned and walked out, slamming the door behind her.

'Oh, Maggie . . . ?'

'What's wrong, Kathy?' Joe saw my face and frowned. 'What has Maggie been saying to you?'

'Billy has been hurt bad. They've taken him to the Infirmary.'

'Hurt – how?'

'I don't know. Maggie said something about a fight.'

'This doesn't have to change anything, Kathy. He beat you earlier and he will do it again given the chance. Men like that never stop once they get a taste for it.'

'But I can't just walk out.' I swallowed a sob. 'I don't know what to do, Joe. I want to leave but, how can I? Billy was good to us when he had money, and he *is* Sarah's father.'

'Don't make up your mind now,' Joe said. 'I'll take you down there in the car and you can see how he is, then you can take some time to decide. If he really is hurt bad he isn't going to be a danger to you or the children for the moment.'

'No, no, he isn't.' I looked at Joe gratefully. 'Thank you. I've been in such a state that I didn't know what to do.'

'You don't have to explain anything to me, lass. Bridget has always been fond of you, and I know Tom thinks highly of you. We're here to help in whatever way you want – not to pass judgement or tell you what to do with your life.'

'You and Bridget have been good friends,' I said. 'I'll just get my coat and then we'll go.'

The woman in charge of the reception desk at the Infirmary gave me an odd stare when I asked to see Billy. She looked me over thoughtfully, then glanced at Joe.

'I'm not sure if you can see him, Mrs Ryan.'

'Why not?' I shivered as the ice spread down my spine. 'Is he dying?'

'He is unconscious at the moment.'

'What happened to him?'

'I am not allowed to tell you.'

'Surely I'm entitled to know?'

'I think Mrs Ryan ought to be told the truth,' Joe said. 'Just what is the matter with her husband?'

'Leave this to me, miss.'

I turned as I heard the voice and then gasped as I saw a man in the uniform of a police sergeant. His eyes assessed me and then he looked at Joe and his expression relaxed slightly.

'Ah, Mr Robinson, if I might have a word in private, sir?'

'Just wait here a moment, Kathy,' Joe said. 'And don't worry. I'll sort this out for you.'

They went to the side of the hallway, talking in low voices for several minutes, and then Joe came back to me. He took my hand and led me to a chair, indicating that I should sit down.

'It's not good news, Kathy.'

'Is Billy going to die?'

'No one is sure for the moment how bad he's hurt. He was knocked unconscious in a fight and he hasn't come round yet.'

'Where was the fight? I don't understand. I thought he'd gone to work.'

'That's the worst part of it in a way, Kathy. He was with some men robbing a warehouse. Apparently, it is usually empty apart from one old nightwatchman, but the police had been warned that the robbery was going to happen and they charged in when the robbers were attacking the old man. Billy was hit over the head by one of the police officers while resisting arrest. Apparently, he hit a policeman with an iron bar and . . . killed him. If he recovers from this he will be arrested and charged with murder.'

'No! You can't mean it!' I felt faint as the floor seemed to come up to meet me and if Joe hadn't been there to steady me I might have fallen from the chair. 'Billy killed a police officer . . .'

I was stunned, too shocked to take in what he was saying at first. How could Billy have done such a terrible thing? I knew he had his faults – but murder!

'It must have been an accident. Billy didn't kill him on purpose. He isn't a murderer.'

'It happened in the heat of the moment,' Joe said. 'It wasn't premeditated, but it's still murder, Kathy. Even if Billy had a good lawyer, he would go to prison for the rest of his life.'

'He would rather die . . . it would be better if he never came round at all . . . better for everyone.'

'You selfish little bitch!' I was startled as Maggie yelled at me and I turned to see her standing just behind us. 'It would suit you if my Billy died, wouldn't it? You could go swanning off with your lover then and forget all about him.'

'Maggie, don't,' I whispered my throat tight with emotion as the tears stung my eyes. Maggie had always been my friend. I didn't want to quarrel with her at a time like this. 'Please?'

'I'll say what I like, you little tart!' She lunged at me and slapped my face as hard as she could. 'You've never cared about him, never! You should be ashamed of yourself wishing him dead.'

I put a hand to my face, staring at her but making no move to strike back. 'I'm sorry, Maggie. Please don't hate me . . . don't say these things to me. I didn't mean it that way.'

'I'll say what I like.'

She was interrupted as the police sergeant came up to us.

'Excuse me, Mrs Ryan, but I've been told Mr Ryan is conscious. He asked for you.'

'Yes, of course.'

'He doesn't know she was going to leave him,' Maggie said bitterly. 'I'm his mother. I'll see him.'

'Only Mr Ryan's wife for the moment,' the sergeant said. 'We want to interview him if he's able to speak – but only

200

one visitor is permitted at a time. You might be able to see him later, if you wait.'

Maggie glared at me but Joe restrained her from following us. He put his hand on her arm and I could hear them arguing as I went off with the police officer.

'I'm sorry I can't allow you to be alone with him, ma'am,' the sergeant said. 'But we have to hear what he has to say – it's evidence.'

'Yes, of course, I understand,' I said. 'Billy isn't a murderer. He has a bad temper, but he didn't mean to kill your officer. I know him. I know he wouldn't murder anyone on purpose.'

Yet I also knew that he had a terrible temper when roused, and he had been in a foul mood when he left the house.

The sergeant looked at me pityingly. 'I dare say not, Mrs Ryan, and if witnesses can be brought to testify to his usual good character in court, it may help his case.'

From his manner I could tell that he didn't really believe anything would help Billy, but he was trying to be kind. He'd seen the bruises on my face and felt sorry for me.

There was no time for more as we entered the small room where Billy was being treated. He had been kept away from the main wards because he was a prisoner, and the police didn't want to risk anyone getting near him. They had stationed a man outside his door, and another was sitting inside. It seemed a lot of security for a man who was badly injured and had never previously been involved in anything violent like this and I felt that Billy had been condemned without a trial.

'Has he said anything more?' asked the sergeant.

'Just asked for his wife, sir.'

I went to the bed. Billy was lying with his eyes closed, his hand on top of the cover. His head was swathed in thick bandages, and it looked as if blood had seeped into them. I reached out and took his hand in my own, my heart contracting with pain as I saw the bruises to his face. He had been hit several times, and I felt for him, whatever he had done.

'Billy,' I said softly. 'It's Kathy. I'm here.'

His eyelids flickered and then he opened his eyes and looked at me. It seemed to take him a moment or two to focus, but then he made a movement with his fingers, as if he had recognized me.

'Kathy.' His voice was a husky croak. 'Kathy love, is it you?'

'Yes, it's me, Billy. I came when they told me. What happened? Why were you there? Why did you do it?'

'I 'ad to,' he said, moistening his lips with his tongue as if he was thirsty. 'It were to pay me debt to . . . Water, can I 'ave some water?'

'Yes, Billy.' I saw a jug of water on the cabinet beside the bed and poured some into a glass, then held it to his lips, my arm supporting his head because he was unable to sit up. He sipped once, then fell back against the pillows as though the effort was too much. 'Are you saying you were forced to do this robbery by someone? Was it those men who threatened you before?'

'Yeah. They were 'is men, Kathy. He sent me a message, told me it were the only way to wipe the slate clean.'

'Was it Maitland?' The police sergeant stepped forward. He had been behind me and Billy had not seen him until he spoke. I saw the immediate flash of fear in his eyes. 'If you tell us what we want to know about Maitland it will help you, Ryan. If your information helps to put him away for a long time, we might even see our way clear to easing the charge against you to manslaughter.'

'It were self-defence. That copper come at me swinging a truncheon.' Billy clutched at my hand. 'I never meant to kill 'im, Kathy. You got ter believe me.'

'I believe you, Billy. We'll get a lawyer and plead self-defence.'

'Nah, no lawyer.' Billy's eyes closed. 'No money fer

lawyers. I've 'ad it, Kathy. Think of yerself and the kids now. I'm finished.'

'I'll help you all I can, Billy.'

'Leave me,' he muttered. 'Go ter Tom, he'll look after yer. I'm sorry I were a bad 'usband ter yer, Kathy. Sorry I 'urt yer, lass. I loved yer but yer made me so mad.'

'You tried some of the time, Billy. We were happy for a while.' My throat was tight with emotion, tears trickling down my cheeks.

'Tell us about Maitland.'

Billy's eyes flicked to the police officer, who had come closer to the bed, and then back to me. His hand gave mine a warning squeeze as his eyes seemed to convey a message.

'I were a fool. Good job I never told you nothin', Kathy. Best you don't know . . . best you don't . . .' He gave a cry as if in sudden pain, then there was a rattling sound in his throat and his eyes rolled wildly as he gasped for breath, his chest heaving. His hand clutched at me desperately and he seemed as if he was trying to say something, then a trickle of blood ran from the corner of his mouth and I saw death in his eyes.

'Nurse!' The police sergeant was at the door, calling urgently. 'Nurse, come quickly!'

Billy's hand slipped from mine and then his eyes closed, his body jerking horribly for a few seconds before he lay still. I stared at him, my chest painfully tight and finding it hard to breathe, as a nurse entered and came rushing up to the bed. She bent over him as I backed away, tears sliding down my cheeks.

'He's gone,' she said looking at the police officer. 'I'm sorry. The doctors thought he might not recover consciousness at all.'

'Billy?' I choked. 'Oh, Billy . . .'

'Your husband said you didn't know anything about his unlawful activities, Mrs Ryan. Is that true?'

I turned to the officer. 'I had no idea what he was doing

this evening. I thought he was at work as a nightwatchman. He told me very little.'

'Nothing about a Mr Maitland?'

I remembered all Billy's warnings about keeping my mouth shut, and I shook my head. There was no point in telling what little I knew and risking retaliation from Mr Maitland's bullyboys.

'No, I'm sorry. I wish I could help you, but Billy was very secretive about his work. He never told me anything.'

'Very well. Please don't think of going anywhere for the moment, Mrs Ryan. We may want to question you again – and we may want to search the house.'

'For what?' I stared at him in dismay.

'For stolen property. Mr Ryan was carrying a valuable ring when he was brought in here last night.'

'That belongs to me. Eleanor Ross left it to me in a will. We were training as nurses together and she was killed in France.'

'Can you prove that?'

'You could ask Miss Maitland – Miss Mary Maitland. Or check it with the solicitors.'

'You have a solicitor's letter telling you about the inheritance?'

'No.' I bit my lip. 'Miss Maitland brought it to me. I can't prove anything.'

'There are records for this kind of thing. If it was in a will, it can be checked,' the sergeant said. 'If it is yours you will get it back one day.'

'It doesn't matter much,' I said. 'It was only a ring, but he didn't steal it.'

'I'll look into the matter,' he promised. 'If the ring is yours I'll make sure it is returned to you.'

'Thank you. What happens now – to Billy? Can we . . . can we take him home? Maggie is waiting.'

'Your husband's mother might like to come in now,' he said. 'And I see no reason why you shouldn't make arrangements to go ahead with the funeral in a few days – when we've finished our inquiries.'

I nodded, turning blindly away as the tears streamed down my cheeks. Whatever Billy was, whatever he had done, he had been my husband and there had been times when we were close. I grieved for him and for what had happened to him.

'It's too late for tears now,' Maggie said when she came in a moment or so later. 'You can weep all you like, Kathy, but I know the truth. It's your fault my boy's lyin' here dead. Your fault.'

'That's not fair, Maggie. I never wanted him to rob people.'

'It was because of you,' she said, her face cold and hard. 'You made him feel inadequate and that's why he had to get more money, so that you would look up to him. He told me once he was afraid you would leave him if he didn't get things for you.'

'That isn't true, Maggie. You know it isn't. I didn't ask him for anything. It was his pride. His pride made him do it.'

'I know you were leavin' him,' she said. 'And I know you were carrying another man's bastard when you married him – that's enough for me. As far as I'm concerned, the sooner you clear off out of the lanes the better.'

'I shan't be goin' until after Billy's funeral.'

She raised her head and spat in my face.

'You're scum, Kathy Cole, that's what you are, just like your mother. I'll tell you now. I'm takin' my boy home and you won't be welcome at his funeral. I never want to see or speak to you again as long as I live.'

'Maggie . . . ?' I walked out of the room, the tears running down my cheeks. How could she do this to me? 'Please don't hate me, please don't be like this.'

She turned her back on me, going to the bed to stare down at the body of her dead son. I knew she would not relent, and I left her to mourn alone.

Joe Robinson was waiting outside the door. He came to me at once, putting a friendly arm about my shoulders.

'Come away, Kathy. I'll take you home. Maggie is upset. She doesn't mean a half of what she says.'

I accepted the large white handkerchief he offered and wiped my eyes.

'Oh yes,' I said. 'She means what she says all right. She means every word . . .'

Eleven

Joe took me back to his house in his car. He said that he and Bridget wouldn't dream of letting me stay at my own home alone that night after what I'd been through.

'You can sleep at ours tonight, Kathy. Bridget will already have put the children to bed and you won't want to disturb them. Time enough to think about what you want to do tomorrow.'

I was feeling too numbed, too dazed to argue. Everything had happened so fast that I was still reeling from the shock. After Billy's threats and the way he'd hit me I had felt justified in leaving him, but seeing him in hospital like that – seeing him die – had affected me so powerfully that once again I was plagued with guilt.

Was Maggie right? Was it my fault that Billy had gone wrong? There was no way I could ever be certain, and it was too late to change things, but her harsh words played on my mind. The waste and the pity of it made my heart ache, and I grieved for the man who had been my husband and Sarah's father.

I slept very little that night, and I was up early in the morning. The police sergeant had warned me not to go away, and I had been told my house would be searched, so I decided to return there as soon as the children had had their breakfast. Mickey asked me if we were going on holiday and I told him I would take him soon.

'Joe told me the police are coming to search the house this morning,' Bridget said when I went downstairs. 'Would you

207

like me to keep the children until they've been? We could take them out for a ride in the car?'

'Thank you, they would like that,' I said. 'It will be a treat for them.'

Mickey was a bit doubtful about going without me, but I reassured him, telling him I had work to do. 'Bridget will look after you and I'll see you at teatime, darling.'

I didn't have long to wait for the police visit. Four of them came, looking very officious and determined. Their attitude made me feel as if I had done something wrong myself. They were very suspicious when they found the bags I'd packed, and got excited when they saw the bulky sacks, but when they opened them and discovered they contained only children's clothes and toys, they were duly embarrassed.

The search they made of the house was thorough, but they couldn't find anything of real value, and after two hours they apologized for disturbing me and went away. It took me another hour to straighten up, and I was just about to make a cup of tea and sit down, when someone started banging at my front door. Before I could open it, it was thrust wide and Ernie Cole staggered in, an evil leer on his face. He was dressed in filthy clothes, his beard unshaven for several days.

'I 'eard what 'appened to yer 'usband,' he muttered. 'I come ter tell yer that it ain't the finish of yer doin' fer me, Kathy. I can still make things unpleasant fer yer if yer break yer word.'

'I don't care what you do or say,' I said anger flaring out of me. How dare he barge into my house like this? The stink of strong drink on his breath was disgusting and I felt glad that he was not my father. 'This is all your fault. None of it would have happened if you hadn't told me those foul lies.'

'What lies?' His eyes narrowed in a crafty leer. 'Yer don't know the truth and that's a fact. Yer mother told me it were Jamie O'Rourke and she's dead so she can't say no different.'

'How do you know she's dead?' I stared at him. 'You can't know that unless you killed her!'

He looked startled for a moment, then growled low in his throat, 'I never touched 'er. She cleared orf and left me. Stands ter reason she's dead years ago. She were a whore and 'er sort don't last long. 'Sides, she'd 'ave come crawlin' back long ago if she weren't dead.'

'Go away!' I cried as he advanced towards me, a menacing look in his eyes. 'I don't want to see or speak to you again, and you can rot in your own filth for all I care. I shall be going away from the lanes soon anyway.'

'Yer a bitch and a whore,' he muttered and grabbed hold of my upper arm, his fingers digging into the soft flesh. A shudder ran through me as he thrust his face close to mine and I saw a certain look in his eyes. 'I've always fancied yer.'

'No!' I was not going to let this horrible man force his will on me, either physically or mentally. I'd had enough of being bullied and intimidated by men who thought they could use violence to get their own way. I wrenched away from him, whirling round to pick up a steel poker from the parlour fireplace and then I turned to confront him. 'You come one step nearer Ernie Cole and I'll hit you with this. I mean it! I'm not afraid of you and I shan't put up with your bullying. I was a fool to listen to you in the first place. Bridget says Jamie was courting at the time my mother must have conceived me and she doesn't believe he is my father.'

Ernie hawked and spat on the floor, his eyes glittering. 'That Bridget Robinson knows too much fer 'er own good. She wants ter shut 'er mouth or someone might shut it fer 'er.'

'You wouldn't dare say that if Joe Robinson was around.' I raised my poker again as he hesitated. 'I'm warning you – come any nearer and I'll hit you.'

'Yer were alus a cold 'earted bitch. But that don't change nothin'. If yer know what's good fer yer, you'll come and clean my place and get me some supper – or everyone will know what yer precious Tom O'Rourke's been up ter.'

'Get out!'

I yelled so loudly and so fiercely that he was startled and went without another word. I was shaking and I felt sick as I sat down, still clutching my poker. He meant what he said. Unless I carried on cleaning and cooking for him, he would spread his lies about Tom and me – and they had to be lies. I was almost sure in my own mind now that he had taken advantage of my uncertainty at the time to fill my mind with his filth.

They had to be lies, because I loved Tom so much. I dropped my poker on the floor, bent my head and let the tears I had been holding inside flow.

It was all so hopeless. I was trapped now just as I had been when I married Billy. Tom said he would look after me, but unless he could find proof that Jamie was not my father, there was no way we could live together as man and wife. Even if we tried to be simply friends the rumours would follow us, destroying us both in time.

I couldn't do that to Tom. I couldn't ruin his life, his career – as rumours of that kind surely would. It would be far better if I took the children and went away somewhere alone.

Bridget looked at me anxiously when she brought the children home that evening. Sarah was sleepy after her day out, but Mickey was full of all the exciting things he'd been doing with his uncle Joe.

'Went for a ride on a train,' he told me. 'Uncle Joe said I can be an engine driver when I grow up if I want. We had ice creams and sticky buns at the teashop, and we went to the zoo to see the animals. It was lovely, Mamma. Can we go there again another day, please?'

'Yes, one day,' I promised and kissed him. 'Go upstairs now, darling. I want to talk to Bridget. I'll be up in a minute.'

'He's a beautiful child,' Bridget said after he had gone.

'And so is Sarah, of course. But Mickey is so bright and clever – and so full of energy!'

'He's that all right,' I said and laughed. 'It takes all my time keeping up with him. Thank you for what you did today, Bridget. I'm glad he wasn't here when the police came; he understands too much and it would have frightened him. They were here for two hours, but they didn't find anything, of course.'

Her expression was serious as she looked at me. 'Have you thought about what you're going to do, Kathy?'

'I'm not sure. I don't think I can stay here much longer. As soon as things settle I shall have to look for somewhere to live.'

'Tom will be home soon . . .'

'Unless we can prove Tom isn't my uncle . . .' I sighed as my voice tailed off. 'Ernie Cole was round here earlier threatening me. I've decided I'm not going round there anymore and he says he'll spread rumours about Tom and me, and I think he means it. He's a vicious, bitter man.'

'If he tries it I'll sort him out,' Bridget said. 'Leave it until after the funeral, Kathy – and then I'll go to see him with you and we'll hear what he has to say to me.'

'He hates you and your family, Bridget. It might be better if you didn't go near. He's so violent these days. He's capable of anything, believe me.'

'He didn't try to hurt you, did he?'

'He tried but I threatened him with the poker.'

'Be careful of him, Kathy.' Bridget looked serious. 'It might be best if we wait until Tom gets home before we speak to him – all of us together. Just be careful you're never alone with him.'

Sarah was stirring in her pushchair. I bent to pick her up and she gave me a sleepy smile and a wet kiss.

'I'd better take her up and give both of them a wash before they go to bed. We'll talk again another time, Bridget.'

'I've got to go and see Maggie,' Bridget sighed and looked

upset. 'Joe told me what she said to you. She didn't mean the half of it, Kathy. I've known Maggie for years and she sometimes flies off the handle, then she regrets it and says she's sorry. I'm sure she will come round and apologize to you before long.'

In thinking that Maggie would soon relent, Bridget was wrong. Maggie was harbouring a deep resentment against me, and she blamed me for Billy's death. Bridget told me about it when she came round again the next day.

'I've never known her to be this way,' she said, clearly distressed. 'She wouldn't speak to me except to say that I was sure to take your side because of Tom – and we've been friends for years. We could always talk things over, no matter what.'

'I'm sorry, Bridget. Sorry you've fallen out with Maggie over me.'

'Maggie has fallen out with me. As far as I'm concerned, we're still friends. If she gets over her paddy we'll go on as if nothing had happened – and I'm sure she will once she's had time to think things through. I know Maggie, she can't go on like this forever.'

'She told me I wouldn't be wanted at the funeral.'

Bridget looked shocked. 'She shouldn't have said that to you. Billy is your husband. You must go, Kathy, of course you will. Joe and I will go with you. Maggie might ignore you, but she won't make a scene in church.'

'What about the children? I can't take them.'

'I'll ask Amy to look after them for you. As you know, she's been away at art college for the past year or more, but her course is finished now and she's finally coming home – though I don't know if she'll settle down here. Joe hoped she would go in for something useful like teaching, but she doesn't seem to know what she wants to do. She likes drawing things, but there's not much of a future in that for a woman. I suppose she'll get married in a couple of years or so.'

'She will find it different coming back to the lanes after that fancy school of hers.'

'Well, she might go and stop with Lainie for a while up west. Amy likes her aunt, and Lainie has her own dress shop these days. I think I did tell you that when I got her letter, didn't I?' Bridget sighed and I sensed that she was unhappy at the idea that her daughter would rather live with her aunt than stay in her own home.

'Yes, you told me Lainie's late employer had left her quite a bit of property. I saw her walking up the lane once with Amy, but she doesn't come to visit often, does she?'

'Lainie hates being reminded of the past. Things were bad for her when she lived around here, Kathy.'

'Gran told me your mother used to get in dreadful tempers. But you came back, Bridget, and you stayed.'

'Joe has suggested buying a house in a nicer location several times, but I like it here. My friends are here.' Bridget's face clouded. 'Anyway, to get back to what we were saying – Amy will look after the children. She likes children, even if she doesn't care much for living in the lanes. You have to go to Billy's funeral, Kathy. No one has the right to stop you, and Mick will tell Maggie so. He'll make her behave decently to you. And whatever happens afterwards, Joe and me will be there with you.'

'Thank you,' I said. 'And I am sorry that Maggie isn't speaking to you because of me.'

Maggie showed no sign of relenting as the day of the funeral drew near, but Mick Ryan came to see me. Mickey was his favourite, and he had brought toffee apples and fudge from the midsummer fair, which had been held by the river earlier that week. The children fell on him with delight, Sarah crawling into his lap to be nursed while Mickey pulled at his shirt and asked him when they were going to play football together.

'Soon,' he promised and ruffled the boy's hair. 'Run away now and take Sarah with you. I want to talk to your ma.'

He was silent as Mickey took Sarah by the hand and led her through the house into the back yard, where we could soon hear him encouraging his sister to play his favourite game with him.

'He's a fine boy,' Mick said. 'We shall miss him when you take him away, Kathy.'

'I could bring him to see you sometimes.'

'That would be a grand thing,' he said. 'We shall be sorry not to see you and the children, Kathy. We've other grandchildren, but their parents have scattered all over the country. It won't be the same when you've gone.'

'I don't think I can stay here, Mick. I had a letter from a solicitor this morning asking what I intend to do about the money owing on the house.'

'You mean Billy never paid for it?' He frowned at me. 'All that money he was throwin' around and he hadn't paid for his house. You didn't tell Maggie about that, Kathy.'

'I didn't tell her because it would have worried her. There are other debts too. The lawyer says that if I am willing to move out of the house all Billy's debts can be settled without further trouble to me.'

'And what if you don't want to move?'

'I'm not sure. I think they would take the house back and throw me out – but it doesn't matter, because I have to go anyway.'

'Yes, I can see that.' He nodded and looked at me thoughtfully for a moment. 'Have you been very unhappy, lass? You can tell me the truth, you know. I've no illusions about our Billy.'

'It was all right some of the time, but I should never have married Billy. Maggie is right. It was unfair to him. I didn't mean to hurt him, but he kept insisting we were getting married and I didn't have the courage to say no. I was sorry afterwards and I wished I'd told him the truth – but it was too late.'

'Billy was too proud for his own good,' Mick said and

looked saddened. 'Maggie is much like him. She's hurting over all this, Kathy. She won't admit it and she won't apologize to you, lass, but she loves you and the children and this is tearing her apart.'

'I want to be friends, Mick, but when she saw me in the street the other day she crossed to the other side to avoid me. I can't force her to speak to me if she doesn't want to. Bridget has tried to make it up with her, but she just refuses to listen.'

'Aye, she's like that – stubborn as a mule when she gets somethin' in her bonnet.' Mick grinned wryly. 'We had some right old barneys when we were younger. I've known the day she wasn't above takin' a rolling pin to me and chasing me up the street with it.'

'I know, Gran told me that once.' I gave a strangled laugh that was half a sob. 'I care about Maggie, too. She was my friend even though she knew –'

'That Mickey wasn't Billy's?' Mick nodded, his gaze sympathetic. 'He knew about it, Kathy. I think he suspected it even before you were married.'

'Did he? I don't see how he could.'

'Men know these things. He still wanted you, Kathy – and he never stopped loving you. Don't blame yourself for what happened. Maggie won't admit it, but Billy had been in trouble before – as a lad. He was caught stealing a couple of times and lucky not to have been prosecuted for it. I took a stick to him and hoped it would cure him, but in my heart I knew it wouldn't. It was always in him, Kathy. Before he went in the Army he was in with bad company. I suspected it and I was glad he'd had to join up – at least it kept him out of trouble for a while.'

'Maggie never told me that.'

'No, she wouldn't. She could never admit to herself that Billy wasn't a good lad – but deep down she knows it. She knows that it wasn't your fault he did what he did, Kathy –

and one of these days she'll be sorry. The only trouble is it may be too late.'

'Oh, Mick . . .' the tears were streaming down my face. 'Thank you so much for telling me all this. I've been feeling so rotten, thinking it was my fault that Billy got into trouble'

'I knew you would be,' Mick said. 'That's why I came to see you. I didn't want you to ruin the rest of your life over something that couldn't be helped. Billy would have slipped into his old ways sooner or later whether you married him or not.'

I went on thinking about what Mick had said for a long time after he had left. If Maggie knew all this then she was being unfair, but I couldn't blame her. Billy's death had hurt her, as it had hurt us all. I hadn't told the children yet, because I wasn't sure what to tell them, but Mickey had asked once or twice where his father was and I was going to have to tell him very soon.

The day of Billy's funeral was cool and overcast, but not as cold as Maggie's icy stare when she saw us enter the church. Any hope that she might relent was squashed as I saw her expression. Mick had said that she cared for me deep down, but from the way she looked at me that seemed unlikely. Perhaps she had once, but Billy's death had hardened her heart against me.

However, respect for the church prevented her from making a fuss during the ceremony, and Bridget, Joe and I left immediately after the coffin was placed in the ground. I hadn't cried, although my heart ached. I didn't love Billy in the way a woman should love her husband, but there had been a warm affection between us for a while. It was only after things had started to go badly wrong that I had begun desperately to wish myself free of my marriage.

Maggie started after me as I walked away from the churchyard, but Mick held her back. I saw him say something to her in a low voice; she glared at him, and then sagged against him, as if her anger had given way to grief.

'I'll go round later,' Bridget said as we walked away. 'Maggie is a fool to herself. I'll see if I can talk her round, Kathy.'

I nodded but didn't answer her. At that moment I was feeling empty and alone. I wished that Tom would come back so that I could talk to him. I needed someone I could open my heart to but I knew it was unlikely that he would be back for some time. He had gone to see if he could find Jamie, but I needed him here.

I tried to explain to Mickey the day after the funeral that his daddy had gone away to a better place.

'Why didn't he take us with him, Mamma?' His eyes were large and serious as he gazed at me. 'Didn't he like us any more?'

'Daddy had to go,' I said. 'Sometimes people are called to a place called heaven and they have to go whether they want to or not.'

'Is he with God? Granny says good souls go to heaven to be with God and the bad ones go to hell to be burned by the devil.'

'Granny tells lots of tales like that because she is a Catholic,' I said. 'I'm not a Catholic, Mickey, and I don't think anyone goes to hell to be burned by the devil. I believe that whether someone is good or bad God forgives and loves him, and we all go to heaven one day.'

Mickey nodded. 'Does that mean we'll see Daddy one day?'

'Perhaps – but not in this life. When we're all good souls with the angels.'

'Then he won't hit you any more?'

'No, he won't hit any of us any more.' I stroked his hair. 'Daddy didn't mean to be unkind – he just got upset sometimes.'

'I'm glad he won't hit you any more, Mamma.' Mickey

hugged me, burying his face against me, his voice muffled by tears. 'I love you and I didn't love Daddy when he was bad to you. You won't go away and leave Sarah and me, will you?'

'Oh, Mickey, no I shan't leave you.' I held him as the tears trickled down my cheeks. 'I love you too, my darling. I love you so much.'

'Will it just be me and Sarah and you, now? Granny and Granny Bridget, too?' Mickey gazed at me, touching the tears on my cheeks with his fingertips. 'Why doesn't Granny love us any more? Granda came to see us, but Granny doesn't love us.'

'Of course she does,' I said and held him close. 'We all love you, but Granny is sad because Daddy went away. She loves you really and I'm sure she will come to see you soon.'

I thought about what my son had said for several days. Maggie had shown no sign of relenting, and I was beginning to feel angry. She knew that Billy had been in trouble long before he married me and yet she persisted in blaming me for everything.

It wasn't fair. I didn't mind her taking her grief and anger out on me, but it wasn't fair to make the children suffer. Both Mickey and Sarah missed her and it hurt me to know that my son believed she had stopped loving him.

A week after the funeral I made up my mind that I'd had enough of it, and I decided to do something. I put Sarah in the pushchair and took Mickey by the hand, marching them up the road to Bridget's house.

She looked pleased when she opened the door, but then a bit anxious as she saw the militant expression in my eyes.

'What's wrong, Kathy?'

'Will you have the children for me for an hour or so please Bridget?'

'Yes, of course, but what are you going to do?'

'I have to see Maggie. I can't let this go on any longer – it's upsetting the children.'

She looked at me doubtfully. 'Are you sure about this?'

'Yes, I am. I have to have it out with her.'

'I've tried, Kathy. She won't listen to me.'

'Then perhaps she'll listen to what I have to tell her.'

I left Bridget to take the children in, then turned and walked back down the road to Maggie's house. I was buoyed up by my anger. I'd had enough of being treated as if I was the wicked witch. So, I'd made a mistake in marrying Billy without telling him the truth, but that didn't mean it was my fault he was dead. I banged the knocker hard several times.

Maggie was a moment or two before she answered, and when she did come her hands were covered in flour as if she had been baking. She stared at me in silence for a moment and I thought she was about to tell me to go away, then she stood back to let me enter.

'You had better come in,' she said icily. 'We don't want to let the whole street hear us.'

'I don't care who hears,' I said. 'I've had enough of hiding and hanging my head in shame. I made a mistake, Maggie. I admit it but I've paid for what I did – a hundred times and more.'

'Billy has paid more,' she said as she led the way into the kitchen. She wiped her hands on a towel and then motioned to a chair. 'You can sit down if you like.'

'I'd rather stand,' I said. 'I haven't come here today to grovel, Maggie. I'm going to say what I have to say and then I'll go. It's up to you whether I come back again or not.'

'Get on with it then.'

'I know you blame me for Billy's death, but it wasn't my fault. I tried to tell him not to get involved with . . . that man, but he wouldn't listen. Billy went his own way, you know that. You know he wouldn't listen to anyone.'

'Aye, I know that. He was always headstrong, but it was your fault that he was miserable, Kathy. You can't deny that it was you that hurt him. He wouldn't have got into bad ways if he hadn't been trying to get things for you.'

219

'I didn't ask him to buy me things. I told him I didn't need all he gave me.'

'He wanted to make sure you didn't go running off with another man.'

'All he had to do was be nice to the kids and me. I wouldn't have left him if he hadn't started hitting Mickey and me.'

'He wouldn't hit the children. He loved Mickey! Don't tell me lies, Kathy.'

'You ask Mickey about it,' I said. 'He was so scared that he pulled Sarah in the cupboard under the stairs, dragging her on her bottom because he couldn't lift her. He was scared because Billy was shouting and hitting me and he thought he might hurt them too. That's why I made up my mind to leave him – not for my own sake, but for the children.'

'You're just saying this.' Maggie stared at me, her face red and then white. 'You know it's your fault and you're trying to push the blame on my Billy.'

'It's the truth – and I'm fairly certain that he put that toy on the stairs hoping I would trip and lose the baby.'

'That's a wicked lie! May God forgive you.' Maggie crossed herself feverishly. 'You're a wicked woman, Kathy Ryan.'

'Don't think I'm saying this out of spite. I couldn't believe it at first either, but I know in my own mind that it's true. Billy was worried about money. He didn't think the fall would hurt me, just cause a miscarriage. When I fell, at first he was worried because he was afraid I'd broken my back, but once he knew I was all right he was glad that I'd lost our baby.'

'I don't believe you. You've a terrible mind, Kathy – a terrible mind, so you have.'

'I didn't want to believe it, but I remembered seeing the toy in Mickey's bed when I went in to kiss him goodnight. I didn't put it on the stairs and Mickey was still asleep when I fell. Think about it, Maggie. That train didn't get there by itself. If Billy didn't put it there – who did?'

Her eyes dropped away from mine and I sensed that she believed me but she wasn't prepared to admit it.

'Billy would never willingly harm you or the children, except when he was in a temper. He shouldn't have hit you.' Her head came up and I saw the anger in her eyes again. 'You drove him to it, Kathy. He knew you wanted Tom and it drove him mad. He just couldn't bear to think of you and his best friend together. No man with any pride could stand it.'

'I wouldn't have left Billy if he hadn't left that toy there – but that destroyed something in me, Maggie. It killed any affection I had for him, and after I knew that Mickey was frightened of him I made up my mind that it was better for all of us if I went away.'

'Better for you if you went off with your lover!' she cried bitterly. 'Well, now you can do what you like, can't you? My Billy's dead and you're free. You must be laughin' inside, kickin' your heels at the thought of him lyin' there in the ground.'

'I can't believe you said that to me, Maggie.'

'You deserve it!'

It was useless to try to reach her. I was wasting my breath trying to persuade her that I was not entirely to blame.

'I don't particularly care what you think of me any more,' I said quietly. 'Hate me if it makes you feel better, Maggie, but don't take it out on the children. They love their granny and they want to see you sometimes. Mickey thinks you've stopped loving him. Don't you think he's been hurt enough without you turning against him?'

'Of course I love him . . .' Maggie stared at me in silence for what seemed an eternity. 'I can't forgive you, Kathy – but I care about the children. You know I do.'

'Then show it,' I said. 'You don't have to come to the house – not that I shall be there much longer. I've had notice to leave by the end of next month.'

'Leaving? Where are you going?'

'I don't know yet. I shall have to find somewhere. Somewhere away from the lanes.'

'Then I shan't see the children.'

'They are with Bridget now,' I told her, giving her a hard stare. 'Bridget has done nothing to harm you, Maggie. It's upset her because you won't speak to her – and none of this is her fault. If you want to see your grandchildren in the future, I'll promise that you can sometimes. But you have to go to Bridget's now and make it up with her – and show the children you still love them. I shan't be there so you don't have to put up with me. It's your choice. If you don't care –'

'Of course I care!' She looked at me oddly. 'Where are you going?'

'I've another problem to sort out,' I said, 'and I might as well get it over. I'm going to see Ernie Cole.'

'He's been saying some strange things about you,' Maggie said and frowned. 'Mick told me he was drunk the other day in the pub and he said you were Jamie O'Rourke's daughter.'

'I know. Mick told me about it when he came to see the children yesterday.'

'Mick came to see them?'

'Yes, he's been once or twice to see us. He doesn't blame me, Maggie, and if you were honest with yourself, you wouldn't either.'

I turned and walked out of her house, leaving her to stare after me. I'd done all I could and it was up to her now. Either she made it up with Bridget and let her grief begin to heal or she went on nursing it and hating us all.

Mick had been upset when he'd called on me that Sunday morning. He'd brought the children sweets as he always did, and spent half an hour playing football with them in the back yard. He hadn't told me what was on his mind until he was ready to leave.

'He was shouting his mouth off about your mother being a whore,' he'd said looking bothered. 'Bragged he knew a secret if he wanted to tell it – about you and Tom

222

O'Rourke – and then he said that Jamie O'Rourke was your father.'

'He told me that before I married Billy,' I said. 'I think it was a lie, but I couldn't be sure. I promised I would cook and clean for him if he kept his mouth shut.'

'And now you've decided you're not going to let him blackmail you any longer. Good for you, Kathy.'

'Yes – but I have to make him stop telling his lies, Mick. It . . . it wouldn't be good for Tom if people thought . . .'

'That you were his niece.' Mick nodded. 'Does Ernie know the boy is Tom's?'

'He suspects it.'

'No wonder he had a hold on you. I often wondered why you went there to clean for him.' Mick shook his head. 'I'd swear it is a lie, Kathy. Jamie O'Rourke wasn't interested in Grace. I saw her make a play for him once in the pub and he just laughed at her, told her he wasn't interested.'

'You heard him say that?'

'Yes. I was sitting right beside him. We'd been havin' a drink together when she came up and tried to sit on his knee. She wanted him to buy her a drink, and he did but then he told her to go away because he wasn't interested. He said he had a girlfriend.'

'Bridget said more or less the same thing.'

'Jamie told me he wasn't daft enough to get caught by Grace. He said he thought she was headin' for trouble.'

'If only I could be certain . . .'

'Don't let Ernie Cole's lies ruin your life, lass. It's time you had a bit of happiness.'

I was thinking about what Mick had said to me as I walked towards the house in Brewery Lane where I had lived for so many years. I had decided that I would have it out with Ernie and see if I could get him to change his story.

The foul smell hit me as I opened the door and went in. The hall was full of rubbish that had been strewn carelessly on the floor and the living room was no better. I was tempted to clear it up, but then I realized it would look as if I had given in to his blackmail again.

As I stood there hesitantly, the kitchen door opened and Ernie lurched out, staggering as if he were drunk.

'So you've bleedin' come back, 'ave yer?' He leered at me through eyes bleary with drink. 'I thought you'd come ter yer senses once I started ter 'int at yer dirty little secret. Yer won't want yer precious Tom O'Rourke getting' inter trouble.'

'We don't have a dirty secret,' I said, my stomach turning as I looked at him. He was disgraceful; a filthy, foul-mouthed, bitter man who was old before his time. 'Tom isn't my uncle and you know it. You made up the lie. Jamie O'Rourke never touched my mother.'

'And who told yer that?' A wary expression came over his face. 'Yer can't prove it, yer little bitch. It's only yer word against mine.'

'There are people who know the truth. Mick Ryan says Jamie wouldn't have anything to do with her when she tried to pick him up. And Bridget says he was courting.'

'That bloody Bridget Robinson.' Ernie hawked and spat on the floor. 'She's a nosy bitch!'

'Bridget tells the truth and that's more than you do!'

'I should 'ave strangled yer at birth,' Ernie muttered. 'Yer bleedin' mother cheated me. Strung me along yer were mine until I married 'er and then she laughed at me, taunted me that the kid weren't mine.'

'She shouldn't have done that. I'm sorry if she hurt you, but you don't have to ruin my life just because she ruined yours.'

'What do you know about it?' He glared at me. 'I give up everythin' fer 'er 'cos I thought it were mine. Give up the woman I loved fer 'er sake and she mocked me . . . called me a fool fer believin' 'er.'

'But she didn't say who my father was, did she? She just told you I wasn't yours. That's the truth, isn't it? You made it up about Jamie O'Rourke because you wanted to punish me, to stop me marrying Tom. Don't you think I've been punished enough now? Please, stop telling lies and let me find a new life for myself.'

Ernie stared at me for a moment, blinking owlishly as if trying to think clearly, then his eyes narrowed.

'You look like 'er sometimes, Kathy – that's when I fancy yer. I fancied 'er when I went with 'er, even though I loved another girl. If she'd given me a kind word or shown she liked me I would never 'ave, but she were too bleedin' proud. She were lookin' fer somethin' better than I could ever give 'er.'

'You mean Bridget, don't you? You were in love with her once, that's why you hate the O'Rourkes, isn't it? You blame Bridget for turning you down, but it wasn't her fault that you went with someone else.'

'What do you bleedin' know about it?' Ernie demanded. His eyes focused on me. 'Yeah, yer look just like 'er, and yer ain't no better than she were neither.'

I took a step back as he lurched towards me, then glanced round for a weapon. I couldn't see anything that I could use to defend myself.

'Ain't got no poker,' he said, a mocking expression on his face. 'Took it up the pawnbroker along with everythin' else.'

'Don't you dare to come near me!' I cried.

'It's about time yer learned a bit o' respect fer yer dear old father,' he muttered. 'Only I ain't yer father, Kathy, 'cos Jamie bleedin' O'Rourke is, that's who!'

'And that's a lie, Ernie Cole!'

Bridget's voice startled me. I certainly hadn't heard her come in and I glanced at her as she came to stand beside me, confronting Ernie. He stared at us, his mouth curling back in a snarl as he saw Bridget.

'Who let yer into me bleedin' 'ouse?'

'I let myself in,' Bridget replied. 'You should be ashamed of yourself, Ernie Cole. Your poor mother would turn in her grave if she could see what you've done to this place. Jean was a good, decent woman and she would be ashamed of you, so she would.'

'Keep yer bleedin' mouth shut or I'll shut it fer yer.'

'I'm not afraid of you, Ernie Cole. You always had a big mouth but you've gone too far this time – telling lies in the pub about my brother. Jamie will sort you out when he gets back.'

'Jamie is coming back?' I stared at her, forgetting about Ernie for the moment in my surprise. 'Oh, Bridget, does that mean that Tom found him?'

'No, I think they must have crossed paths as Tom went out to America. I had a telegram from Jamie this morning to say that he had arrived at Dover and would be coming to see me in the next day or two.' Her eyes went over me anxiously. 'I wrote to the last address I'd had for him and someone sent it on to him.'

'Oh, Bridget!' My heart began to race wildly. 'Jamie will know the truth.'

'Are you all right, Kathy love? Maggie told me you were here.'

'She came then?'

A roar of rage from Ernie alerted me as he moved towards us. I hadn't noticed what he was doing, but now I saw that he had fetched a heavy cudgel from somewhere and was charging at us from the direction of the kitchen. He must have gone to fetch it while our attention was diverted.

'Yer an interfering bitch, Bridget O'Rourke. I should 'ave taught yer a lesson years ago.'

His intention was clear. He was going to hit Bridget and the chances were that he would injure her badly.

Without thinking, I moved in front of her, putting out my hands in an attempt to wrench the cudgel from him. He was so strong, so very strong, and he was in a terrible temper.

'I'll kill 'er,' he muttered as I wrestled with him. 'Kill yer an' all. Yer a bleedin' whore like yer mother . . . ought ter 'ave killed yer years ago an' 'er an' all.'

'You're a fool,' Bridget cried from behind me. 'Put that thing down, Ernie. Put it down now before you hurt somebody.'

'I intend to 'urt yer.'

I was holding on to his weapon with all my strength, trying to pry it from his grasp. Bridget rushed at him from the side, joining in the struggle and kicking at his shins. He gave a growl of rage and threw me off, then struck out at her with his stick. It glanced off her shoulder, sending her staggering back. Ernie went after her again, clearly about to hit her even harder, but I rushed between them, shielding my head with my arms as I tried to fend off the blow.

It caught me on my arm and I gave a cry of pain. He laughed and turned his attention to me, lifting the stick to rain blows down on me wherever he could as I tried desperately to fend him off. I was caught by his ferocious attack, unable to get away as I staggered and then fell to my knees and he went on and on hitting me like a mad thing.

'Stop it, Ernie!' I heard Bridget screaming at him. 'You will kill her. They'll hang you, you fool. Stop it!'

The pain was more than I could bear as I sank in a heap to the floor, but I was conscious that for some reason he had stopped hitting me and I thought I heard Joe Robinson's voice and very faintly someone else just behind him. And then the blackness began to drag me down, down, down into the pit of pain and forgetfulness . . .

Twelve

The blackness was all enveloping for a long time, blotting out the pain and the fear. Then, very slowly, the pain came back to tear at me and torture my poor beaten body. Through all this time I was aware of the voices and sometimes the touch of a hand, caressing me, telling me that it would be all right.

'He can't hurt you anymore, my darling,' the voice said. 'I'm here with you now and I promise you're safe. The children are safe and there's nothing to worry about. I'm going to look after you. All you have to do is to get well again.'

'Tom . . . ? Is that Tom?' I croaked and my voice was no more than a whimper of pain. My senses were telling me that Tom was with me, but I knew it couldn't be true. Tom had gone to America and it might be months before he came home. But I wanted him here, I wanted him so badly. 'Tom, I love you . . . tell Tom . . .'

'Yes, I know, my love.' A gentle hand soothed the damp hair from my brow. 'I love you. I'm here. I'm with you. Rest now, Kathy. You're safe, my darling. No one is going to hurt you any more and I shan't leave you ever again. I promise I won't go away.'

Tears trickled down my cheek. I wanted Tom so much, but I was married and we could never be together. Tom was my uncle . . . someone had told me that but I couldn't remember who had said it. I couldn't remember anything except the pain. Had there ever been a time before the pain – a time when I was happy?

Oh yes, I remembered being happy. I was strolling along a beach and the sun was shining. Tom was with me and he kissed me, later we lay in the sand and talked of how happy we would be when we were married, but we could never marry, never . . .

A whimper broke from me as I realized it was hopeless. I could never be with the man I loved. There was no future for me so why should I struggle against the pain? Why not just let go and slip away into that place of dark oblivion?

'She is wandering in her mind,' a voice said from somewhere beyond the mists. 'Remembering. I think she has forgotten what happened.'

'That's just as well,' another voice said. 'That was a terrible beating, Mrs Robinson. The man who did it deserves to hang!'

'He will be punished,' Bridget's voice said. 'I can assure you, doctor. The police will catch him eventually and then he'll hang for what he did. He tried to kill her, I saw it all and tried to stop him but there was nothing I could do until the others came.'

The voices were fading now and the pain was easing. I was drifting into a place where there was no pain and no fear. Drifting . . . drifting . . . drifting.

When I opened my eyes the sun was shining in at the window and I was aware that the fever and the worst of the pain had gone. I still felt very sore and I had a headache, but the terrible soul-destroying pain, that I had not been able to bear without help, had gone.

'Are you better now, my love?'

I turned my head as someone came to stand by the bed. The light from the window was behind him and for a moment I couldn't see his face, then I gave a glad cry of recognition. It was Tom and he was smiling down at me, reaching for my hand to take it gently into his own. I had longed for him so much and he was here. For a moment I thought I must be back in my nightmare world of mist and fantasy.

'Tom . . . is it really you? I thought you had gone to America?'

'No, I didn't go,' he said and raised my hand to his lips to kiss the palm. 'I told Bridget that was where I was going and then I heard that Jamie had been seen in Ireland so I went there instead. I discovered that he had been there for a while but then he left and no one knew where he'd gone. I was going to get the next boat for America, and then I had a telegram from a friend who told me I was wanted urgently at home – and I arrived the morning that man did this to you.'

I put a hand up to my head, feeling the bulky bandages and beneath them the soreness. 'What happened? I'm not sure. Someone hit me . . .' Suddenly a vague memory came into my mind and I shuddered. 'Was it Ernie Cole? Did he do this to me?'

'Yes, he was the one.' Tom bent to kiss me on the mouth, his hand trailing my cheek tenderly. 'Don't try to remember, Kathy. Sometimes it's better to forget.'

'I can't remember much, Tom, but I think Bridget was there too.'

'You tried to stop him attacking her and then he turned on you instead,' Tom said. 'You were very brave, my love.'

'I can't remember that, just that someone was hitting me and it hurt. It hurt such a lot, Tom. Then I went away somewhere . . .' I was still feeling weak and a little dazed, my mind hazy as if I had just awoken from a long, deep sleep.

'It was the pain,' he said. 'Sometimes the body does that to protect itself. You had a fever and you were wandering in your mind. For a while we thought you might die, but the doctors were very good. You were lucky, Kathy, but it's going to take a long time to get you well again.'

'How long have I been ill?'

'Three weeks.' He saw my look of bewilderment and smiled. 'I know. It seems impossible, but you were hardly conscious at all. Your mind was wandering for a lot of the time.'

'I thought you were here sometimes but it seemed like a dream.'

'I've been with you as often as I could, and Bridget was here when I had to sleep. We've kept a watch over you, Kathy.'

'The children? What happened to the children?'

'Maggie and Bridget have been taking turns to look after them. I've been teaching Mickey to play cricket on the grass by the river. He says he's not sure it's as good a game as football, but he likes it when it's his turn to bat.'

'Mickey always wants to be the best,' I said. 'He's a bright, intelligent boy, Tom, but he does like his own way. And he is very strong-willed – like his parents!'

'Yes, I've discovered that,' Tom said and laughed softly. 'I think we are going to have to teach our son to be a little more thoughtful of others, Kathy.'

'Perhaps I've spoiled him, but he was all I had of you.' I caught back a sob. 'I do love you, Tom.'

'And I love you, my darling. When you are well again I shall ask you to marry me – and this time I am hoping you will say yes.'

'But?' I stared up at him. 'What if . . . ?'

'It's all right, Kathy. Jamie told us – it was a lie. Ernie made it up just to stop you marrying me, to have a hold over you. He knew that if you married me you would go away, and he wanted you to cook and clean for him – and he hated the O'Rourke's because of something that happened between him and Bridget years ago.

'Jamie has told us that he never went with Grace, not even once. He said she was after him even before he went away to work for Joe, but he didn't make love with her. And after he met Mary Robinson he never looked at another girl for years. He isn't married now. He says that he will never love anyone the way he did Mary, and he has remained true to her memory.'

'Oh, poor Jamie,' I said. 'It's so sad that he should be alone.'

'He isn't exactly alone,' Tom said and smiled as he stroked my hair back from my forehead. 'I believe he has lots of friends, ladies included. He is rather popular at dinner parties apparently – valued for his single status – and could marry if he wished. Jamie has made quite a name for himself in America, Kathy. He owns a ranch and a string of racehorses, and I think he has a wonderful life out there. He wants us to go and live near him when we are married, and I've said I'll ask you.'

'Can we talk about it – when I'm better?' I asked. 'I'm not sure . . .'

'Of course we shall talk,' Tom said. 'You know I wouldn't force a decision like that on you, Kathy. I'm not Billy. I don't take things for granted.' He made a wry face. 'I know I may have pushed a bit for marriage and kids when we were going together before, but I was in love and impatient – and I've learned the hard way. I've seen what Billy did to you, and I shan't make the same mistake. I promise you that. In America it might be possible for you to work as a nurse – even if it's only in my own clinic.'

'Oh, Tom,' I said reading the love behind that simple statement. 'Perhaps one day when our children are grown up, I may want to do some kind of work outside the home – but for now all I want is to be your wife and be happy.'

'I think we've both learned a lot, Kathy.'

'It's been a hard lesson,' I said and held his hand to my cheek. 'I can't think now, Tom. I'm so tired . . .'

I closed my eyes, drifting away to sleep.

When I woke again I was alone in my room. For the first time I really thought about where I was and realized that I must be in hospital, but not in the Infirmary. This was a private room in a proper hospital, and as I looked around at the flowers and the bowl of fruit on the bedside cabinet I knew that Tom and his family had paid for all this luxury.

I sat up in bed as a nurse came in. She smiled at me and after a moment I realized that I knew her.

'Is it Sally?' I asked. 'Sally Baker? We were at the hospital together during the war?'

'I thought it was you,' she said and grinned as she came to sit on the edge of the bed. 'Yes, I went on with my nursing after the war. I felt I had to do something.'

'I didn't know. You went home just before I left?'

'My brother was ill for a long time, but he recovered in the end.'

'I'm so glad, Sally.'

'Yes. Unfortunately, my fiancé wasn't so lucky. He was killed just after I went home that time. I couldn't face coming back for a while, but once my brother was over the worst I asked for a posting to another hospital and then I took up nursing as a profession at the end of the war.'

'I got married and had two children,' I said. 'Ally is married too and expecting her third baby soon.'

'I should love to see her,' Sally Baker said. 'Would you give me her address?'

'Yes, of course. I shall write to her soon, and I'll tell her you are a nurse here. I am sure she will be thrilled to hear from you.'

'I heard about Eleanor,' she said. 'It was in the paper the other day – they are going to give her a posthumous medal.'

'I didn't know that, but she deserves it.'

'Yes, I think so too,' Sally said. 'Well, I've been sent to see if you would like any help – washing or eating? There's a bathroom just through that door. I could help you if you wanted? Run the water for you and give you a hand in or out?'

'I should love a bath,' I said. 'I think I can manage if you help me get there and back. I'm still feeling a bit weak.'

'Are you hungry?'

'Yes, starving.'

'Right – I'll bring you something to eat first, and then we'll see about that bath.'

I was sitting in a chair by the bed when Bridget came in. She was carrying a bag of large luscious black grapes and a magazine, which she placed on the table at the side of my bed.

'You look much better, Kathy. Are you feeling better?'

'I had a bath and the nurse washed my hair for me. It felt so awful because of all the blood, but she took the bandages off and said the wound had healed enough for me to wash it very gently.' I put a hand to touch the bald spot at the side, where the hair had been cut back to stitch the wound Ernie had inflicted. 'Does it look awful?'

'It shows a bit at the moment,' Bridget said being truthful as always. 'But it will soon grow round again, Kathy. I could bring you a pretty scarf to wear round your head until it does.'

'Thank you.' I laughed. 'I know it's only vanity, but I would rather Tom didn't see me like this.'

'Silly girl! He won't mind – he's just glad you're alive. We all are, Kathy. We were very frightened for a while.'

'What has happened to Ernie? Have the police arrested him?'

'Not yet.' Bridget frowned. 'He must be hiding somewhere – but don't worry, Kathy. They will catch him eventually.'

'I'm not frightened of him. I suppose it was our fault for talking about Jamie and not watching what he was up to.'

'You've remembered it all now, then?'

I shivered and closed my eyes for a moment. 'Yes, I've remembered – most of it, anyway.'

'Well, don't dwell on it,' she said. 'Ernie is a hunted man and not a danger to you any more.'

'I think it was you he wanted to kill most, Bridget.'

'I'm well protected. Joe hired someone to keep watch over me wherever I go – we've had to deal with this sort of thing before.'

'What do you mean? Has someone threatened you before, Bridget?'

'It was a long, long time ago,' she said. 'There was a man . . . a very dangerous man, but that's an old story and best forgotten.'

'Where are the children today? I wish they would let you bring them to see me.'

'You've been too ill, Kathy – but I'll ask and see if they can come next time. Mickey misses you, but Joe and Mick and Tom have kept him busy between them.'

'And Maggie? How does Maggie behave with them now?'

'The same as she always did.' Bridget smiled at me. 'She wants to come and see you, Kathy, but she's afraid you might not want to see her – after the way she behaved.'

'Tell her to come,' I said. 'I should like to see her. All I want is for her to forgive me.'

'I'm sorry, Kathy. I know I was a bitch to you – and I've wished the words unsaid a thousand times since that terrible man hurt you. If you had died I should never have forgiven myself.'

Maggie looked thoroughly chastened as she sat by my bed, and I realized that it had shocked her when she heard how ill I'd been.

'It wasn't your fault, Maggie. My going to Ernie's house had nothing to do with you. I wanted to sort it out, to stop him telling his lies.'

'But I shouldn't have let you go there alone,' she said. 'I knew he was a bitter, revengeful man and I should have stopped you.'

'You couldn't,' I replied. 'My mind was made up and nothing you could have said would have changed it. So don't feel guilty for what happened – because it wasn't your fault.'

'And it wasn't your fault that Billy was killed in that fight with a policeman,' Maggie said. 'I shouldn't have blamed you, Kathy. The sergeant came to tell me they think it was a put-up job – the constable that killed Billy has disappeared.'

'What do you mean, disappeared?' A trickle of coldness ran down my spine, spreading through my body like ice. 'Has something happened to him? I don't understand, Maggie.'

'They reckon it was gangland stuff,' Maggie said. 'Billy had upset one of the big bosses and the raid was set up so that he would be killed resisting arrest. But whoever was behind it didn't reckon on him killing a copper himself, and they must have had a fright when he was taken to hospital. If he'd lived he might have spilled the beans. The copper that hit Billy was new to this area – and now he's gone. Disappeared without trace. Maybe he wasn't even a policeman? No one seems to know who he was.'

'Oh, Maggie . . .' I stared at her in horror. 'I knew that man was dangerous but I never thought . . .'

'Did Billy tell you anything about the man he was working for – the one that set him on that job?' Maggie looked at me intently. 'Anything at all? The police said they suspect who is behind all this, but he's too clever – they can't touch him.'

'Billy told me he worked at a club for someone – a very rich, powerful man – and he used to drive him around sometimes, but I don't know any more.'

'What was his name – did Billy tell you that?'

'Yes – yes, he did, but he told me not to repeat it. He warned me several times.'

'Would you tell the police, Kathy? Would you help them to catch my Billy's killers?' She looked at me with such appeal in her eyes that I understood how much it meant to her. 'Please?'

'Billy said it was dangerous . . .' I took a deep breath, knowing that I owed her this at least. 'But if you want me to, I will, Maggie. I'll tell them what little I know, but it isn't much.'

'Even a little might help,' she said. 'I want that man caught and punished, Kathy. I'll never rest easy in me bed until I know he's finished.'

'Tell that police sergeant to come and see me,' I said. 'I don't know much, but I will tell him what Billy told me.'

'Bless you,' she said and bent to kiss my cheek. 'You did your best to be a good wife to Billy, and I'm sorry I said them dreadful things to you, Kathy love. I want us to be friends again, if you'll forgive me?'

'We'll forgive each other,' I said. 'What's past is past, Maggie. Let's put it behind us and look to the future.'

'I came as soon as I heard,' Ally said when she came to visit me later that same day. 'I'm sorry for what happened to you. You always did say your father could be violent. It was a daft thing to do – going there to confront him alone. You might have known he would attack you.'

'I thought I could handle him and it was only when Bridget arrived that he went mad,' I said. 'I think he really hates her now. He loved her once and everything went wrong for him after she finished with him. I suppose in his own mind he blames her for all his troubles, but it wasn't her fault that he had an accident and lost his job. He had been drinking when it happened, and when they gave him a menial job sweeping floors and the yard it took his pride away, making him bitter.'

Ally nodded, her eyes thoughtful as she looked at me.

'I was sorry about Billy. I couldn't get to the funeral. There's always so much to do, and my lazy husband never turns a hand unless he's forced.' She pulled a wry face. 'Men! I sometimes think we would be much better off without them.'

'It didn't matter about you coming to the funeral; it wouldn't have helped anything. I'm sorry for what happened to Billy too – but we hadn't been happy for a while. If I'd been sensible I would never have married him.'

She nodded, a faint echo of the old jealousy in her eyes. 'I suppose you'll marry Tom O'Rourke now?'

'He has asked me and . . .' I smiled at her. 'Of course I shall marry him, Ally. I love him. I always have.'

'Then I wish you luck,' she said and bent to kiss my cheek. 'I used to be so jealous of you, Kathy. I thought if you married a doctor you wouldn't want to know me any more.'

'That's daft, Ally. I'll always want to know you – you're my friend.'

'I don't suppose I'll see much of you if you go off to America – but write to me sometimes, won't you?'

'Of course I will – and maybe you'll come on a visit one day?'

'Pigs might fly!'

'They probably will one day – in an aeroplane,' I said. 'Don't look like that, Ally. We're friends and we'll keep in touch somehow.'

'As long as you don't get too posh to know me?'

'Don't be silly,' I said and laughed. 'Wherever I go I shall still be Kathy Cole from the lanes.'

'I'm sorry, Sergeant Green, but that's all I can tell you. I know it isn't much – but Billy wouldn't say any more about that man. He was very frightened of him and he owed him money. I warned him to be careful, but he didn't listen. He was told he had another chance to make up for whatever he'd done to upset Mr Maitland – and, well, you know the rest of it.'

It was two days since Maggie's visit and I was beginning to feel very much better. I was dressed now in clothes Bridget had brought to the hospital for me and the doctors had told me that I would be going home soon.

'I only wish we did know the rest of it, Mrs Ryan,' the sergeant said. 'We suspect a great deal, but unfortunately we can't prove anything. Now that we know Billy was working for him it will give us a chance to question Maitland, but I'm not sure that will get us anywhere. We need some real proof – proof that he was behind a lot of the robberies and other rackets we suspect he has a hand in over a long period.

We've known about Maitland for years, of course – but there has never been proof. Men who might have testified have disappeared without trace or been murdered.'

'Yes, I know. Maggie Ryan told me the policeman who hit Billy has disappeared.'

'If he can't be found, he can't testify. If we'd proved it was deliberate and not just in the line of duty, it would have been murder, Mrs Ryan. Billy was known to us as a petty criminal, but he'd never been involved in anything violent before. We suspected that something dodgy was going on from the start – and then we had a tip-off, but still nothing that lays the blame at Maitland's door.'

'Billy warned me not to say anything. He was afraid of what might happen to the children and me.'

'We shall keep an eye out for you, Mrs Ryan – but I don't think you need to worry too much. Your name won't be mentioned. I give you my word.'

'Thank you.' I smiled at him. 'I'm sorry if you thought I wasn't helpful the night Billy died.'

'I didn't expect anything else. Most people haven't the courage to tell us what they know, even if they wanted to – and the majority of them aren't interested in helping the police. They despise us – until they need us. It's only when they're in trouble themselves . . . but I shouldn't grumble at you. You've come forward and that may be of help one day.' He reached into his pocket and then handed me a small box. 'I checked this out myself, Mrs Ryan – and the ring belongs to you just as you said.'

'Thank you.'

'No, thank you for your help.'

'I did it for Maggie Ryan,' I said. 'I did it for my friend.'

'Maggie had no right to ask it of you,' Bridget said. 'If only you'd spoken to me first, Kathy. You should never have told the police what you know . . . not about *him.* You don't realize what you've done.'

The four of us were sitting in Bridget's parlour. It was my first day back from the hospital, and I had just related to them what Sergeant Green had told me about his intention to question Mr Maitland.

'I haven't done anything much,' I said. 'I only know that Billy worked for him sometimes – and that he said he was being given another chance. That doesn't prove anything.'

'It doesn't have to,' Bridget said and shivered. I realized she was really alarmed, frightened for me. 'You don't know that man . . . you don't know what he's capable of doing.'

'He hasn't done anything to us,' Joe said frowning at her. 'He could have, Bridget – but he's left us alone all these years.'

'He left us alone because he knew you could cause trouble for him, Joe. He banked on you letting it go after the man who murdered Mary was executed. Hal Burgess was killed on Maitland's orders. He was executed because he had made a terrible mistake and Maitland had to have him silenced. We knew that . . . everyone knew it, but the police could never prove it.'

'Are you saying that you and Joe know this man?' Tom asked, looking from one to the other, his eyes narrowed and thoughtful. 'Was he something to do with the fire that killed Mary? I remember that – and the look on Jamie's face when he came in that day. It should have been his wedding day.'

'Yes. It should have been their wedding day.' Bridget looked at him, an old grief in her eyes. 'We didn't tell you, because you were too young and it had already upset you. We were all devastated by what happened. The fire was set to punish Joe and me – because I knew something about Maitland, and Joe was trying to find out more in the hope of having him caught and punished for his crimes. Joe was supposed to die that night but Mary was staying in the rooms over the shop instead.'

'And my mother never forgave me for letting it be Mary instead of me,' Joe said. 'She tried to forget but she never quite forgave me to her dying day – and I can't forgive myself.'

'It wasn't your fault, Joe.' Bridget reached for his hand and held it. 'I was the one who discovered what he had done to Lainie and I went to his hotel and pried into his things. I took that letter and he told me he would make me sorry. I should have killed him that day when I had his gun in my hand . . .'

'Maitland is a crook,' Joe said, looking at Tom and me in concern. 'But he's too clever, too powerful to get caught. He has other people to do his dirty work for him. I thought his empire had begun to crumble after the fire, and perhaps it did in some areas, but he's built his fortune in secret ways, grown richer and more powerful, if anything. He seems to be a respectable man, though I know he's been dropped from the gentlemen's club he used to belong to – and he was thrown off a charity committee only recently, though they hushed it up. Nothing seems to touch him; he's like a huge fat spider in the middle of a web of evil which he controls through fear and greed.'

'He sounds a thoroughly nasty piece of work,' Tom said, looking anxious. 'Does this mean that Kathy might be in danger?'

'She might,' Joe admitted. 'But only if Maitland suspects that she knows something important – something that could link him to Billy or crime.'

'Kathy doesn't know anything – at least, nothing that could put him away.'

'Maitland doesn't care about *what* she knows,' Bridget said. 'If he thinks she's a danger to him he might . . .' she stopped as we heard a loud knocking at the door. 'I'll see who it is.'

'We should go away,' Tom said after Bridget had gone out. 'Jamie has gone over to Ireland to look at some horses. When he comes back we should tell him that we accept his offer to stay with him at his ranch in America until we get settled in a home of our own. This Maitland fellow won't bother about you once you're out of the country and no longer a danger to him.'

'Oh, Tom?' I stared at him uncertainly. 'That seems such a drastic solution . . . to run away.'

Bridget had come back into the room. She looked at me oddly, as if she didn't quite know what to say.

'That was the police, Kathy. They asked for you, but I took a message and sent them away.'

'Something about Maitland?' Tom asked, suddenly alert.

'No, it's Ernie Cole,' Bridget said and her face was as white as a sheet. I could see that she was shaken, her hand trembling slightly. 'They found him hanging over the banisters in his house.'

'Dead!' I stared at her in horror as the shock hit me. 'That's terrible . . .'

Ernie probably wasn't my father, and I had no affection for him whatsoever after what he'd done to me, but it still made me feel sick to think of him dying that way. From what Bridget had told me, I knew that he hadn't been violent when he was younger, and I understood that disappointment and a feeling of being cheated had made him into the bitter man he had become.

'Good grief!' Joe exclaimed. 'He must have killed himself.'

'Yes, that's what the police seem to think,' Bridget said, the words coming slowly, deliberately. 'They believe he was so desperate that he decided to take the easy way out.'

'It isn't easy to hang yourself,' Tom said. 'There was a soldier in France, he hung himself because he was too scared to go back into battle. I had to cut him down while he was still kicking. He died in my arms. I can assure you it isn't easy.'

'You don't think . . .' Bridget was staring at me and she looked frightened. 'You don't think it might not have been suicide?'

'What do you mean?' Tom frowned. He stared at her in silence for a moment, and then nodded. 'You think it might have been Maitland's men, don't you?'

'No!' Joe shook his head. 'Why? It makes no sense. Ernie wasn't even Kathy's father. He tried to kill her. I can't see why Maitland would do it. No, Bridget, I'm sure you're wrong. Ernie realized that he was finished and that there was nothing left for him to live for – and he took his own life.'

'I'm not so sure. Maitland might not have known the full story,' Bridget said. 'Even if he did, he may still have seen it as a way of warning Kathy to keep her mouth shut in future. It worries me, Joe. I don't trust that man.'

'The children . . .' I reached for Tom's hand. 'Supposing he harms the children next?'

'He won't do that,' Joe said, his face grim but determined as if he had reached a decision. 'I'll see that he knows you're going away, Kathy. You and Tom, and the children. You'll be safer in another country, and I think you should go as soon as possible. If Maitland hears that you told the police what you know . . . Yes, Bridget may be right. You should go away.'

'What about the wedding?' Bridget asked, torn between relief and distress at the thought of our imminent departure. 'Kathy will want to be married with all her friends about her.'

'Just you, Jamie, Joe and the family – and Billy's parents,' I said, looking up at Tom. 'That's all we want, isn't it?'

'Why don't we have the wedding in Ireland?' Joe asked. 'I'll get a message to Jamie. He can set it up for us – and we'll all go over together. You've always wanted to have a holiday there, Bridget.'

'So I have,' she said smiling at him. 'Trust you to think of it, Joe. Maggie will love the idea and so will Mick.'

'Yes,' I said and looked at Tom as he held my hand tightly. 'I think that's a wonderful idea. We can go on from there to America.'

Tom looked at me as we went outside to his car later that evening. He was driving us out of London to stay with friends until we caught the ship for Ireland, where our friends and family would join us for the wedding in another three weeks.

'We'll tell the children it's a holiday,' he said. 'We don't want to frighten them.'

'I've been promising Mickey a holiday for ages,' I said. 'He's excited about it. Besides, I'm sure there's nothing to be anxious about – it's just a precaution.'

'It will be an adventure as far as they are concerned – and the start of a new life for us, Kathy.'

'All it means is that we are leaving a little sooner than we might have,' I agreed. 'It doesn't matter, Tom. I'm looking forward to a new life – with you.'

'You look lovely,' Maggie said, wiping a tear from the corner of her eye as she saw me in the cream silk dress and coat I'd bought for my wedding. It was the fashionable shorter length, and showed an expanse of pale silk stockings. My shoes were a deeper shade of cream and I had a small cloche hat, which I wore over my new bobbed hairstyle. I knew I looked very different, and I felt as if the dark clouds had fallen away. 'And so happy. I can see it shining out of your eyes, Kathy.'

'I am happy,' I said. 'Not just because I'm marrying Tom – because we are all friends again.'

Maggie gave me a hug then laughed and apologized. 'Silly me! I'll mess all your fine clothes up so I will.'

'No, you won't,' I said. 'And Mick has promised to bring you over to America for a long holiday soon – so don't be thinking that you'll never see me or the children again, because you will. Even if I have to come back to see you.'

'That daft husband of mine is thinking of emigrating to America at his time of life,' she said with a little scoffing noise. 'If he thinks he's getting me to move to a new country and leave all me friends, he's got less sense than I thought – but I wouldn't say no to a holiday.'

'Bridget has promised to come out, too,' I told her. 'Jamie wants her and Joe to stay with him for a few months, but she wants to get Amy settled first.'

'That girl will be a trial to her mother before she's settled,' Maggie said and frowned. 'You mark my words, Kathy. Bridget has spoiled her – and now she's off to stay with her aunt Lainie. And who knows what will come of that?'

'What do you mean, Maggie? Lainie has done well for herself.'

'If you mean being left that dress shop and bit of property in her late employer's will . . .' Maggie sniffed. 'Well, I suppose she's respectable now, but I've got a long memory and I remember the trouble she was to Bridget when they were younger.'

Maggie's dark hints intrigued me, but before I could ask her to tell me more Bridget poked her head round the door and asked if she could come in. She exclaimed over my clothes, told me I was as pretty as a picture and then it was time to leave for my wedding to Tom.

Once again my wedding was to be a civil one, but not because of a difference in our religions. Tom had told me that he was no longer a practising Catholic.

'It's not that I don't believe in God,' he said, 'but I've discovered that to practice medicine as I want to I need to be free in my thinking and not bound by any doctrine. To my mind there are times when a patient's well-being is more important than the teaching of any church.'

'You're not an atheist?' I was slightly shocked, knowing how devout his sister was.

'No, I'm not that either,' he said. 'I believe, but in my own way.'

'That's how I've always felt too,' I told him and he kissed me gently on the mouth. 'It's the way you behave to others that counts. Lead a good life and you've nothing to be ashamed of. I did a bad thing when I married Billy without telling him I was having a child and it taught me a lesson.'

'Try to forget all that now, Kathy. It's over, my love. You don't need to think about it any more.'

I had tried to forget, but Billy had been a part of my life and I had only to look at my darling Sarah to remember her father. I could think of him now with regret, and try to remember only the good times.

'Are you happy, Kathy?' Tom asked as I lay in his arms that night, content after our lovemaking. 'You are sure you want to go to America? We could always go somewhere else, even back to London if you like? I doubt that there was any real danger from Maitland. Bridget can't forget what happened all those years ago, but Joe thinks she was probably worrying for nothing.'

'Yes, I think there was a lot more to her story than she told us,' I agreed. 'But it doesn't matter to me, Tom. I'm looking forward to seeing a new country. When I was nursing I had a taste of what life could be like away from the lanes. I was happy enough there sometimes, but I'm glad our children won't be brought up in that environment. I want more for them than I had – much, much more.'

'You didn't have much of a life as a child,' Tom said, pulling me closer to kiss my hair as his hand stroked the arch of my back. 'I can remember what it was like for us when Ma was alive – all the fighting and bickering, and the times when she was drunk. I was scared of her most of the time.

'I hated it when Bridget said I had to go away to hospital, because I thought I was being punished. Ma fell down the stairs and hurt herself when she had that first stroke. I was haunted by guilt for a long time afterwards, and it was partly my fault because she was shouting at me and I shouted back at her, but while I was away I learned that things could be better and I was determined to do something with my life. Bridget marrying Joe made it a lot easier for me; he paid for me to go to college and supported me through medical school. All I had to do was work hard.'

'And you have,' I said, snuggling up to him. 'That's why Billy was so jealous. You escaped and he didn't. He never would have even if he hadn't become involved with Maitland.'

'But you have and Sarah has – I think Billy would be pleased about that if he knew, don't you?'

'Yes, I do,' I said. 'Mick is still swearing he wants to emigrate to America, and Jamie has offered him a job. They might end up escaping too.'

'Not if Maggie has her way,' Tom said and laughed as he looked down at me. 'They used to have some royal battles in the past and I can see it happening again.'

'Oh, Tom, we're so lucky,' I said as he bent his head to kiss me. 'So very, very lucky.'

'I'm lucky to have you,' he whispered as he drew me closer, kissing me and caressing me in a way that made my body sing with pleasure. 'I thought I had lost you, Kathy. You'll never know how much I regretted that stupid quarrel.'

'You couldn't have regretted it more than I did,' I said. 'We both made mistakes, Tom – but we shan't make them again. We'll make a promise now never to let the sun go down on a quarrel. We'll always end the day like this, talking to each other, loving each other.'

'I like the sound of that,' he said and drew me to him in a passionate embrace that drove all other thoughts from my mind.

It was only long after, when Tom was sleeping and I lay content but wakeful at his side, that the thought came into my mind. In America I would be safe, beyond the reach of Maitland and his bullies, but what of Bridget and her family?

And there was Lainie, too. Bridget had hinted that she was somehow caught up in the old story, though she had never explained what she meant. Perhaps the story was not hers to tell – but it made me wonder. I knew about the fire that had cost Mary her life, but what else had happened all those years ago that was so terrible it still had the power to make Bridget tremble? A shiver ran through me and I was suddenly afraid for my friends. I felt that there was a shadow hanging over them, and that fate had yet more twists in the saga that had begun so long ago.

'Be careful, Bridget,' I whispered. 'Please be careful . . .'

I was not sure what I was trying to warn her of, but an icy feeling at the nape of my neck seemed to be a premonition of danger for Bridget and her family. I lay for some minutes aware that I was uneasy but not knowing why. There was surely no reason why they should be in danger now?

My fears were foolish, of course they were – a leftover from the tragic events that had led up to Billy's death. It was all in my mind, merely shadows. As Joe had pointed out, Maitland had left them in peace for years – why should they be in any danger now?

I was letting my imagination run away with me. As the feeling of apprehension receded I smiled in the darkness. I was foolish to let anything spoil my happiness. Bridget had Joe to look after her and I had a whole bright new future to enjoy.

I turned to snuggle into the warmth of my beloved husband, and soon I too was sleeping.

.